Near Death

Near Death

The Experience . . .

Steven Cox

Grateful Steps
Asheville, North Carolina

Grateful Steps Foundation
30 Ben Lippen School Road #107
Asheville, North Carolina 28806

Copyright © 2018 by Steven Kilner Cox
Library of Congress Control Number 2013931798

Cox, Steven
Near Death:
The Experience

Cover design by Sundara Fawn
Cover art from Dreamstime

ISBN 978-1-935130-58-1 Paperback
Printed in the USA
at Lightning Source
FIRST EDITION

www.gratefulsteps.org

To Sky,
the reason I do everything

Acknowledgments

I would like to thank God, Jesus, Judas, my mom, your mom, everybody's dads, all our siblings, cousins and ex-roommates or mates. All the guys I was locked up with. Most of the people I've ever met, and all the ones I haven't. Plus warm regards to anyone's deity that differs from my own. I'm thankful to anyone who takes the time to read this book. But then there are the ones who helped me write this book. God already knows the depths of gratitude I have for his help, but I haven't told those who follow:

Micki Cabaniss . . . without you, there is no book period! Lindy, Stephanie, Chris and the rest of the staff at Grateful Steps, I would not be the writer I am today if not for y'awl's influence.

Chaplain Steve Plemmons . . . thank you for the subterfuge. Doug Simonson . . . the lynch pin.

Wheelchair Chris . . . thank you for securing the package . . . by the way I still owe you eighty dollars. The English professor at Lees-McRae College . . . told me about screen-play formatting disk.

Jerry Burgan for saying, "Your ideas will never work."

Prologue

SOMEWHERE A PHONE begins to ring. The lady has no idea where her call is connecting, but she waits, listening to the sound—torn between hoping it is answered and fearing what will happen if it is. *God, I should hang up . . . before it's too late!*

"Hello?"

The woman is frozen by the male voice at the end of the line. She sits in silence, struggling with tears of pain and anguish.

"Hello? Mrs. Crane, we trace all incoming calls. We know it's you."

The tears fall; she closes her eyes and roughly wipes them away. "He did it again! He said he wouldn't, but he did. And this time the kids saw it all. I didn't know what to do! I don't think I can take this anymore!"

"It's going to be all right, Mrs. Crane. We'll do what needs to be done."

"He's not really a bad person!"

Click, the line is broken. She clutches the phone to her chest as she succumbs to the pain and tears. She is lying on her bed, crying, still holding the phone when her husband barges through the door.

Will Crane is a large man with a well-hidden mean streak. You would never guess what the youth minister at the local Baptist church is capable of behind the closed doors of his two-story farm house. He is also a smart man. That is why the closest neighbors aren't close at all. He keeps a tight leash on his family in order to protect his carefully cultivated good name. It wouldn't do at all to have the community find out that one of their city council members, and—many people think—next mayor, is in fact a cold-blooded beast.

Daddy taught him well. That's why he gets so irate when he walks in and sees his wife lying on the bed with the phone in her hand. Will lunges forward and grabs the phone, jerking it roughly from his wife. He puts the phone to his ears and listens to the dial tone. He looks the phone over and hits the redial button. He waits as the phone begins to ring. It seems like an eternity before the line picks up. He listens with relief when a recording begins to spout out the date, time and weather. Will jerks the phone from the jack and hurls it into the corner, shattering it against the far wall.

"Who the hell did you call?" Will looms over his wife and snarls at her. "So help me God, woman, if you called the cops and they show up, I'll paint these walls red with your blood before they take me to jail!"

Tina Crane looks at her husband with dread, knowing the consequences of the mistake she's made. Why didn't she just put the phone back? "I didn't call anybody, Will. I swear it!"

"Then why did you have the damn phone in your hand when I came in?"

"I'm sorry. It won't happen again!"

Will laughs cruelly, glancing at the shattered phone lying in pieces on the floor. "I know that, Tina. Now we have to make sure you know that too!"

Tina Crane's bruises will remind her of the fact she could have avoided the brutality of the next couple of hours, not to mention the recovery time.

Will looks at his wife with anger mixed with pleasure. *"I'm going to enjoy teaching you this lesson!"*

ONE

PHILLIP STEVENS IS not a bad looking man; in his mid 40s, he looks more like his early 30s. He likes to hike and works out regularly. He also jogs a couple miles several times a week. Add his dark hair that refuses to show any gray and his brown eyes, and, while nothing about his facial features makes him stand out, there is nothing that takes away from his overall handsome appearance. When women pass him on the street, some don't give him a second glance, but most of them do . . . not that he would notice. And even the ones who do wouldn't today. Phillip is very hyperfocused. If it's not about his work, it doesn't exist. Which can be good in Phillip's case; he's got a very important job.

Phillip's normally immaculate appearance is ruffled this morning. He didn't go home last night, too wound up about his upcoming schedule.

He sits dozing behind his desk. A TV across the room shows an old man giving an interview, trying valiantly to raise money and awareness for some noble cause or another. If Phillip were awake, he would smile and applaud the man's effort. But he's not. He sleeps in relative comfort as far as his surroundings go. His office is nice and airy, sparsely furnished with a desk and chair, along with the flat screen television mounted on the left wall. The right wall is nothing but moderately tinted windows letting in an abundance of sunlight. A door at the far end of the office allows access to the balcony running the length of the room. A black leather couch and a small conference table are positioned next to the windows. Had Phillip thought about it, he could have stretched out on the couch and avoided the stiff neck awaiting him. The only other things in the room are a computer and phone on his desk plus a few nature pictures on the opposite wall—places Phillip has hiked.

At this particular moment, the phone beeps. Phillip stirs from his nap and leans forward, pushing the speakerphone option. "Yes?"

Sandra St. Clair's voice fills the room. "I have this month's reviews."

"Good, bring them in." The line goes dead. Phillip smooths out his shirt and wipes the sleep from his eyes as his attention wanders to the man on the screen.

***

The door to his office opens and in walks Sandra St. Clair, a stunning brunette in her early thirties, who, if she chose, could be a well-paid model. But that's not going to happen. Sandra loves her job and the challenges that come with it. Truth be told, she loves Phillip, too, not that he knows it. For such a brilliant man, he can miss the blatantly obvious. Phillip continues to watch the man on TV as Sandra crosses the room, carrying the monthly reviews. She stops in front of the desk and looks from Phillip to the TV and back.

"You didn't go home last night, did you?"

Phillip glances at Sandra for the first time. "Is it that apparent?"

"You need to take a break, Phillip. You're working too hard."

"I just had a nap."

Sandra shakes her head. "That's not what I mean. You need a vacation. When's the last time you took one?"

Phillip shrugs. "We're too busy right now, too much going on."

Sandra sits on the edge of the desk. She crosses her legs provocatively, showing them off, yet she does this absentmindedly, her gaze returning to the man on TV. She lays the folder on the table. "That's what you always say."

Phillip takes the folder and opens it. "It's always true."

"He's one of ours, isn't he?" Sandra says, tilting her head toward the TV.

Phillip looks up from the first file then reaches into the top drawer of his desk, grabs the remote for the television and turns it off. "You know the rules, Sandra."

They both speak in unison. "No spreading any information without due cause."

Phillip looks back at the file. "Exactly. You know, this folder is a little light. I thought we had six reviews this month."

"We did, but Mr. Dobbins died last week in a skiing accident."

Phillip looks up at Sandra and raises his eyebrows at the news. He leans back in his chair with the file. "Good for him, the lucky bastard."

"I suppose you're right."

Phillip continues flipping through the pages, then comes to a stop and lays the last file on the table. "This one could get real tricky!"

Sandra looks down at the file and nods in agreement. "Yeah, too tricky if you ask me."

"What are you saying, Ms. St. Clair?"

Sandra rises from the desk and paces in apprehension. She smooths out her suit, then crosses her arms while Phillip looks on. "I think we should table this review for at least the next three years."

Phillip shakes his head. "That's not an option; you know the rules. Everyone comes up for review after twenty years. There are no exceptions."

"I don't know why you just can't talk to the senator. I'm sure he would agree that in this precarious situation, we would be justified in a postponement."

Phillip continues with his rigid stance. "There's no reason to include Higgins in the loop. He doesn't have the authority to make that decision."

Sandra goes back to her pacing. "Well, who does?"

"Nobody. The board phased out, as planned, after rules of order and financing were established. Higgins is only responsible for personnel and oversight."

Sandra stops pacing and stares at Phillip. "Well, Phillip, I think it's apparent what we have to do."

"What's that?"

"We have to break the rules."

Phillip refuses to show his surprise and distress. "Sandra, because you mean so much to me, I'm going to ignore what you just said. But know here and now I won't be so gracious in the future. Everything we do and everything we stand for is based on an impenetrable integrity. I simply can't risk that for any reason."

Sandra looks at Phillip with resignation and acceptance. "Phillip, I knew you would say that; you're such a noble man. I think that's why I love you."

Phillip registers his surprise at her admission. He doesn't quite know how to react to her words.

"Don't say anything," Sandra says. "That would just make what I have to do that much harder."

Phillip looks confused. "What do you have to do?"

Sandra pulls a gun from the small of her back and points it at Phillip. "You're so predictable! Remember, Phillip, checks and balances."

Phillip stares at the gun. "Sandra, you don't have to do this!"

"Yes, I do." Sandra pulls the trigger before Phillip throws up his hands. A tranquilizer dart protrudes from his neck. He looks around, not understanding how or why. Sandra holds the gun upright, and a lone tear runs from the corner of her eye. Phillip falls limp in his chair, unconscious from the effect of the drug. Two large men in black, low-key suits enter the room. They move briskly toward the desk as Sandra turns and greets them. She flips the gun to the closest man. "You know where to take the body and what to do."

Both men nod. Sandra exits the office, leaving the men with Phillip's inert form.

TWO

Tina Crane takes her seat at the dining table of the old farmhouse. She loved the place when they first bought it right out of high school. She was 18, and big, tall, handsome Will Crane was 26. The starting quarterback on their school's only state championship football team, he drove a nice, red, Chevy Silverado 4x4 with huge tires. She never stood a chance when he walked up to her at the local movie theater and asked her out. All she could say was yes.

Six months later she was pregnant and they were standing in the front of a courtroom getting married. She had not dreamed it would be that way, but at least she had the man of her dreams—and the farm, too.

Will's dad, president of the local bank, got them an incredible deal on a just-foreclosed property. Tina felt bad about the family who lost their house over such a small amount of money. Will said they were being relocated to a more affordable home, which turned out to be the local homeless shelter, although eventually, the family was able to move into a rundown single-wide in the trailer park down below the local paper mill. The old man, who had lost the farm that had been in his family for three generations, made quite a scene at Will's father's bank, waving a shotgun around, demanding to see the manager. The cops showed up fairly quickly, and the old man ended up with three slugs in his chest. He didn't return fire— simply because the gun wasn't loaded. His family was a tough bunch but knew there was nothing they could do. The old man had made it to his late sixties, and they figured if he hadn't been killed, he would never have made it out of prison anyway. All in all, they were proud of what he had done; they just wished he had remembered to load the damn gun first. They had started keeping all the guns unloaded after their youngest daughter and her three young boys moved back home.

Tina did not feel bad for long after she and Will moved in. She spent several months redecorating the place as her pregnancy progressed. She had all the rooms repainted and had a breakfast nook added onto the kitchen. They had new appliances installed. Will's parents had even paid for their furniture, and, though Tina would have chosen different styles, she was thankful for the gift.

Will was completely supportive about everything and never acted out of the way toward her. He spent time at home overseeing the landscape project. He had a nice fountain built and a walk-through garden planted in the front yard. Tina still loved to walk through and admire the various plants and flowers, although now she spent more time on her hands and knees maintaining the garden than she did admiring it.

Apparently, Will's plan had involved her doing gardening maintenance all along. Tina had to admit she had learned more than she had ever imagined there was to learn about proper plant maintenance and upkeep. One thing she would always be able to say was that being married to Will had opened her eyes to a strength and depth of resiliency she never would have dreamed she possessed.

It seemed very important to Will that when people visited their home, they left with an impression of wealth and happiness, however false the impression might be. When she had finally had Kelly, their first baby, Will's true personality surfaced. After she came home from the hospital, Will beat her severely. He said it was her fault that Kelly wasn't a boy. "The next time you get pregnant, it had damn well better be a boy."

Ever since then, the only way she could avoid the beatings was by getting pregnant. Will never laid a hand on her during her three pregnancies.

Tina thinks of all of this as she grimaces with pain from two cracked ribs.

***

Little Tony is 9 years old and looks at his battered and bruised mother, barely holding back his tears. He wants to tell his mom he loves her and that she should go to the hospital, but he knows better. He is old enough to realize his dad would not allow it. If he says anything, his father is liable to flip out and beat his mom even worse. Little Tony has a couple of bruises of his own, so he holds his tongue and looks over at his older sister.

Kelly is 11 and doesn't say much anymore. For the last year or so, dear old Dad has taken the kind of notice and liberties with Kelly that can really damage a child. Kelly will barely eat her food, then will run upstairs to her room and spend the rest of the evening hoping and praying Daddy doesn't follow.

Jody, the 1-year-old baby boy, is still too young to know the kind of hell he's in. Talk about "born into sin," baby Jody is neck-deep in it and doesn't even know it.

Big Will Crane sits at the table, wolfing down his food with gusto. Will is in a hurry. He's got to get to church, and he's running late. Big Will had to teach his wife a lesson, and now if he doesn't leave in the next ten minutes, he'll be late for the church budget meeting. Will looks at his wife as he finishes his meal. "You overcooked the meatloaf, woman."

"I'm sorry, Will. The timer on the oven is broke, and I was trying to change Jody's diaper."

Will gulps down his drink and slams his glass on the table. "Save it, Tina. There you go blaming someone else for your mistakes! You're trying to tell me Jody burned the meatloaf?"

"No I was—"

"Enough! I don't want to hear any more of your lies." Will pushes back from the table and gets to his feet. "It's you lying about that damn tire on the van that got all this started! Hell, I'm out busting my ass, trying to provide for this family, and you're out whoring all over town!"

Tony looks up from his food to his dad. "She ain't lying about that tire, Dad. She barely kept us from wrecking when it blew."

Will grabs his coat. Throwing it on, he turns toward his son. Tony cringes as his dad looms over him. Will grabs his son and shakes him vigorously. "Boy, I'll beat the skin off you. Your mom's a liar, and I'll be damned if any son of mine is going to be corrupted by her evil ways. So, when I get home, you be ready for a lesson on the dangers of lying."

Tony breaks down in tears while Tina watches in horror and Kelly tries to ignore it all.

"Dad, I'm sorry. I won't lie anymore. Please don't beat me."

Will looks down at his son somberly and moves his hand to one of his shoulders. "Lessons must be learned, son. Never doubt that." Will leaves his son in fearful tears and heads from the dining room through the well-lit country kitchen and opens the back door. Will yells back to his wife as he leaves, "Tina, have this place cleaned up before I get back."

Tina sits in defeated silence, listening to the door slam shut. Jody begins to cry at the sound of the door. Tina does too.

Kelly looks up from her plate for the first time. She leaves her seat, takes Jody in her arms and tries to calm him down. She rocks him gently back and forth. "Don't cry, little Jody, because in this family, once you start, you never get to stop."

THREE

PHILLIP STEVENS AWAKENS with a start to the beeping of his desk phone. He looks around his office in confusion, with an intense feeling of déjà vu. The phone beeps again. Phillip shakes his head to try to clear it, then slaps the button, activating the speaker phone. "Yeah?"

Sandra St. Clair's voice flows over the line from her office down the hall. "Phillip, are you all right? This is the third time I've tried to reach you."

Phillip stretches, and then stifles a yawn. "I think so; I must have been sleeping pretty hard. I had the craziest dream."

Sandra's voice conveys her concern. "You didn't go home last night did you? Damn it, Phillip, you can't work twenty-four hours a day. Even *you* need a break!"

"Yeah, you already told me that."

"No, I didn't."

Phillip leans forward in his chair and grabs his TV remote and flips it on. The man from his dream fills the screen in a repeat performance. Phillip stares at the image with wary confusion.

"Hello. Earth to Phillip. I'm still on the line, you know."

Phillip tears his attention from the screen. "Sorry, Sandra, I can't seem to get myself together this morning. What can I do for you?"

"It's the first; I have this month's case reviews ready for you to sign off on."

"Bring them whenever you're ready."

"I'll be there directly."

Phillip leans forward and kills the line. He immediately turns his attention back to the old man on the screen. He listens in fascination, remembering everything the man said from his dream the night before. Phillip mentally steps back into the dream, which he remembers more and more as a nightmare. He thinks about the moment Sandra pulled out the gun and shot him. So deep in thought is he, he sits up with a jerk when his office door opens and Sandra St. Clair glides through the door and across the room toward his desk, carrying the folder—again just like his dream.

Sandra stops at the desk and looks Phillip over. "Phillip, you look so pale! You're not sick are you?"

Phillip shakes his head. "No, but I had this dream last night, and so far everything that happened in it is happening this morning."

Sandra tosses the folder in front of him, then takes a seat on the desk, crossing her legs. Phillip leans back in his chair.

"See, that's exactly what you did in my dream!"

Sandra eyes Phillip skeptically. "Come on, Phillip, this is where I sit every time I come into your office." She glances quickly over her shoulder, then back at Phillip.

"You have the only office I have ever seen without chairs for other people to sit in."

Phillip throws his hands up in frustration. "You don't get it." Phillip points to the TV. "You see that man there? Everything he's saying is exactly what was in my dream!"

Sandra watches the man speak for a moment. "You probably saw this on the news last night and then dreamed it. I've seen this man a couple of times myself."

Phillip grabs the remote and turns off the TV, cutting the man's speech short. He looks at Sandra suspiciously.

She looks back at him with confusion. "What? Why are you looking at me like that?"

Phillip leaves his seat and comes around the desk to where a very perplexed Sandra still sits. "There is more to the dream than what I've told you."

Sandra eyes Phillip warily. "Like what?"

"You did something to me."

Sandra stands up and places her arms over Phillip's shoulder seductively, then whispers in his ear. "You know all this isn't necessary; if you want your dreams fulfilled, you can just ask."

Phillip fails to notice the bait for what it is. Rolling his eyes, he removes her arms from over his shoulders, spins her roughly around and pushes her forward so she has to catch herself from falling face-forward onto his desk.

"Oh, my, Phillip, I wouldn't have guessed you had this in you!" Sandra's mood quickly changes from one of seduction to utter confusion as Phillip pats her down. Not finding anything, he steps back from her, then glides back around the desk, takes his seat, grabs the folder and begins to flip through it. Sandra stands up from where

Phillip pushed her over his desk and smooths out her suit. "And what the hell was that about? Did you just pat me down?"

Phillip doesn't look up from reading one of the files. "You're right, it was only a dream."

"And what made you change your mind?"

"You're not packing heat."

"Of course not, why would I be?"

Phillip finally looks up. "You shot me in my dream."

Sandra steps back and her jaw drops. "I shot you! Why, I thought we had . . ." Sandra shuts her mouth with a snap; her face turns red with embarrassment.

Phillip smiles knowingly. "You thought what, Ms. St. Clair?"

Sandra recovers her composure and quickly changes the subject. "It doesn't matter. I think we've wasted enough time this morning on false realities."

"Indeed. This folder seems a little light; shouldn't there be six case reviews this month?" Phillip places the folder on the table and leans back in his chair.

Sandra takes the documents and quickly looks them over. "No, Phillip, the folder's accurate. We only have five this month . . . but with the potential for disaster one of them has, I would think five is more than enough."

"You telling me we didn't have a client die in a skiing accident last week?"

Sandra shakes her head no. "That is something I would have been aware of, Phillip. Where did you get your information?"

"Never mind that I said anything. I must have read it in the paper and thought I recognized the name."

"I can double-check if you want me to."

Returning his attention to the file, it is Phillip's turn to shake his head. "No need, we've got plenty to keep us busy right here."

Sandra retakes her seat on the edge of the desk so they both can look over the file. She has often thought to suggest they make a second copy of the case reviews so each would have one, but she enjoys the closeness involved with sharing one file. *A girl can't help the way she feels.* The two sit head-to-head, looking at the third review on their list. This is the one that kept Phillip in his office all night.

"Well, San, we'll earn our pay pulling this one off."

"Maybe we should consider postponing it."

Phillip looks up at his colleague. "How did I know you were going to say that?"

Sandra returns his gaze. "The same way I know that you're not going to do it."

FOUR

Will Crane stomps across the driveway toward his shiny black Beamer. When a man works as hard as he does, he's allowed to splurge on himself every now and again. It's murky outside and hard to see; the sun has been down a good ten minutes by now. Will doesn't see the damn cat till he steps on his tail, causing the little black fur ball to screech in pain and dart away. *Serves the cat right; maybe next time he'll learn to stay out of my way.*

It's getting dark outside, but it's not so dark that Will can't see the donut tire on his wife's much older and beat-up minivan when he walks around the front of it. Will can't help but be a little impressed at the length she'll go to in order to cover up her sins and transgressions. He also thinks it might be time to upgrade her ride as well. Too many more trips around town in that clunker and people will start to gossip. That's the problem with small towns: people always snooping around in your business.

It had been more than luck that had landed him such a sweet deal on this house way out in the country where people couldn't poke into his family affairs. His dad had known the value of privacy and had kept his eye on this place for years. He had known the old owners were struggling to stay afloat, and when he talked them into refinancing all those years ago, he knew it was only a matter of time before they lost their home. It had actually happened faster than anticipated, and Will's dad had deferred several payments on the loan in order to keep them in the house . . . until Will was financially stable enough to buy the place out.

Sliding into the front seat of his sleek ride, Will turns the ignition, starts the car and takes off, spinning a little gravel in his wake. He hits the blacktop and turns left toward town, fishtailing slightly. He fiddles with the radio, adjusting the dial till he finds his favorite gospel station. The church choir hymn hour is not quite over. Will sings along with one of his favorites: "Amazing grace how sweet the sound—"

Cut short by the ringing of his cell, he reaches over and grabs the phone from where he had thrown it onto the passenger seat. He looks at the caller ID and quickly answers. "Hello, Mike. How ya doing?"

"Well, we're about ready to start the meeting, and we were wondering if you were going to make it."

Will turns the radio down so he can hear the caller more clearly. "Yeah, I'll be there in about ten minutes. If you think you need to, you can start without me."

"No, no, that won't be necessary. Just making sure you were coming."

Will smiles into the phone, sensing the other man's hesitation. Mike knows Will is an up-and-comer in the church as well as the community, and Will knows Mike doesn't want to get on his bad side. "Well, I'm on my way. I would have been there twenty minutes ago, but Tina had a blowout, and I had to go and change her tire."

"You're a good man, Will, and we'll see ya when ya get here."

Will hangs up the phone without saying goodbye. He turns the radio up just in time to catch the end of the song. *Damn.*

"Will Crane, you're such a liar. You should be ashamed, lying to Mike like that." Will spins his head around, staring dumbfounded at his wife—who sits in the passenger seat, scolding him and pointing her finger at him. "What the hell, Tina? How did you get here? I left you at home!"

Tina Crane ignores Will and just keeps talking. "You didn't change my tire; I did. Then when you got home, you beat me for it. You blackened my eye and cracked two of my ribs."

Will stares in disbelief at his wife. He watches in growing horror his wife's skin begin to fall from her face, revealing the blood, cartilage and, finally, bones underneath. He begins stuttering, trying to comprehend what's going on. "What in the name of God? I must be losing my mind!"

"No, you're not. Tell him, kids."

Tony, Kelly and little Jody speak in unison from the backseat. "Mom's right, Dad. You're a wife beater."

Will turns and notices his children in the backseat for the first time. *Jody can't talk yet!* Will looks at his family slack-jawed, his mind bending from trying to comprehend the impossible. He can't turn away as the skin on his children mimics his wife's and begins to fall from their faces. "Jesus, this can't be happening—"

"Will, watch the road."

Will tears his attention from the grotesque form of his children and focuses on his wife, who is little more than a skeleton by now. "Wha . . . what?"

Tina points a skeletal finger toward the windshield. "The road, Will. Watch the road."

Will jerks his head back forward just as he crosses the center line and hits a black SUV head-on.

FIVE

THE TWO EMTs move in harmonic unison that comes only from working together for several years. They go through the process of trying to stabilize Will while transporting him in an ambulance to the hospital.

Harry, a 27-year-old father of two, has wanted to be an EMT since a young boy, when the efforts of an ambulance driver saved his mother's life.

Taylor, his mom, had been driving home from dropping his dad off at the airport for the start of a week-long business retreat. She had not been happy about the prospect of her husband being gone so long. Neither had her husband, John, Harry's father. The trip couldn't be avoided though; John needed the training in order to continue his upward march within the company ranks. The young couple had left their two small boys with a babysitter. They had decided to spend the evening before the trip at a fairly upscale hotel near the airport. John had an early flight out, and, instead of having to wake up well before dusk to make the commute from home, they could use the early flight as an excuse to spend a romantic evening together. The couple had hardly slept at all by the time the morning came around. After a very intense session of love-making, they had spent the remainder of the night resting in each other's arms, basking in the knowledge of their brightly burning passion and occasionally whispering in each other's ears of the love they shared. Needless to say, Taylor was fairly tired for the hour and a half drive home.

Clyde has been an EMT for over twenty years. When he saved the life of Harry's mother, he had thought of it as just a part of the job. He had no idea the profound effect he had over the lives of so many people other than the victims.

Harry had come onboard six years ago and specifically asked to be a part of Clyde's crew. Clyde had resisted the brash young kid at first, but he finally gave him a chance, and, after a couple of weeks of awkwardness from Harry's hero worship, Clyde learned to appreciate the constant reminder of the good he was doing in the world. Harry brought him out of a depression—from the negativities of such an emotionally draining job—Clyde didn't even know he suffered. It didn't take Clyde long to start to believe the comments from his friends and family of how much brighter and happier he seemed to be.

Clyde and Harry exist in a self-propelling positive cycle. Clyde loves Harry like the son he never had.

***

Will clings to consciousness and observes the men working frantically to save his life.

Suddenly, the pulse monitor linked to Will's body flat-lines—his heart stops. One EMT quickly grabs the defibrillator and the other checks the machine, then urgently feels for a pulse from Will's inert body. "We're losing him!"

"Clear!" The first EMT hurriedly backs out of the way, allowing the second to press the pads to Will's chest, sending an electric charge flowing through his body.

Will watches everything but feels nothing. He has time to notice—with thankful satisfaction—how hard the two men are trying to save his life. Will hovers over his own body for a moment before he feels a hidden force pulling his soul away. Will never thinks to resist; it just feels too right. He turns his attention from his inert form and the activity surrounding it as he flows up through the roof of the ambulance into the night sky. He relishes the feelings of peace and acceptance coursing through his soul and enveloping him in a white light. Straining his eyes, he catches a glimpse of what could only be the gates of Heaven above him. "Lord, I'm coming home!"

Suddenly, Will feels a new force, equally as strong as the first. But this force pulls him downward and fills his soul with ice cold fear and menace. Will cries out in pain and anguish, feeling the two forces battle for supremacy. He is enveloped in fear and dread; the new force begins to win the tug-of-war over his soul. He reaches toward the light in vain. "Oh, God, please. No!"

SIX

DANIEL MOORE, JR. stands behind the podium on a collapsible stage. On a clear, crisp fall day, he addresses the crowd gathered in front of the White House with the enthusiasm spurred by a profound belief in the cause he champions. Daniel does not look his 56 years of age. His salt-and-pepper hair goes well with the depth of his pale blue eyes. If he had been asked when he was 25 if he thought he would ever be President of the United States, he would have laughed the questioner out of the room. Sometimes life throws a curve ball, and a man ends up in places doing things he never would have dreamed.

Twenty years ago, life's curve ball was more like a fast ball, and it hit Daniel right between the eyes. Daniel thinks back to that day often, without ever failing to wish that the fast ball would have killed him instead. Most people dream of being president; Daniel is just fighting his way through a nightmare. Twenty years ago, Daniel was given a job to do, and he will not rest until it's done.

He is on the cusp of being arguably the most profound president in America's history. Depending on political affiliation, people either look at Daniel as heaven-sent, as most of the world's poor do, or, like the rich elite, they look at him as the devil himself.

***

The crowd hangs on his every word, never missing a chance to burst out in applause.

"The number of children dying from hunger and disease worldwide has dropped to a sixty-year low. And with the continuing efforts of the people of this great nation, they will continue to drop—until we can say there are no longer people in this world who don't get the basic chance at life that every one of God's children deserves!" Daniel concludes his speech with a wave of his hand toward the crowd. The people respond with intense applause and cheers of approval and affection. Michael Miles, the Mayor of D.C., meets Daniel as he steps away from the podium. The two men shake hands and trade positions.

Michael takes the podium. "The President of the United States, everyone." The crowd erupts again when Daniel leaves the stage. Daniel waves one more time before sliding from view behind the stage where he is quickly flanked by secret service agents. Walking toward the White House, Daniel is met by his chief of staff, Josh Weedy, who is followed by John Powers, a new intern.

"Wow, Dan, that was a hell of a speech." Josh shakes his hand. "Congress will be hard pressed to block the additional funds for the hunger coalition. Did you see that reaction from the crowd? The people are really getting onboard this thing!"

Daniel smiles with a shrug. "Josh, it's like I've always said, 'The best speeches contain the truth.'"

John Powers seems unsure of himself around such powerful men. He trails behind the others, carrying a sealed document, waiting for a break in their conversation to present the file without interrupting.

Daniel stops before a side entrance with Josh beside him and waits on the trailing intern. The president winks conspiratorially at Josh, who pretends not to notice. "What's on your mind, John?"

John abruptly stops and stammers a nervous response, "Uh, M-M-Mr. President, sir, sorry to bother you."

"How many times have I told you to call me Daniel?"

John's nervousness escalates as Daniel faces him, hands clasped behind him in casual observation. "Sorry, sir," John says.

"I guess that will have to do. What do you have for me?"

John holds the file out in front of him, face-up toward Daniel. The words:

PRESIDENT DANIEL MOORE'S EYES ONLY

are clearly visible in big, bold, black letters on the cover.

Josh watches amused. Daniel looks expectantly from the file back to John without taking it. John looks uncomfortably confused, waiting to be relieved of the awkward document.

"Well, what's in it?" Daniel asks.

John stammers in apprehension. "I don't know! I didn't open it, Mr. President . . . I mean sir . . . I mean, Daniel . . . sir."

Daniel waits a long second before he smiles and breaks the tension. He playfully slaps John on the back, then takes the file. "Just messing with you, John. Believe it or not, we like to keep things light and have a little fun around here."

"Uh, understood, sir, I mean, Daniel." John abruptly turns and flees from the two men who burst out in laughter at the new intern's struggles.

"Jeeze, Dan," Josh said, "you're going to have to take it easy on the interns; you're going to give that man a heart attack!"

"They have to learn the ropes sometime; it might as well be sooner than later."

Josh nods his head in agreement, then both men simultaneously turn their attention to the file resting in Dan's hands. Josh looks at Daniel questioningly. "What do you think this is about?"

Daniel shrugs in bewilderment. "You know, I usually have some kind of idea what's in these things, but this one is completely out of the blue. I don't have a clue."

"That's a bit unusual."

Daniel fingers the document while the two men contemplate its contents. Slapping the file against his other hand, Daniel breaks the silence. "Well, there's only one way to find out what's inside. If I don't get too tied up, I'll meet you for lunch, and, if I can, I'll let you know what's in this thing."

"Sounds good." The two men nod goodbye and enter the building. They head in opposite directions.

SEVEN

Angie Peoples grew up hard. She came from a broken home in a poor neighborhood in Louisville, Kentucky. She was barely noticed by her mother, who was too involved with drugs and alcohol to see the abuse Angie suffered at the hands of her stepfather.

Angie ran away from home when she was 13. She spent a couple of dark weeks on the street, clinging precariously to her sanity, dodging other streetwalkers, whose morals were corrupted enough to see an obviously underage girl as an easy target.

When she left, she had taken some money from her stepfather's wallet while he was passed out on the living room couch. She had managed to eat enough to survive for a while. But that money was almost completely gone when she got lucky and found a home with an older couple who came across her sleeping on a park bench early one morning.

***

Sam and Betty Jones saw right away that this girl came from a bad place, so instead of trying to find her parents, they took her in and decided to raise her as their own. They were a loving Christian couple with firm beliefs in the importance of education, both being retired school teachers. Though it took a while, they were able to complete the process of adopting her as their own. They home-schooled Angie, so it didn't take them long to discover just how intelligent this girl was. They taught her everything at an accelerated pace—from foreign languages to political science. They treated her like their little experiment. Angie had an unquenchable thirst for knowledge, equal to their desire to teach her. The three of them spent most of their waking moments in various discussions and debates on different subjects and current events.

Sam and Betty took Angie on countless trips around the world to show her first-hand the things other students only experienced in books or on television. By Angie's 18th birthday, she tested well enough to get scholarship offers from any university she wanted to attend. She got a degree in anthropology from Tulane.

***

Angie didn't really know what to do when she graduated; all she did know was she wanted to help people who grew up like herself.

After college in New Orleans, she went back to her adoptive home to visit for a while. She couldn't help but notice the new senator when he held a rally in town. Angie went with Sam and Betty to the event and found herself deeply moved by the man's passion and message. She left the event with the idea that this senator was someone she could support. She got her resume together and emailed it to the senator's office along with a detailed cover letter. She was more surprised than anyone when a couple of months later she found in the mail an invitation for an interview. She landed a job as a secretary for the senator's personal assistant. Karen was an older lady nearing the end of her career. Angie stepped in and made an immediate impression on everyone.

Karen didn't take long in deciding this young woman would be her ideal replacement. When she suggested it to Daniel, he was at first hesitant; they had already targeted another staff member as a future replacement. Karen knew this but pushed anyway. In the end, it came down to the fact that Angie showed herself to be too indispensable in too many areas not to get the job.

It was with mixed feelings that Daniel took her on, but those were quickly resolved. The two became inseparable. Angie considered Daniel a saint, and he considered her an angel sent from above to organize and keep track of the otherwise impossible schedule of his office.

***

Angie notices the file as soon as Daniel arrives from the rally. Never missing a beat, she assimilates the file into her mental calendar of today's schedule. She falls in step with Daniel who enters the Oval Office and removes his jacket. He carelessly lays it on a chair before sliding behind his desk. Angie takes a seat on the opposite side of the desk. "Your four o'clock with Senator Benson has been moved back to 4:30, so I moved your 4:30 with the Defense Council back to five o'clock."

Daniel doesn't suppress his laugh. "I bet they loved hearing that."

Angie rolls her eyes in response. "Not really. General Huntingworth was irate. He says we knew good and well he has to be on a plane to San Diego by 6 p.m. and that we moved the meeting back just so he couldn't attend."

"Did you tell him we're not that smart?"

Angie gives him a coy smile. "Speak for yourself. The last thing I want to have to do today is book him on a later flight, while at the same time having to listen to him bitch and moan about how the meeting went long. It is scheduled to last over two hours, but you always have them out in an hour and a half."

"So you're telling me you didn't move it back because of the fact that the general is the lone voice of dissent keeping the arms treaty from moving forward."

Angie blushes slightly at the playful accusation. "Is he? I had no idea."

Daniel smiles at the little lie. He turns his attention to the file on his desk. Angie follows his gaze and then rises to leave. "Listen, Ang, I need a few minutes."

Angie opens her planner and quickly scribbles in the time. "I'm already on it. I can push back your appointments for twenty minutes, any longer than that and I'll have to cancel someone."

"That shouldn't be necessary." Daniel takes the file and examines the outside of it as if the cover will reveal the contents without having to be opened. Angie finishes with her notations and heads for the door. Just before she leaves the office, the president calls her. "Angie."

She peeks around the door, looking back to where Daniel sits holding the file. "Yeah?"

"You know, you don't surprise me anymore."

"I know, but I still amaze you. Now get to work; the clock is ticking." Angie turns and leaves the office, shutting the door behind her.

Daniel lets his attention linger on Angie. He can't help but think how helpless he would be without her. Shaking the thought from his mind, he returns his attention to the unopened envelope and feels a little apprehension. He tears open the seal that ends up on a document only after it has been thoroughly screened for potentially harmful substances. *When has classified information ever been good news?* He pulls out the lone sheet of paper and reads over it, not really understanding what it pertains to at first glance.

The following is classified for Daniel Moore, Jr., only:

Case # 00119290- Daniel Moore, Jr.
Review 9 a.m. Oct-25-2038

Please make proper arrangements to keep this appointment.

You will be contacted with further instructions.

Thank you in advance for your cooperation in this matter

Agent # 421 - N.D.E.C.

Daniel rereads the memo. He is at a complete loss. *Review? Review of what? And what the hell is the N.D.E.C.?* Daniel reads the piece of paper one more time; this time he concentrates on every word, mulling each one over. He reads the date, October 25, 2038. *October 25th!* Daniel turns in his chair and grabs a picture of a young woman, smiling, holding hands with a pretty blond girl of about 7, also smiling. He stares at the picture with an intense pain mixed with regret. Talking to himself, he grips the picture. "Why that day of all days? Twenty years to the day of the accident!" Daniel turns in his chair suddenly and hits the call button on his phone.

Angie's voice fills the office. "What's up, boss?"

"Angie, I need you to check my schedule for October 25 in the a.m."

"Just a sec."

As he waits, Daniel looks from the picture to the file and back again. "Why October 25th?"

"What's that, sir?"

Daniel hadn't realized he has spoken aloud. "Nothing, talking to myself."

"You know what they say when you start doing that."

"How about that schedule?" Angie quickly recovers from the slight Daniel's tone conveyed to her. "Right here. You're completely clear in the morning all the way up to two in the afternoon."

Daniel shows his surprise to the empty office. "Isn't that kind of unusual?"

Angie's voice reveals her concern at Daniel's abnormal behavior. "It would be if you hadn't left a note on my desk on Tuesday, requesting me to clear the morning with no exceptions."

"Did I?"

"Daniel, are you all right? You seem a little distant and strange."

Daniel tries to shake off his confusion. It wouldn't do to have Angie suspicious of his lack of knowledge of what's going on, even if he was completely in the dark. He had a hunch that whatever this thing was, he wanted to keep it under wraps. Daniel responds with a renewed, if unreal, sense of confidence. "No, Angie, I'm fine. I just couldn't remember if I had left the note or not."

"Do you still want to keep the morning open?"

"You know, I'm not sure if I'm going to need it or not. Let's keep it clear for now."

"Will do."

"Thanks, I'll be ready to go in ten." Daniel cuts the line and leans back in his chair with the picture in one hand and the file in the other. He loses himself in memories he has struggled both to forget and to hold onto.

EIGHT

Will Crane slowly regains consciousness. He opens his eyes to find himself sitting upright in an odd-looking chair. He groggily looks around what seems to be a gray room. There appears to be a fog surrounding him. He is alone. The room, if that's what it is, stands completely empty except for the chair he resides in.

Will calls out, "Hello?"

The room swallows his voice. Will looks around once more with a growing fear. He cannot remember how he got where he is, but his gut tells him he is in trouble. Will tries to rise from the chair, but cannot. He is restrained by bindings that only become visible when he tries to struggle. Will strains with all his might against the bonds. His eyes register horror as the bindings begin to cut into his skin. Will lessens his straining for fear the bonds will sever his hands from his body. When he relaxes, the bonds disappear along with the wounds inflicted with his struggle. "*What the hell?*"

"Exactly, Will Crane. Would you leave so soon?"

Will looks around the room frantically for the source of the powerful booming voice.

"Who's there?"

"And where would you go?"

Will pulls against the bonds again but quickly stops after they cut back into his wrists. He continues to look around the room with a growing since of unease. "Show yourself, and untie me for Christ's sake!"

The room disappears revealing the owner of the voice, a dark figure in a hooded cloak, hovering in front of Will. Also revealed are the fire and brimstone that completely surround Will's suspended chair. An incredible roar fills the air, causing Will to quake with dread. The cloaked figure points below Will to where a hideous-looking horned demon flies toward him. Will screams in terror. The creature reaches out as if to grab him while closing the distance between them. Just before the demon can rip Will from his chair, the walls return, leaving the blubbering and quivering Will paralyzed by the roar of disappointment echoing in the room from the demon.

"The next time the unworthy utters the Son's name the walls won't come back."

Will stammers a reply. "But I'm a man of Go—" The deafening roar from the demon returns and the walls flicker in and out of existence, revealing the beast circling just below."

"Speak not, fool. We know of your deeds in life. A man of our Father would never treat his family like you have treated yours. Your words are as empty as your head. You are of a vile and evil heart. If it were not for the love of that same family you so carelessly destroyed, then your fate would already be sealed."

Will cries again as the cloaked figure slowly paces in a circle around the chair. "But I left them all at home."

"You would waste the time with meaningless blather that I would spend explaining your penance. Utter not one more word, for if you do, then I shall not, and you will be left to your fate." The cloaked figure continues to circle Will. The walls flicker in and out, once again revealing the hell that currently surrounds them.

Being the smart man that he is, Will says nothing more. The room re-forms around Will and the mysterious messenger, creating an illusion of safety. Will remains silent and motionless while the messenger waits patiently to see if Will speaks and seals his fate.

"Very well, this is what you must do."

NINE

HARRY PERFORMS CPR on the inert form, trying valiantly to revive his patient. Clyde stands poised with the defibrillator, ready to send more volts through the body if needed. Both men turn to the heart monitor, hearing it beep, signaling the success of their efforts as the pulse restarts, shaky at first, but quickly steadying into a weak but continuous pattern. Harry and Clyde share a smile and the elation that comes with saving someone's life.

"Nice job, Harry," Clyde calls out. "This man might make it yet!"

"Yeah, if we ever get him to the hospital." Harry nods at the heartfelt praise, and then turns his attention toward the front of the ambulance. "Hey, step on it will ya? We got him back!"

Both men grab for handholds just before the ambulance driver accelerates quickly into a turn, threatening to send them tumbling onto Will's body. As the two men continue to hang on, they speak of their plans for the next day. "So, Clyde, can I tell Sally to set a place for you for supper tomorrow?" Harry asked.

"What's she fixing?"

"What else but your favorite!"

Clyde rubs his pleasantly plump belly with his free hand in anticipation. "Lasagna! Count me in, Harry. That little lady of yours makes the best damn sausage lasagna this side of Italy!"

Harry laughs. "Thought you'd say that."

TEN

Eddie Smithfield sits alone on one side of the conference table. With calculated suspicion, he eyes the man and woman sitting across from him. He wonders briefly about the three men at the back of the room who could only be security. *"What do they think I'm going to do, freak out and start shooting the place up?"* Eddie has been a public defender for the last 18 years; before that he was considered one of the best young attorneys in Chicago.

Most people considered it inevitable that Eddie would someday become one of the most feared D.A.s in the history of the state. Eddie had many nicknames during his ten years in the D.A.'s office, and he liked them all, but his personal favorite was "The Death Dealer." Eddie wielded the death penalty like a sword, and as often as not, he could slide it home into the heart of whatever defendant found himself unlucky enough to be in his reach. In the ten years he spent in the D.A.'s office, only two defendants had left the courtroom with less than ten

years, one because of severe and blatant police brutality—
the guy will never walk again—the other because of the
man's political connections with the federal government.
He was able to go over Eddie's head. That's what made
Eddie's jump from the D.A. to the public defender's
office so unusual.

He caused quite an uproar when he did this complete
180, and it took him awhile to earn the trust of so many
who considered him a mortal enemy. Before long his
doubters became admirers. As good a prosecutor as
he was, they quickly understood he was an even better
defense lawyer. Once his colleagues saw the results of
his almost maniacal effort, they learned to appreciate
his assistance whenever they could get it. Eddie soon
became the go-to man for all the toughest cases.

On top of all that change was the incredible pay cut
he took overnight. Eddie jumped ship from his six-figure
salary and landed squarely into the middle of poverty.
Eddie's take-home should have been in the midnineties,
but if a client couldn't afford to pay, then Eddie let it
slide, and when working in the public defender's office,
all the clients arrived there because they couldn't afford
to hire their own.

Eddie stays out of the homeless shelter by moon-
lighting on the side. He'll take one or two cases a
month to pay his bills. In fact, he feels he has been
misled by these two people in front of him; otherwise
he would have never agreed to this meeting. As Eddie
contemplates opening the folder that has just been slid
across the table by the man who calls himself Phillip,
Eddie senses this is one meeting he would have been
smarter to have missed.

Eddie reads his name off the cover of the file, then glances up with suspicious confusion. "This file has my name on it. I showed up for this meeting under the impression you were in need of an attorney."

Sandra's face shows regret. "Mr. Smithfield, we're sorry for misleading you, but in our profession, secrecy is paramount. It would not do for a client to possess too much information before their scheduled review. If it's any consolation, you will be paid for your time."

"It is not, Ms. . . . did you say St. Clair?"

Sandra nods. Eddie places the file on the table in front of him. He clasps his hands together over the file without opening it and assumes an air of confident superiority, spawned from years spent negotiating deals in his favor.

Phillip and Sandra convey their own confidence in the relaxed manner of people who already know the outcome of the events unfolding around them. Eddie breaks the silence. "Well my time is valuable, so if we can get down to business, I think you should start by telling me what this is all about."

Phillip motions to the documents. "Everything is in your file; please read it over. When you're finished, we'll be glad to discuss any and all questions and concerns you might have."

Eddie takes the folder and flippantly opens it. "Very well, have it your way, but I sincerely doubt there is anything in here that should cause me undue concern. I tend to walk the straight and narrow."

Eddie begins to read in silence. Phillip and Sandra watch the contents absorb his attention completely. Phillip can't help but be impressed with the man's outer calm when he knows the file contains information that could emotionally cripple him.

However, with the turning of each new page, Eddie's mood appears to darken. This is what Philip has always considered one of the most critical points in the review process. He has learned through experience that if a client is going to become violent, this is the moment when it will happen.

At first Eddie reads without comprehension; he views the contents as some kind of record of his life. Then he begins to understand the true nature of the information he's reading and begins to sweat. He becomes restless, hands shaking by the end of the document.

Eddie drops the file on the table, repeatedly shaking his head in disbelief. He is finally able to utter his first words. He looks at Phillip and Sandra with an emotional mix of pain and anger. "Is this some kind of joke?"

Phillip slowly shakes his head. "Everything in the file is true."

"What the hell is wrong with you people? This is unbelievable." Eddie paws at the file with anger and frustration; tears of fury begin to trickle from his pain-filled eyes. "Where do you people get off thinking it's okay to do something like this to someone? What am I, the unwitting subject of some sick social experiment?"

Sandra leans forward with compassion. "Mr. Smithfield, we know this can't be easy to accept, but if you will let us fully explain, then by the end of this meeting, we think you will feel a lot better with a full understanding of your case."

Eddie jumps from his seat and looms forward with anger and menace. His emotions threaten to engulf him completely. Sandra sits back in her chair, moving out of Eddie's potential reach. The three men in the back of the room glide quickly forward, taking up defensive positions directly behind the enraged man. "Understand? I would like to understand where you get the fuckin' right to look me up one day out of nowhere and decide I'm in need of some kind of sadistic torture program. What did I do, win a who's-the-government-really-going-to-screw-with lottery?"

Phillip has had about as much of Eddie's anger as he is willing to take. He leaps from his chair and points at Eddie accusingly. "We didn't pick you at random. You were submitted as an optimal candidate."

Eddie freezes at this, looking at Phillip in bewilderment. "What? Who would do this to somebody?"

"Someone that knew you well enough to know you deserved it."

Eddie's face shows the fear of all the negative emotions swirling inside him. He realizes he doesn't want to know the truth of his situation. "That is impossible . . . Beth couldn't . . . she . . ." The whole truth comes crashing down on him like an unbearable force. He slinks back down into his chair with no trace of his recent anger. Eddie looks into his hands. Phillip signals the three men to move back to their previous positions and then returns to his own seat. After a moment Eddie looks up at Phillip with defeat and hope mixed in his bloodshot eyes. "How is she?"

"Why don't you ask her yourself?"

Eddie's face registers saddened hope. "You mean she's here?" Sandra motions to a darkly tented window with a door beside it.

"She is."

"And she's willing to see me?" Eddie looks longingly at the door before taking his head in his hands. As often as he's dreamed and prayed for this exact moment, now that it's unbelievably upon him, he doesn't know if he can face her.

Phillip understands the man's dilemma; he's seen the struggle many times before. Sliding the two pieces of paper across the table to the emotionally devastated man, Phillip already knows the choice Eddie will make. "But it's up to you. Beth is sitting just outside that door, hoping you decide to join her so you two can begin to get to know each other again. Or you can refuse to renew the past, and in that case we can reintegrate you permanently." Motioning to the two pieces of paper, Phillip explains Eddie's options. "Sign the one on the right, and Beth's back in your life, and you can talk to her immediately. Sign the one on the left, and you go back to what you were before you came to this meeting, and Beth is gone forever."

Eddie doesn't even try to control his emotions and tears. He fumbles with the pen lying between the two pieces of paper.

Sandra gasps, watching Eddie go for the form on the left. "Mr. Smithfield! That's the wrong form. If you sign . . ."

Phillip reaches over and grabs Sandra's wrist, silencing her with a look. "He knows which form he's signing."

Eddie hesitates for a moment. With the pen hovering in midair, he looks at it as if it might make the decision for him. "I'm just not strong enough!" In a flurry he quickly signs the form, drops the pen and then pushes the paper back across the table.

Phillip takes the form, then nods to the men in the back of the room. They quietly come forward and surround the chair of the defeated man. "Mr. Smithfield, if you will come with us."

Eddie looks at the three men standing around him, then drags himself to his feet and, without looking back, allows them to lead him to a door on the opposite side of the room from the one where his forever-lost love waits in vain.

ELEVEN

BETH WATCHES THE three men lead Eddie away from her. Never overly emotional, she doesn't cry, and though it hurts to see her high school sweetheart walking away for what she knows is the last time, she's been through worse. She never really expected to see him again. One thing she always knew about Eddie was if he was offered an easy out, he was going to take it. Besides, how would they overcome the monumental changes of the last twenty years? She had remarried years ago and had two children, one 17 and the other 15. She loved Jim, her new husband, with all her heart. The only reason she had even shown up for this meeting was a sense of obligation she felt toward Eddie. If nothing else, he deserved to at least confront her after all these years.

***

Though she would not apologize for what she had done, she felt she had no choice. She had known Eddie since the second grade. They had started dating in the sixth and had married right out of high school. Eddie had wanted to go to law school, and she supported that completely. He had excellent grades and was accepted at Duke. She had noticed a change in him after his first semester away. She asked Eddie about it, but he dismissed her concerns as frivolous. Whereas before they always talked about the good they were going to do to help others, now when he came home, all he talked about was the fraternity he had been accepted into. He would go on and on about his fraternity brothers and what a lot of them planned to do after law school. She would bring up their plans about mission work in poverty-stricken countries. He told her it was time to grow up and put away those childhood fantasies. He spoke of all the criminals and how best to make sure they got proper punishment.

Beth couldn't relate to this new Eddie. Her own father had been a small-time pot dealer in their hometown. He had been busted with two ounces of pot divided into eight quarter-bags. By the time the local police were done with him, her father was in prison serving a ten-year sentence and her mother lost their house to seizure. Beth had never felt that the crime fit the punishment, and, until Eddie went off to college, he had wholeheartedly agreed with her. Now when they spoke of it, Eddie would say her old man had to "do the time if he did the crime." When she asked about her mom losing the house that had been willed to her by her parents, all Eddie could say was that there were unfortunate casualties of war. Beth didn't know what war Eddie was talking about. As Eddie progressed through law school, he only got worse, becoming more and more adamant about the need for harsher penalties and stricter government. Beth knew Eddie still loved her and would remain dedicated to their marriage; unfortunately, she didn't feel the same way. The one time she brought up the possibility of divorce, Eddie flipped out and made all kinds of threats about legal repercussions that could be brought to bear on her lawless family. Beth quickly forgot that option.

She spiraled into a deep depression after Eddie finished law school and took a position within the D.A.'s office. Her depression worsened when he would come home and tell her the stories of his smashing defeats and merciless tactics, often bragging about how the deal he forced a defendant into was far worse than the poor fool should have taken. She actually considered ending it all when she found that cryptic little ad in the classified section of the newspaper.

As she thought about it, she was glad Eddie had made the choice he made. Things would be easier. She felt a genuine pride in the new path Eddie's life had taken. It made her shudder to imagine the monster he would have become had she not intervened, and he had stayed on the course he had started out on. Death-dealer indeed. Beth was well versed in the rules of not contacting the clients, and she would have no problem following them.

Beth turns and walks guiltlessly through the door of her choosing as Eddie is guided through a door not *really* of his choosing,

TWELVE

Senator Anthony Higgins studies Phillip intently as the younger man gazes out over the city. He loves Phillip like a son and knows when something is bothering him. He also knows Phillip is fiercely independent, and if he pries, it will only make him less likely to share what's troubling him. So the senator waits patiently. He didn't make it this far in life and politics by being a bull-headed ass . . . although he can think of more than one man who has. That was never his style, thank God.

Anthony got his start in politics on the local level almost fifty years ago. Anthony's dad, sheriff of their tiny mountain town tucked in a small corner of Arizona, instilled in him growing up the importance of working to make a positive difference in the world around him. Anthony really looked up to his dad, and he took his lessons to heart. He went to work for his father right out of high school, patrolling the back roads of their large, sparsely populated county.

Late one night, during Anthony's rounds, he had noticed a glow in the distance. Only one piece of occupied land was out that way. The Olsen family lived on a big ranch that ran from a dead-end road to a small canyon that bordered it on three sides. Anthony usually turned around a mile from the house so he wouldn't risk disturbing the Olsen family's sleep. Old man Olsen and his two sons got up before the crack of dawn to start their daily chores. The Olsens also had three daughters, one less than 2 years old.

When Anthony noticed that glow, he did what came naturally. He hit the siren, turned on his blue lights and gunned the engine. The Olsens slept light and they heard Anthony's sirens approaching. The whole family rushed into the yard just as he pulled into the drive. Smoke and flames were quickly engulfing the house. Anthony jumped from the vehicle and immediately got a head count. The only one missing was baby Zoe. Suddenly, they all heard the little girl scream. Anthony looked up and saw right where the scream came from. Like a flash, he climbed up a corner of the wrap-around porch onto the second floor balcony. He jumped right through an open window into a smoke-filled room.

The whole family watched in silent horror, hoping like crazy he could save their little baby. And just when they started to think it had been too long and that he couldn't possibly make it out alive, Anthony burst from the window with little Zoe. He suffered a couple burns but that little girl made it out without a scratch on her.

***

The rest is history. Whether he wanted it or not, he received credit for the quick thinking that saved the lives of an entire family of eight. It became pretty easy-sailing as far as political advancement was concerned. Everybody loves a hero, and on top of that, Anthony turned out to be a pretty darn good representative of his people.

After becoming mayor of his town at the age of twenty-five, he made the kind of moves and decisions that got him quickly noticed by the state Democratic Party. One thing led to another, and another led him to his present position.

***

Anthony has always held true to the principles his father taught him. He has a deep-seated belief in the project he secretly started so many years ago, and he has never regretted the day he put Phillip in charge of the N.D.E.C. The senator takes a moment to enjoy the view of the city as well. It's windy this high up, and he likes the feeling of the wind whipping around his long white hair. The senator may be pushing 70, but he doesn't look it, and more importantly, he doesn't feel it.

Both men enjoy the shared silence, but Phillip finally breaks it. "I never get tired of this view."

"The world from a distance is always better for the eyes and the soul."

"But why? Why can't it be this pure up close?" Phillip questions.

"The answer to that is easier realized than spoken," Higgins replies.

Phillip looks over at Higgins. "I don't follow."

Higgins chuckles warmly at a joke only he understands. "Exactly!"

Phillip continues to look at Higgins, not understanding.

Higgins quickly recovers his thoughtful demeanor. "Sorry. I think what I mean is when a person looks at the world from afar, it's purer because he sees it without his influence. But when he looks at the world up close, he sees a view obscured by his own connection to his surroundings. Which simply means we go through our day seeing everything around us through the view of how it pertains to us."

"I should know better by now than to ask you rhetorical questions."

Both men chuckle. After a quick moment, Higgins' demeanor turns somber. "As much as I hate to end our philosophical wandering, I think it's time we got down to the business at hand."

Phillip refocuses his attention back over the balcony. "The oral report that follows is as true to the facts as I know them to be."

Higgins casually leans against the rail, listening to Phillip's report. "Heard and understood."

"We have five reviews this month. Of the five, one has been concluded."

"Did everything follow due course and process?"

"Completely."

"What about the other four?"

"Of the four, three fall within all normal preset parameters."

Higgins turns his head and gives Phillip his complete attention. "And the other?"

Phillip continues to stare out over the city. "The last has a quality that falls outside the normal established parameters."

"How so?"

Phillip finally turns to face the senator. "Noted public figure."

The senator nods his head in understanding. "Influential?"

"Very."

Higgins removes himself from the rail while he considers this, and Phillip follows suit. "We both know you can't disclose personal information of the clients. But if this person could destabilize the program in any way, you are obligated to seek my counsel."

"I'm aware of that."

Higgins looks at Phillip expectantly, waiting to see if he is going to disclose the information. "Well?"

"I have followed protocol exactly and, having weighed all the facts, determined that at this point, I shouldn't approach you for counsel."

Higgins relaxes slightly at Phillip's statement. "Phillip, you've run this operation for over ten years now, and I must admit it's never run smoother. So I think you've earned my trust."

Phillip smiles in appreciation at the senator's compliment. "Thank you, senator. That means a lot."

Sharing a warm handshake, the two men say their farewells. "Just promise me at the first sign of trouble you'll let me know."

"You have my word."

"Good enough. Now if you'll excuse me, Phillip, I've got a meeting with the Arizona Teacher's Union rep, and I'm already ten minutes late."

"Don't let me hold you up."

Senator Higgins leaves the balcony to Phillip, who watches the senator leave, then returns to the view. He thinks back to when he first met the senator as a field man in the F.B.I. Phillip had been following a lead on a terrorist operating in the D.C. area. He followed a tip he had picked up from one of his local informants. The man had a line on everything of any size going down in the city. Phillip kept the man out of jail on small-time drug charges in exchange for information on major gun transactions. The man kept Phillip in the loop because he never wanted to know who sold the guns. Phillip wanted to know who bought them. The man's tip led Phillip to a warehouse where the F.B.I. caught the terrorist red-handed with enough guns and explosives to equip a small army. Phillip also found detailed plans to blow up the office building of his now-good-friend Senator Higgins—a small building where a few other offices were filled with low-level political appointees. Everybody assumed but never proved Anthony was the target. When Phillip approached the senator with the information, the two men had formed an immediate bond. After a couple of years of the senator's good-natured pressure, Phillip had finally agreed to take a position in the ultra-secret N.D.E.C. After his initial debriefing, he fell in love with the job and quickly worked his way through the ranks to the position of director of operations. Phillip had been top dog in the N.D.E.C. for the last ten years.

Phillip leaves the railing and heads back into his office only to find the senator in quiet conversation with Sandra. Both look up surprised by his intrusion. The senator quickly says his goodbyes and leaves. Sandra covers her slightly guilty look with one of exasperation. Phillip casually walks across the room to where she is standing. "I thought Anthony had left five minutes ago."

"I stopped him on the way out. I hadn't seen him in a while, so I wanted to catch up."

Phillip nods, then pauses, remembering Sandra is supposed to be at the dentist. "Didn't you have a dentist appointment this morning?"

Sandra throws up her hands in frustration. "Yes, I did, and wouldn't you know it? I get to my appointment and sit there for twenty minutes before the receptionist thinks to tell me Dr. Keagan is sick and won't be in today. She is 'so sorry.' She thought she called everyone and rescheduled but somehow must have missed me."

Phillip gives her a quick squeeze as he heads toward his desk. "Tough break; I know that tooth has been giving you fits. Did the receptionist reschedule your appointment?"

"Yeah, for next Tuesday."

Phillip looks up with concern. "You won't be here next Tuesday."

"I know. I'm going to wait till Tuesday morning then call and reschedule."

"Nice."

Sandra follows Phillip to his desk. "By the way," he asks, "have you set up the next review?"

"Everything is in place for Friday. The subject will be present." Sandra looks at Phillip hopefully. "Though I must admit the one after is looking far more difficult. Did Higgins have any suggestions?"

Phillip looks at Sandra with surprise. "You know Higgins can't help. He would have to know who the subject is."

"I know. I just thought maybe in this case we might make an exception."

Phillip's look turns stern. "We've already been through this. There are no exceptions to our policies. They've been in place since the very beginning back in 2012."

"I know, Phillip, but we've only been doing case reviews two and a half years, and we've never encountered a situation close to this explosive!"

"Listen, Sandra, if you don't think you can get the job done, then let me know, so I can find someone who can."

Phillip's mood softens after he sees the hurt on Sandra's face from his harsh words. He moves closer to her and takes her hand gently in his own. "I'm sorry. I shouldn't have said that. You have been the rock I have leaned on for the last ten years. And in all that time you have never let me down once." Sandra looks into Phillip's eyes with emotion. "I would be a fool to think I could ever replace you!" he continues. "And I know I'm asking you to do the impossible. But who else could I ask except the person I've seen do the impossible over and over again?"

Sandra lowers her head slightly. "Now you're just buttering me up."

Phillip raises her head gently with his hand and looks into her tear-filled eyes. They both smile warmly. "Maybe so, but everything I said is true."

"Yeah, I guess you're right." Sandra laughs slightly.

Phillip laughs too. "There's the girl I know and love." He looks at her with concern. "You got this?"

Sandra brushes away her tears, and nods yes. "Yeah. Yeah, I got this."

Phillip smiles widely. He then turns and grabs his jacket and throws it on. "Great, because I have a meeting I'm going to be late for if I don't get my ass in gear!" He moves to the door.

Sandra turns and follows him. "Well, then let me help you." She playfully kicks him in the rear as he leaves the room.

"I guess I had that coming," Phillip calls over his shoulder.

And that's not all either," she calls back, grinning. But the smile Sandra wears at the end of their playful banter, fades to a look of apprehension.

THIRTEEN

From the backseat of the White House limo, Daniel Moore watches Angie go over his upcoming appointments. He wonders if he has ever had a more dedicated colleague and friend. He has thought more than once about what the two of them might have had. Daniel felt no attraction toward Angie when he first met her. Hell, he was too preoccupied with his political career to notice any woman. He had politely turned down the advance of more than a few. A couple of them had taken his refusal as an insult, but that was their problem. Unlike the vast majority of politicians, he did not take advantage of the many beautiful women willing to advance themselves any way possible. When he thought about it, he never blamed the women or had any less respect for them. Any man who had a problem with a woman's sexual tactics used to get ahead suffered from the intense jealousy of not being able to duplicate them. *Any means necessary is the golden rule for political advancement.* If more politicians thought a little more about their ideals instead of dwelling on their fanatical drive to get to the top, they would have a better chance of eventually reaching their goals. How many had reached the summit only to fall to the scandals of the wrongs they committed to get there.

No, Daniel's attraction to Angie had grown over time really without his knowledge. The positive qualities of the woman's personality, coupled with her unfailing loyalty, showed up in everything she did. Plus she was one of the few women in his life who hadn't made advancements toward him. *Apparently, being president is a hell of an aphrodisiac.* Angie just kept on being Angie, and the more she stayed the same, the deeper his feelings became. Daniel had come to love her truthfulness, determination and belief in the greater good. And unlike him, she had come by her attributes honestly. Daniel lately had to fight an internal battle with himself over whether to tell Angie his feelings. More than once he had made up his mind to approach her. Then he would remember the truth of his life. He would remember that moment out of time he had spent all those years ago, face to face with his true self and his failures. In an instant, he would know Angie deserved more.

Angie looks up from her note and observes the melancholy smile on Daniel's face. "What's got you so introspective?"

Daniel snaps out of his wanderings and shakes off the transparency of the unguarded moment. "I'll never tell."

***

With a frown, Angie sighs at what she fears is the truth. In all the time she has known Daniel, she has never seen him with his guard down, and she seriously doubts she ever will. She has often thought to herself, *What a beautiful but tormented man!* She has never come close to finding out exactly what happened to cause his unfair treatment of himself. As much as she would like to take the time and try to convince Daniel to open up, she knows from past experience the effort would be futile. So she lets it go and returns her mind to the tasks at hand. "Well, I've got the rest of your day organized, and it looks like you're going to be tight trying to get from the children's hospital to the Arms meeting at 3 p.m. You might have to leave the hospital a few minutes early."

"Not going to happen. Those children deserve far more time than we already have for them. If anything, the meeting can start a little late!"

Angie nods and begins to write in the planner. "I'm not sure how happy that's going to make the other attendees."

"I don't care if they're happy or not. If they want the President of the United States to be there, they will have to wait the extra 15 minutes."

Angie can't help but smile. "I knew there was a reason I voted for you besides the cool job and rocking benefits."

They both laugh.

The limo comes to a stop, and the door is opened by a secret service agent outside. Angie exits the limo, then turns. "Remember your 6:30 with the Prime Minister. The last time you were late, and I played hell trying to placate the poor man's ego."

Daniel throws his hands up in mock surrender. "It won't happen again."

"I've heard that one before." They share a smile before the driver shuts the door. Angie steps back and watches the limo pull from the curve and pick up speed. She turns and heads into the Capitol. If she hurries, she can set up tomorrow's timeline and be out of the office before nine for once. *Who knows? Maybe I'll be able to watch that movie I picked up last week.*

***

With a sigh, Daniel watches Angie dash up the stairs. Reluctantly, he turns his attention to some briefs. The limo picks up speed, leaving the Capitol behind. He lets the documents absorb his full attention. Early on in his career, he learned the need to read at a very high speed. He received one-on-one lessons from an accomplished speed reader. No man sitting in the oval office could personally read everything put in front of him, but Daniel always made the effort to cover as much as humanly possible. And, thanks to the techniques he learned, the amount he does read would surprise and impress even his most critical constituents.

The phone in the car rings and startles him from his concentration. With slight irritation, he picks up the phone on the second ring. Less than ten people have this number, and Angie is the only one who ever uses it. Everyone else calls her, and she relays the messages to him. Though bothered by being disturbed, he can't help but be impressed by her efficiency. She left the limo less than five minutes ago! "What is it, Ang—"

"Mr. President, my name is Sandra, and I'm calling you to verify you will be on time for your case review this upcoming Tuesday at 9 a.m."

Daniel snaps to attention and leans forward, realizing what the call is about. "Case review? I'm not showing up anywhere until I know what in the hell this is all about!

What's your last name, and who do you work for? If this is some CIA bullshit, there's going to be hell to pay!"

"All that will be explained to you on Tuesday. And Mr. President, Emily will be there."

The phone line goes dead before Daniel has a chance to respond. He sits in the back of the limo in extreme agitation and disbelief. *Emily! It's not possible; she's been dead twenty years! Who the hell are these people?* Daniel buzzes his driver. "Lucas, where did that call come from?"

The driver's voice fills the back of the limousine. "I'm sorry to say this, sir, but for some reason there was no trace on the call. I can't tell where it originated from."

"Don't we trace all incoming calls?"

"That is the standard procedure. Sir, do you want me to have an investigation started?"

Daniel sits in silence, thinking over the situation. As much as he would like to know where the call came from, he doesn't want the contents of the call divulged.

The driver's voice comes back over the line with a hint of concern. "Sir?"

"No, Lucas. No investigation will be necessary. In fact, I would like this conversation kept completely confidential. I don't want any of this going any further than the two of us. Do I make myself clear?"

"Yes, sir."

Daniel nods to himself in satisfaction. He lets the speaker disconnect and sits back, lost in emotion-filled thought.

FOURTEEN

DIRTY DOUG HAS seen enough undercover cops in his life to know right away who occupies the black Chevy sedan that pulls to a stop in front of the building he's currently propped up against. He still takes the bottle of cheap vodka that is being drunkenly offered to him from his present drinking partner. Smiley, who never smiles, is slobbering drunk and will probably pass out any second. Dirty grabs the bottle before it falls from Smiley's grasp, and he casually slides it into the inner pocket of his dingy and well-soiled trench coat.

Dirty is the exact opposite of Smiley in that his nickname describes him accurately. In fact, he might be the most soiled man in the city. He is like this with intent—it keeps the cops as well as others from messing with him too much. People are afraid to get the unidentifiable gunk on them that is all over him.

Truth be told, it's all a front—Dirty isn't even homeless. He's actually quite wealthy and owns a fine apartment in the nicer part of the city. His problem is he suffers from a mild form of schizophrenia, and he has always struggled with the social hypocrisies he sees all around his cocoon of family wealth. He comes from old money, and the rest of his family has no problem being incredibly rich while all around them people live in various levels of poverty.

Dirty finds his peace by coming down to the homeless shelter he is currently leaning against and dwelling with the lowest class of the citizenry, made up of mostly drunks, junkies and the truly insane. He hangs out for a couple days at a time, then wanders his way home before his family starts to search for him. He has donated thousands of dollars to the homeless shelter over the years, all anonymously. He also buys all the booze when he hangs out. The only reason he took the vodka is to keep from having to try to move his drunken ass from where he's sitting and having to stumble down the block to the liquor store and buy more.

Dirty knows he sits in a relatively safe zone as far as the cops go. They don't harass the drunks who stay close to the shelter. Max Willingham runs the place and will vouch for any man the cops try to run in. Dirty looks up to "the old man,"—that's what all the homeless people affectionately call Max. Dirty has never met a better man. Max has been in charge of the shelter for as long as Dirty has been coming around. Max tries to save everyone—he leaves no man behind.

Dirty looks over the two men smoothly climbing from the vehicle. These guys are coming from way up the cop ladder. Watching the two walk past him to the entrance of the shelter, he wonders who they're here for. He looks over his shoulder at the sound of Smiley's head hitting the sidewalk. Forgetting the two men, he watches the blood leak from Smiley's forehead. Dirty pulls a bandana from a pocket, folds it, reaches over and clumsily lifts Smiley's bleeding head. He looks at the wound and sees it's not too serious. He places the tattered cloth firmly against the small laceration, then looks at his handiwork.

Smiling with satisfaction, Dirty removes the vodka from his coat and sloshes it around, seeing it's only a fourth full. He turns the bottle up and kills the remaining liquor, then drops the bottle beside him, fighting to keep the vodka from ejecting itself from his stomach and spewing from his mouth. He squirms and sweats from the effort, but slowly the intense compulsion to vomit subsides. He wipes spittle from his mouth and then looks drunkenly around.

Dirty just passes the threshold with that drink. He goes from drunk to hammered. He tries unsuccessfully to stand. After a couple failed attempts, he uses the building behind him for support and slowly struggles to his feet. He notices the black sedan for what he thinks is the first time. Dirty suffers from alcohol-induced dementia, a symptom of his illness. He's in for an eventful evening. "Shit, ninjas have to be in that car! I better get out of here before they spot me." Dirty takes off at a stumbling run. It is amazing how much ground a drunken man can blindly cover when ninjas are chasing him.

FIFTEEN

KEVEN IMMEDIATELY SPOTS the two dark-suited men enter the cafeteria. Keven is a nervous man and instinctively steps behind a column in the dining section to continue watching the men. He begins to worry after they approach one of the volunteer servers in the food line. The two men forcefully break into the line moving to the front. Linda, the server, looks up at the commotion and eyes the two rude men.

***

Linda used to frequent the shelter, back when she was on drugs and homeless. The staff at the shelter were always kind and understanding when she came in. They never failed to offer her any help they could to break her drug habit.

After she overdosed and came to in the hospital, the doctor told her how close to death she had come. She made a vow to get clean. She went from the hospital straight to the shelter and asked for help. The staff immediately entered her in a ten-week program that got her clean. They helped and guided her every step of the way. Linda has been clean for six years now, and she volunteers at the shelter three times a week so she can give to those in need as was given to her in her time of need.

Linda doesn't like the way the two men have pushed their way to the front and demanded her attention. She looks the two over without hiding her displeasure. "Is there a reason you two find the need to push through my line of patiently waiting patrons and horn your way to the front?" Linda is surprised when the two men look apologetically at the people surrounding them. Their facial expressions briefly reveal a depth of understanding she would have never guessed existed.

Chad stands with Mark and looks the server over. He knows from the experience of his job that the people who care the most tend to be the people who have suffered the most. He sees in this woman's eyes a person who truly cares for the people she is trying to help. Chad smiles at her, revealing an alliance of purpose, otherwise well hidden. "Ma'am, I'm sorry for our perceived rudeness and line breaking. It's just that my colleague and I are here on urgent business, and to this point you're the only person we've identified in the room who works here."

Linda lowers her guard and returns the smile while she motions across the room. "Well, that's understandable considering Keven is hiding behind the post over there." The two men look briefly over their shoulders to where Linda points at the not-very-concealed Keven. "Well, what do you fellas need to know that's so urgent?"

The two men return their attention to Linda who awaits their answer. "We need to speak with Max Willingham, and we were hoping you could tell us his whereabouts." Keven breaks from hiding and scurries from the dining hall through the doorway leading to the rest of the shelter. Linda, Chad and Mark watch him go. Mark speaks for the first time.

"Not very subtle is he?"

Linda shakes her head, agreeing with the understatement. Linda frowns at the two men. "I could never forgive myself if I felt I did or said something to betray the old man. Tell me you're not hit men or, God forbid, here to arrest him."

Chad and Mark share a good-natured laugh. "None of the above. You can rest assured our business with Mr. Willingham, while strictly confidential, is noble in origin."

"You fellas look smart enough to find your way through that door and down the hall to Max's office whether I tell you or not, and unless Keven has convinced Max to skip town, then that's where you'll find him. Now if you'll excuse me, I've got a line to serve."

Chad smiles his appreciation, then follows the already-departing Mark. Linda watches them go, then returns to serving the food.

SIXTEEN

THE OLD MAN sits behind his desk in what would better serve as a closet for a janitor than the director of the Hope and Help shelter for the homeless. And from the looks of the old can wash in the corner with dried and rusty spigots, that's exactly what it used to be. Old Max doesn't mind a bit though. If he wanted, he could have kept the big corner office the old director had before he came. But if he had done that, they couldn't have expanded their service to include a nurse and examination room. From the moment Max arrived at the shelter, he had wanted a nurse on staff. The problem was finding space for her to work. Max took one look around his office and thought, *"Problem solved."* Max never thought twice about the small cramped space he now worked from.

Max leans over the ledger in concentration; the hardest part of his job is keeping the shelter finances straight. Once upon a time they had an accountant do this. That guy had proved more than willing to take from the poor to enrich himself. He had stolen almost a hundred grand over a four-year period, from which the shelter has still not fully recovered. The man had received a much deserved six years in prison. Nowadays Max trusts the books to no one but himself.

Max continues to work, unsurprised by Keven bursting into his tiny office. Keven hops from one foot to the other, waiting for Max to acknowledge him. This isn't the first time Keven has come charging into his office, and Max takes it for granted it won't be the last.

The old man finishes the calculation he is in the middle of before he looks up. "Keven, calm down before you give yourself a heart attack."

Keven fidgets uncontrollably while he tries to tell Max what's wrong. Keven has been at the shelter for nine years. He has no family and no friends to take him in. The court system recommended him to the shelter. He had been arrested repeatedly for loitering around the local parks. He never drank or did drugs . . . or anything else for that matter. But he made the parents who took the children to the parks nervous because he seemed to always be there. He just liked to swing and had no place else to go. Keven wouldn't be considered the smartest guy in the world, but his real problem was a complete and utter lack of social skills. He had all this nervous energy and would walk up to anyone and start talking a mile a minute about whatever was on his mind—usually cars or movies he just saw.

Max couldn't turn the kid away. He let Keven do maintenance around the place in exchange for living at the shelter permanently. In truth, Max loved him like a son and often worried what would happen to him once Max passed on. Max's only son had died twenty years ago. Max hadn't told Keven, but in his will he left everything he had to Keven. He just hoped it was enough.

Max can't help but smile watching Keven struggle to tell whatever has him so riled up.

"No, Max, you don't understand. There are a couple of . . . I don't know . . . F.B.I. agents outside, and they're looking for you!"

Max laughs at this and tries to steady his friend. "I'm sure you're mistaken; what would the F.B.I. want with an old man like me?"

"I'm telling you they're coming. They're going to be here any second!"

Max eyes open wide in surprise when the two men come to a stop in the door of the office behind the still frantic Keven.

Keven sees Max's expression and looks over his shoulder at the two men. "I tried to warn you." Turning, Keven shrugs, slides past the two men and leaves.

Max absently thanks Keven after he is already gone. The two men approach his desk.

"Uh, can I help you?"

"Mr. Willingham, we're going to need you to come with us."

SEVENTEEN

Phillip sits side-by-side with Sandra in a small observation room. He sips water from a glass as the two look through the two-way mirror into an unoccupied room. The room is large and airy, set up to seat comfortably five people around a rectangular table. Sandra seems slightly apprehensive and at odds with Phillip's cool, unemotional demeanor.

I can't help but feel a little nervous."

"I don't know why, as many times as we've done this," replied Phillip.

"Yeah, but this is our first time observing. I feel less in control of the situation from in here."

"We're not in control. Chad and Mark are the controlling members of the team on this review."

Sandra looks over at Phillip. "You think they're up for it?"

"I wouldn't allow them to participate if I didn't." Phillip looks at his watch, then returns Sandra's gaze. "I think I know what this is."

"Yeah, and what's that?"

"I don't think you like the idea of someone else being able to do our jobs."

"And should I?"

"No you shouldn't—that's one of the many qualities I like about you. You and I should always feel that way. But you should also keep in mind that just as Chad and Mark take on more responsibilities, so do we."

Sandra perks up, waiting for the news she now knows Phillip is about to share. "And what might those new responsibilities entail?"

Phillip returns his attention to the room. The door opens and Chad and Mark escort Max Willingham in and to a seat. Sandra ignores the three in the room and keeps her attention attuned to Phillip. "You're not getting off that easy. You got a secret. Spill!"

"Expansion. All the way across the board. Fill in all the details later."

"I knew it. This is so exciting."

Phillip motions to the room. "Let's watch. We're dead in the water if these guys don't pan out."

Chad and Mark take their seats on the opposite side of the table from Max. Max's look of bewilderment only increases after the two men show him a file and debrief him on why they brought him there. Sandra and Phillip watch the unfolding events intently.

"Look at him. Do you think he's okay?"

Phillip shrugs, not overly concerned. "It's a lot to handle. I don't think there's anyone alive who wouldn't have trouble accepting what he's hearing."

"I know, he just seems so old and fragile."

More time passes as Chad and Mark go on and on, with Max never saying a word. He just sits there looking lost and helpless. Finally Mark motions toward a door opposite the observation room. Watching the door open, Max becomes visibly tense. He struggles successfully to stand when a man in his early fifties comes through the door. "Joey!"

"Dad!"

The two men are overcome with emotion. Joey hurries to his father and embraces him. Both men openly weep at the incredible reunion.

"Son! I can't believe it. I never would have dreamed I would see you again!"

"Dad, I've watched you for so long; I've seen everything you've done and all the people you've helped. I'm so damned proud of you."

"I did it all for you, son!"

Sandra clasps Phillip's hand, watching the two men embrace. She shares their jubilation. "God, I love the happy endings!"

Phillip squeezes her hand and smiles slightly, more relieved than anything at the positive outcome. "Certainly makes the bad ones more bearable."

EIGHTEEN

Daniel Moore, Jr. sits behind his desk going over some documents. He signs one and lays it to the side. He takes the next sheet of paper and begins to scan it as well. He doesn't look up at the knock on the door.

"Enter."

Josh Weedy, his chief of staff, enters the room and casually takes a seat across from Daniel.

Daniel looks up briefly and acknowledges his friend and colleague.

"You wanted to see me?"

"Yeah, just give me a minute to finish this." Daniel motions to the small stack of documents. Josh nods for his friend to continue. He takes the moment to look his president over. Josh has known Daniel for fifteen years now. He can tell when something is bothering him. And it's written all over his face now. Something is weighing heavily on the president's mind, and Josh Weedy has no idea what it is.

Josh waits, thinking of the past, back to when he first came across the man sitting in front of him. In '23 they stood on opposite sides of a senate campaign. Josh stood firmly in the corner of the Democratic incumbent for the seat in the senate. The man he backed came up for reelection for the fourth time. Dan, a Democrat, ran as an Independent in order to get on the ticket. No one knew much about him, but everyone considered him an up-and-comer. The seated senator had given Josh the job of digging up dirt on this guy in order to discredit his political run. Josh jumped in with both feet and came up empty. No matter where he looked, this guy was clean. Josh couldn't believe it and neither did the senator. Dan kept campaigning on his own merits for office. He completely ignored Josh's man; he just went out and told the state what he planned to do and exactly how he planned to do it. He spoke in terms regular people could understand and about things they could relate to. He told the media he would never take one dollar from any lobbyists and put his financial records on public display on the Internet. He did exactly what he said he would do and won the election by a small margin.

The pundits called Daniel's campaign the cleanest race ever run. Josh's side had no mud to sling, and Dan's side refused to sling any. Josh knew first hand there were plenty of things Dan's team could have brought up. But they never did. Josh would have been fired anyway for his inability to uncover dirt on his opponent even if his side won the election . . . and they came close.

That's what impressed Josh the most. Daniel could have brought up a long list of inconsistencies in the senator's past if he had chosen to. Instead, he stayed true to his word and campaigned solely on his own merits. Josh had approached Daniel after the election about a job. The new senator lacked people with political experience on a national scene for his staff, so after a long interview, in which Daniel explained what he would and wouldn't tolerate in his team, he offered to hire Josh. A very awed Josh Weedy felt grateful for the opportunity.

So with some trepidation, Josh watches his friend work, wondering what it is that has the man bothered and hoping he will share it with him.

Daniel places the last piece of paper to the side then finally looks up at his friend. The two men share a calculated silence, one wondering what's wrong, the other wondering if he should tell him.

"So what's up?" Josh asks.

Daniel makes his decision. He reaches into a drawer on his desk and pulls a document from its depths.

"It's complicated." Daniel passes the document to Josh.

"What's this?"

"You remember the classified folder I received from John at the rally last week?" Josh reads the cryptic message Daniel received.

"Yeah, I meant to ask you about that. This it?"

"Yep."

"Seems kind of obscure. What's this review about?"

"I'm not sure. I was hoping you might have some insight on this N.D.E.C."

Josh looks from the document to Daniel and shakes his head. "I've never heard of it, but it could easily be in the black."

"Yeah, that's what I was thinking."

"You want me to see what I can find out?"

"Yes, I do, but, Josh, I want you to be very passive in your inquiries. I don't want to spook them and send them underground."

Josh hands the paper back across the desk to Daniel and starts to stand. "No problem, I'll let you know what I find out."

"Josh, before you go, I need one more thing from you."

"Name it."

"I need some hardware."

Josh stands up at this and straightens his suit with a look of surprise. "You don't really think you're in danger do you? I mean we can always raise the alert level."

Daniel chuckles and waves the notion aside. "No, no, nothing offensive. What I want is a wire, the best we got, something undetectable."

"You're not thinking of actually going to this meeting are you?"

Daniel sits back in his chair. "Let's just say there are some facts about this so-called 'review' that I find intriguing, and I want to be prepared for anything."

"Daniel, I must object to any action that might put you in danger."

"Listen, Josh. Your objections are duly noted, and you can rest assured every precaution will be taken." Daniel goes back to his papers on his desk. "Now I have to get back to the old grindstone."

Josh reluctantly accepts the dismissal.

Just as he reaches the door, Daniel speaks to him. "Josh, I'm sure I don't have to tell you this conversation never happened."

Josh looks over his shoulder and briefly nods. "Of course not." Then he turns and leaves.

NINETEEN

SANDRA SITS ACROSS from Phillip, watching him eat. She sips at her wine, thinking it remarkable that a man in his position can carry himself with such a clear conscience. Some things she'll never understand.

Sandra looks around the restaurant, remembering the countless times they had come here in the past. She thinks about her first time sitting at this exact table—in a corner next to the tinted windows overlooking the busy street outside. It had seemed like such a blur, like she was being swept away in a roaring tide.

Fresh out of college, she wanted more than anything to join the bureau and follow in the steps of her father. But that was not to be. She had received a cryptic message about an opportunity in a fairly new, cutting-edge, ultra-secret corporation. And if she had an interest, she should be at this restaurant at a certain time on a certain day. She had tried to dismiss the summons and told herself right up till the day of the rendezvous that she had no desire to set off into such uncharted waters. But these guys had done their homework, and they knew from the research she had the kind of personality and adventurous spirit that would compel her to make an appearance. And sure enough, she showed up.

Once filled in on exactly what she would be doing within the N.D.E.C., she couldn't sign up fast enough. From that very first interview, she had recognized the potential for developing feelings that went beyond professional for this man sitting across from her. But that reckless streak the corporation had so accurately identified within her also compelled her to sign on regardless of any future repercussions.

Sandra's walk down memory lane is broken by the approach of their waiter; he seems to have timed his arrival perfectly. Phillip has just laid down his fork after devouring a fairly large piece of meat. The waiter hands dessert menus to each of them, then passes the soiled entrée plates to a nearby busboy. The waiter clasps his hands together, shifting his attention from Sandra to Phillip then back to Sandra. "Would you like a few minutes to decide?"

Phillip shakes his head no as he flips the menu shut. Sandra takes a moment to quickly scan over hers, then flips hers shut as well. "I'll have the Baked Alaska, please," she says.

"Very good, madam." He turns his attention to Phillip. "And for the gentleman?"

"Just a scoop of vanilla ice cream."

"Would you like it topped with anything? Chocolate syrup, or crushed nuts and caramel?"

Phillip hands the waiter the menu. "No, just a scoop of plain old vanilla."

"Very well, sir. Will there be anything else?"

"No, I think that will do it."

The waiter turns to leave, but Sandra stops him by touching his arm.

"Yes, madam?"

Sandra holds up a nearly empty glass of red wine. "Another glass of wine, please." Phillip raises his eyebrows as the waiter bows slightly.

"Of course, madam." The waiter turns and leaves.

"We have a case commit on the Key Largo couple."

Sandra refocuses with the sudden change in topic. This is the first time they've spoken of work since they sat down. Phillip usually weaves work into the entire meal. She had begun to think they would get through the rest of the evening without broaching the topic. "I know. I've already debriefed the field team."

Phillip nods his approval. "Do we have a firm location?"

"Not yet, but Thanksgiving weekend is looking promising. It looks like all the players will be together for a snorkeling trip."

"Good. Let me know when we have confirmation." Phillip looks around for the waiter. "I'm ready for that ice cream." Sandra looks at Phillip coyly. Phillip looks back, comfortable and content.

"A scoop of vanilla. You know, Phillip, that's what you remind me of."

Philip straightens up in his chair. "Oh really, do tell."

"Well, you're so straight-laced, so completely by the book. It's like nothing ever fazes you. You never show any emotion." Sandra becomes slightly animated. "Doesn't anything ever excite you, or cause you to get angry? Hell, you're always so damn cool, calm and collected!"

"Cool, calm and collected is exactly what our job calls for."

"I'm not talking about work only. I mean, just look at you now—we're having this nice romantic dinner, and there you sit, so formal with your Diet Coke to drink and vanilla ice cream for dessert."

Phillip looks slightly hurt by this. "This is supposed to be a business dinner."

Now it's Sandra's turn to be slightly hurt. She quickly brushes away the look of pain as the waiter arrives with their dessert.

"For the lady."

With forced anticipation, Sandra watches the waiter lower the Baked Alaska to the table. She claps her hands. "Yummy, yummy. I can't wait. Thank you."

The waiter puts down the wine with a smile and then turns to Phillip. "And for the gentleman."

As the waiter lowers the ice cream to the table, Phillip claps in sarcasm. "Nothing I like better than plain old vanilla ice cream."

After the waiter departs, Phillip takes a huge spoonful of ice cream. "Yum, this is so good."

Sandra ignores her own dessert, smirking at Phillip's display between swallows of her wine. Dropping his spoon, Phillip suddenly groans and grabs his head. Sandra looks on with concern. "Oh, my God, what's wrong?"

"Brain freeze!"

Sandra bursts out laughing.

Phillip starts laughing too. "I guess that's what I get for being a smart ass."

They both become silent as they stare at each other. Sandra finishes her wine and looks at Phillip over the glass. She puts the glass down, then collects herself. "So, Mr. Vanilla, what are you doing later on tonight?"

Phillip laughs and wipes his face with a napkin. "You're drunk."

"Is that what you think?"

The two stare briefly at each other.

Maybe Phillip thinks for the first time about Sandra as something more. Then his phone rings, killing the moment. Phillip reaches into his jacket pocket for his cell phone.

Sandra picks at her dessert.

"Hello? Hi, Anthony, what's up?" Listening, Phillip's mood darkens. Sandra stops picking at her food.

"I understand. I'll be on a plane first thing in the morning." Phillip hangs up the phone.

"What's wrong?"

"I'm not exactly sure. Anthony wouldn't get into it on the phone. So, it looks like I'm on a plane to Flagstaff tomorrow." He pulls out his wallet and leaves a credit card on the table. "Listen, I need you to hold down the fort till I get back. Here—this is for dinner. Just hang onto it till I get back."

Sandra nods. "Call me and let me know what you find out."

"As soon as I can. You won't have a problem getting home will you?"

Sandra waves him away. "No, I'll be fine. I'll just have the waiter call me a cab."

Leaving in a hurry, Phillip brushes past the approaching waiter.

"Can you call me a cab?" Sandra asks.

"Of course, madam."

Sandra calls after him, "And another glass of wine."

TWENTY

PAUL STANDS SILENTLY in the doorway of his mother's dressing room as he has countless times before; he knows each step in her cosmetic ritual. He has been coming to his mother's bedroom since before he can remember. When he was a young boy, his mother dressed him while she dressed herself. After they were both adequately clothed she made him a bowl of his favorite cereal. He ate breakfast while she finished getting ready. Once he spilled his milk on her bed. After that she got him a stool, and he sat beside her at the old dresser that had a cracked mirror propped carefully on its top. Paul and his mom talked about their upcoming days and all the things they had to do. After Paul outgrew the need for his mom to dress him, he dressed himself and made *her* breakfast, then came to her room and ate with her. His mom always thanked him for the meal, but rarely ever touched it. Eventually Paul stopped making her breakfast, but he never stopped coming to her room.

After his mother remarried, they moved into much nicer accommodations. Now, instead of a small cramped bedroom in a rundown West Palm Beach apartment, they spent their mornings together in his mother's ultra-nice changing room off the master bedroom of their huge Miami mansion.

***

Kim looks at her son in the mirror as she sits fixing her mascara. Paul always stands at the door instead of taking the seat beside her when something is bothering him. He used to always sit beside her, but in recent years he's spent more and more mornings watching from the doorway. Kim longs to comfort her son but knows the effort would be in vain. Paul used to enjoy time with his stepfather when she had first married him. But as her son grew older, he became less and less involved with Alfonzo. Her son had even approached her on several occasions to try to convince her to leave her husband. When she asked him why, he had told her Alfonzo sold drugs. Kim never pretended to know everything about her husband's business activities, and, truth be told, she figured Paul's accusation had some merit. But Kim told her son simply that she had come to terms with their life, and he should too.

She applies her lipstick for the final touch, slides the cap back on, lays it on the table and looks back at her son, worrying about his lack of attention. He usually never fails to comment on the color she chooses. "What's up, sweetie?"

Paul crosses his arms, refocusing on his mother. "You don't have to put up with this."

Kim turns to face her son in anticipation of his well-worn argument. "With what, honey?"

"You know what. The lies, and the way he treats you like property. Hell, the only reason he married you is so he wouldn't get deported!"

"That may be, but it's not that bad. And besides, look how well we live. He provides all this."

"Yeah, with his drug money." Paul steps through the door, takes a seat on the stool beside his mother and picks up the lime green lipstick she just applied.

Kim turns back to the vanity. "You don't know that."

***

Alfonzo, Paul's stepfather, walks silently to the door and watches Paul and Kim talk for a moment. Paul glances up and catches sight of his stepfather. Paul pops the top off the lipstick and examines the color. "I like this color on you, it's bold and fun."

"He doesn't know what?" asks Alfonzo

Kim and Paul turn and look at Alfonzo simultaneously. Kim rises from her seat smoothly and glides across the short distance to her waiting husband. She gently kisses him on the cheek.

"Can't tell you; it's mother-son stuff."

Alfonzo raises a questioning eyebrow. "Is that so?"

"It is." Kim continues on into the bedroom.

Paul quickly follows his mother, ignoring the look of suspicion Alfonzo aims at him as he slips by.

Kim grabs her purse from the bed after she slips on a pair of high heel shoes.

Alfonzo swivels in the doorway to face the bedroom but continues with his casual lean against the door frame. "It's not good to keep secrets from your loved ones," he says.

Kim laughs lightly at Alfonzo's remark. "Ol' Fonzie, don't be so sensitive. We don't have any big secrets. We just keep tiny harmless ones, so small they can't be seen with the naked eye." She throws her free hand up and pinches her thumb and index finger together to show him the tiny size of the secrets Paul and she keep.

Paul interrupts his mother, mimicking her sarcastically. "Yeah, Fonzie, tiny harmless secrets like the ones you keep from the police."

Kim looks at her son with an exasperated shock. "Paul, don't be rude to your stepfather! You apologize this instant!"

Alfonzo removes himself from his post and waves off any forthcoming apology with one of his patented carefree smiles. He motions for his wife and walks toward her. Kim meets him halfway, and he kisses her affectionately on the forehead. "No need for apologies. All is forgiven. It was my fault for prying into the affairs of a mother and her son."

"Such a good man." Kim kisses Alfonzo firmly, while Paul looks on. If he is bothered by the display of affection, he does not show it.

Alfonzo breaks the embrace and eyes his wife questioningly. "Don't you have an appointment this morning?"

"Yes! A hair appointment!" Kim erupts into action. "And I'm running late." She quickly turns and gives Paul a kiss on the cheek, taking the lime-colored lipstick still in his hand.

"Mom, I'll go with you."

Alfonzo interjects before Kim can agree. "Not this time, Paul. I would like you to have breakfast with *me* this morning."

"I'm not hungry."

Kim, with her son trailing, crosses the room and heads for the door.

Alfonzo reaches out and stops Paul who is attempting to pass. "Be that as it may, I would like you to join me anyway." Paul looks to his mother for a rescue that is not coming.

"Have breakfast with your stepfather," Kim says. "You two don't spend enough time together as it is." She turns and vanishes through the door, leaving the men alone.

Alfonzo watches her go, then turns to eye his stepson intently. "Paul, it's time you stepped up to the plate."

TWENTY-ONE

Paul Carter Rodriguez sits on the balcony of his home, mindlessly sipping a mimosa. He looks over Alfonzo's shoulder to the ocean. His attention shifts to the present for a moment as his stepfather grabs the local paper and flips it open. Paul sighs in acceptance, knowing from previous experience he will be sitting here a while longer, waiting for the man to finish his reading before the unwanted conversation can begin.

Paul lets his mind wander to the distant past as it so often does. He thinks back on his life, studying the events that led to his present existence. He goes over the course of childhood carefully in search of something he can't identify.

He thinks back to his boyhood, when his mother always woke him early in the morning, and they got ready together in their small cramped apartment on the outskirts of West Palm Beach. Paul's father, Tony, had been long gone for the day, already working on the grounds crew of one of the many golf courses in the area. Kim completed all the necessary tasks in order to get Paul off to school and herself off to work by seven a.m. She walked Paul down to the school bus stop and caught a city bus to her own job as a waitress for the early shift at a country club—a different one from the one where her husband worked.

Spending so much time together with his mother, Paul loved to listen to the stories she told him of his parents' early relationship. Kim, a very attractive woman, had learned from experience it was better not to work with her husband at the same club.

Tony and she had met each other when they were coworkers at a club in Palm Beach. Tony was a handsome man with golden Latin American features. An instant attraction formed between them. They had married after only dating a year. It was not long before problems arose from the fact that the male members of the club would constantly hit on Kim, wedding band or not. Tony couldn't sit idly by while some drunk old rich guy fondled his wife. After Tony confronted a particularly persistent member of the club, he and Kim both quit and decided they would be better off working at separate establishments.

Life was otherwise good for the young couple. Kim enrolled in night classes at the community college and made good grades. Already well on her way to an associate's degree in business management, she found out she was pregnant. Kim finished the semester she had started and planned to go back. She gave birth to Paul and decided to take a couple years off in order to give her baby the love and attention he needed. Tony supported the idea by working overtime at the club, parking cars as a valet in the evenings several nights a week. He worked a lot but managed only to pay the bills, as well as put a little money aside each month for savings.

Tony and Kim shared a profound love for each other and their son. They didn't have much and lived in a rough part of town, but, slowly and surely, they were improving themselves. Their savings were increasing to the point of several thousand dollars. When Paul started school, Kim went back to work.

The young couple was very close to having the down payment on a small house in a better part of town when tragedy struck. Tony had been parking cars at a club function and was getting home pretty late on a Saturday night. About a block from his front door, he was approached by Dangle, a local junkie. Dangle knew Tony and often stopped him and asked him for money. More times than not, Tony gave the man a few dollars. Sometimes when he didn't have any cash, he had to tell him no. Tony had cash on him that night—a couple hundred dollars in his billfold—and when Dangle stopped him, Tony pulled out his wallet to give the man a few dollars. Tony had done well parking cars that night. But when Dangle saw all that cash, he acted without thinking. The junkie snatched the wallet and ran.

Tony couldn't believe it. He knew exactly where Dangle stayed. The man had a room with his crippled mother two streets over. Tony followed him right to his doorstep. Dangle didn't realize he had been followed; he stopped on his front porch and started counting the money. Tony snuck up behind him and snatched the wallet back. Dangle pulled out a knife and stabbed Tony nine times right on his front porch.

Dangle ended up with life in prison. Tony ended up dead and Kim ended up a widow at 24.

***

Kim struggled as a single parent after Tony's murder. It hurt her deeply to lose her husband; she mourned his passing for several years. She never let what happened to Tony make her bitter; she loved Paul with all her heart and refused to raise her son in a sad home. She doted on him and smothered him in love and attention. Paul loved his mother just as much. As Paul got older, he came to understand how hard she worked to support the two of them.

Paul did everything he could to make it easy on his mother. Before his seventh birthday, he had asked his mom for a new video game system a lot of the other kids at school were talking about. Kim couldn't refuse her son. On his birthday a brand new gaming system waited for him when he got home. Paul thanked his mother and gave her the kind of hug only little boys can give their mommas. She took him in her arms and squeezed him tightly back. Paul put his arms around his momma's neck and immediately noticed something missing. He pulled back and looked at her.

"Where's your necklace, Mommy?"

Kim tried to play off the question as unimportant. "I just didn't feel like wearing it, sweetie."

"Daddy gave you that necklace, Mommy. You never take it off."

Kim tried in vain to hold back her tears. She had never lied to Paul, and she did not want to start now. Kim held her son and looked him in the eyes. "Mommy didn't have the money to get you your birthday present . . . so Mommy pawned her necklace for the money."

Paul returned his mom's gaze and began to cry too. He had grown up in a tough environment, and, as is usually the case, he had learned more of the grown-up world than most kids his age. Understanding the sacrifice his mom had made, he was hit hard with a feeling of guilt. Paul looked over his shoulder at the video game, then looked back at his mother with determined resolve.

"Take it back, Mom."

Kim looked at him in confusion. "Take what back?"

"The video game."

Kim wiped away her tears and shook her head no. "Take it back? But it's what you wanted."

Paul crawled from his mom's lap and walked across the small living room to where the game rested on the coffee table. He grabbed his birthday present and carried it over to his mother and flopped it in her lap.

"Take it back, Mom, and get back your necklace. Even if you don't, I'll never play it." Kim smiled through her now freely flowing tears. She nodded her head and ruffled his hair.

"Okay, son, I'll take back the game and go get the necklace first thing tomorrow. There's birthday cake in the kitchen, and there's no way I'm returning that, so let's go get a piece."

From that moment on, Paul never asked for anything for birthdays or Christmas. Whenever his mom asked him what he wanted, he would say he couldn't decide, so she should surprise him.

As Paul got older, he came to understand the struggle his mom went through daily on his behalf. He knew she was a pretty woman. He saw her turn down dates several times. Paul came to worry about her, and, as much as he liked being the entire focus of her affection, he began to wish she would find someone for her own happiness. So when his mom approached him not too long after he turned 9 and asked him how he would feel if she went out on a date with a member at the club where she worked, Paul told her she should.

At first it had been as if their dreams had come true and all his prayers for his mom had been answered. Alfonzo Rodriguez, a new member at the club, was a dark-skinned, tall, handsome man with a charisma that quickly won over men and women alike. He always seemed to be the center of attention in any arena. Alfonzo had often told the story of how he took an immediate liking to Kim when he met her at the club. He felt somewhat surprised when his initial advances were declined.

Alfonzo, born and raised in Colombia into a very wealthy family with connections and influence, grew up knowing when he wanted something, he got it. He said Kim was the first person to ever tell him no. When Kim had finally brought Alfonzo home to meet Paul, the boy thought he had seemed like a nice guy. Alfonzo talked with the Latin accent of many of Paul's classmates and possessed an easy, warm smile that he flashed often. Paul's uneasiness with the distant look in the man's eyes was eventually laid to rest by his mom's apparent happiness.

After a while, Paul let his guard down and started to really enjoy the gifts that were bestowed upon him. A year passed before his mom succumbed to the relentless pressure of Alfonzo's requests to marry him. She finally agreed as much for Paul as for herself. She had noticed the amount of attention Alfonzo paid her son and felt encouraged by it. Alfonzo decided to sell his home at the club and moved them to his house in Miami.

Just like that, Paul became a rich kid. He spent the next several years living among extreme wealth, but never embracing it fully. He had always been a curious boy, and soon he started to notice things that seemed odd. He often wondered why so many of Alfonzo's partners carried guns and were accompanied by scantily clad women, some of whom paid his stepfather a little too much attention. This was compounded by the fact that Alfonzo would take Paul with him to a lot of his after-hours business transactions and introduce him as his son to all his associates. Paul watched everyone and everything closely.

Paul confronted his stepfather after one such occasion when he walked in and found a woman performing a very sensual massage on Alfonzo. Alfonzo recovered quickly, slapped the woman for her actions and sent her crying from the room. Paul wanted Alfonzo to tell him why they had snuck off in the first place. Alfonzo complimented his stepson's keen observation.

"I'm proud of you, son," he said. He told Paul that the treacherous woman had told him she had something to tell him in private. When he had found himself alone with her, she threatened to cry rape if Alfonzo didn't comply with her demands. If it were not for Paul coming in when he did, the woman might have been successful in her devious attempt to compromise Alfonzo and Kim's marriage.

The first five years or so in their new home were mostly positive, but Alfonzo always left Paul with the feeling he was grooming him for something the young boy did not want to be a part of. Paul tried to avoid his stepfather's attention as much as possible, but this proved difficult with his mother supporting the interaction. Paul refused to disappoint his mother, so he quit resisting. The older Paul grew, the more aware of Alfonzo's world he became. Paul didn't understand everything he was privy to at first, but around the age of 15, he came to fully realize what it was his stepfather did. Alfonzo's operation served as a very important relay point in the Colombian drug trade. His stepfather's responsibilities included establishing a reliable alternate route of entrance for his family's cocaine industry. What Paul still couldn't figure out was why Alfonzo insisted on including him in his business.

***

Alfonzo studies Paul's features from over the top of his newspaper. He likes what he sees. The boy has matured into a very handsome, young man. Paul's dark skin and eyes definitely came from his Puerto Rican father. The blond hair stands out because of how unusual it is for a boy of his descent.

Alfonzo reflects on the difficulty he has when his wife is not with them, introducing the boy as his son to family members. Paul's naturally blond hair always portrays him as an outsider. One look at Kim's almost-white blond hair would alleviate most suspicions of Paul's lineage. Alfonzo told Kim from the beginning of their marriage that when his family was involved, they would be best served if they didn't mention the fact that Paul is not Alfonzo's biological child. Kim resented this to the point she almost backed out of the marriage. As a last resort, Alfonzo had approached Paul on his own and explained to him the situation, how his very religious family would not consent to the marriage if they knew Paul had a different father. Paul wanted more than anything for his mom to be happy, so he told his mom it was okay. The part about Alfonzo's family not consenting to the marriage was completely true, but religion had nothing to do with it.

TWENTY-TWO

THE RODRIGUEZ FAMILY roots ran strong and deep into the Colombian cocaine crop. They had been growing the coca plant for almost a hundred years. Alfonzo's great-great-grandfather, Javier, had been a gardener at the Escobar Colombian estate.

Javier liked to wake up by 4 a.m. The other servants would sleep till 5 a.m. and then jump from bed to get ready in a flourish, pushing and shoving, trying to get in and out of the two small washrooms. Javier enjoyed the quiet and privacy that the early wake-up afforded him.

He had just been coming from one of the wash houses, dressed in only a well-worn pair of sandals and his underwear when he had witnessed a set of legs slide out of view through a first-story window into the main house. Javier thought for a moment about what he should do. He figured whoever just climbed in the window should not be there. He also knew that the time it would take to go get help would give the intruder more than enough time to accomplish whatever devious act he came to perform. Javier decided to follow the man. He slipped through the same window as the intruder. After landing rather ungracefully on his rear-end, he jumped quickly to his feet. He thought that whatever the man was up to, Pablo was undoubtedly his target.

Javier had worked at the estate for the last twelve years, but he could count on one hand how many times he had been inside the house. The only reason he even had an idea of how to get to the master bedroom he would rather not share. Juanita, a pretty young maid, had once shown him the master bed as well as what she considered to be its primary function. Not that long after their rendezvous, the head of security along with Pablo's niece had walked in on Juanita and one of the other guards retesting the bed's durability. Both were executed shortly afterward.

Armed with this limited knowledge of the layout of the house, Javier continued his pursuit. He found the steps and took them two at once. By then he had time to begin to comprehend the situation, and he felt a profound sense of urgency intertwined with the butterflies that were rapidly multiplying in his belly. After one wrong turn into an empty bedroom and another into an occupied one, Javier finally arrived at the door of the master suite. By this time his racing thoughts had turned his brain into a jumbled mess. He never thought twice as he burst through the door with a mix between a snarl and a scream emitting from his throat. It was a good thing too because nothing he would have thought to do would have worked better, or been done in time.

Pablo became instantly alert as Javier flung himself through the door; the intruder had his gun aimed directly at his now awake target. The assassin did not see Pablo slide a very large handgun from under his pillow because his attention and weapon had both turned, along with his head, and were now set fully on the crazed man in the sandals and underwear. He realized his mistake an instant too late. The assassin considered himself a professional, and with thirty-five successful kills, that's exactly what he was. He knew his death was imminent, so he decided in an instant to shoot the man who acted just dumb enough to succeed in his goal of saving his employer's life. He squeezed off one shot that just missed the heart of Javier. The impact of the bullet spun Javier around and deposited his body firmly on the floor. The assassin then moved with incredible fluidity and speed as he turned his head and gun back to his target. The last thought through his mind was the realization that he could have still beat his target to the punch if he had not wasted that instant it took to shoot the lunatic . . . two mistakes . . .

***

Pablo had awakened to one of his gardeners making a ridiculous noise bursting through his door and then forgot about it quickly upon seeing the man with the gun. To his consternation, he fumbled his gun as he brought it around from behind the pillow. He recovered his grasp of it quickly, aimed and fired an instant after his gardener took the bullet meant for him. *If that man lives,* he thinks to himself, *I'm going to make sure when he does die, it's as a very wealthy man.*

Alfonzo's grandfather had not died. Javier had recovered from his gunshot wound. True to his word, Pablo had given Javier the means to fulfill his lifelong dream of owning his own plantation. While Javier had always imagined fields and fields of coffee beans, he warmed quickly to the idea of the hundred acres of coca plants that were deeded to him. Escobar gave the land on two conditions. One, never bite the hand that feeds you, and two, always keep the business strictly in the family. Javier had stuck to those conditions adamantly, as had each of his descendants on down to Alfonzo's father, Hector. The Rodriguez family had become quite wealthy over many years of partnership with the Escobar cartel.

They would have been content to carry on in this manner indefinitely, but that was no longer possible after the brief-but-bloody Colombian civil war of 2020. The government had made a power move to take full control of the cocaine production and exportation from the old families. The ensuing conflict had led to the annihilation of most of the cartels and the deaths of hundreds of soldiers, as well as several high-ranking government officials. By the time the conflict ended, the government claimed a hollow victory— the mass majority of the population never supported the war or its outcome, and the severely weakened governing body never stood a chance against their political usurpers. They were quickly removed from office. The new regime understood the advantages of letting the families operate their drug cartels while the government took enormous payoffs in the way of bribes and taxes.

The issue they faced was the fact that very few of the original families still existed with the resources and personnel necessary to operate anywhere near their previous profit levels. One solution was the partnership among the leftover pieces of the old families. This solution proved unworkable, as each partner would invariably vie for superiority over the other, causing so many problems these ventures took years to come to fruition, if they ever did. The other major issue with the partnerships was the fact that most of the old families had feuded covertly or openly for many generations, each trying to raise its stature and influence in the drug trade. The feuding wouldn't be set aside, regardless of the harm to the parties involved. Another solution was desperately sought, and it was not long before the new government approached the Rodriguezes, as well as several other families left unscathed by the drug war. These families only *grew* the coca plant, then sold it to their established buyer. Neither side in the war wanted to end the production of the drugs; they just wanted to be the one producing them. The plantations were no-fight zones throughout the conflict.

The government presented the family with a simple and straightforward proposition: expand their operations to include exporting the product, or face losing their land holdings to a governmental takeover. The Rodriguezes had no choice but to agree.

Renaldo, Alfonzo's grandfather, had been the patriarch of the family and had immediately moved forward with the establishment of a reliable export route into the United States. Renaldo had the smarts to know where to get the personnel needed to begin exporting—he simply hired the leftover members of the old cartel's stateside people. A lot of them had thought it wise to avoid the risk of returning home to the uncertainty of their country's conflict. They had simply gone to ground in the U.S. and nervously awaited the outcome. The majority of these men were without a family; some because theirs had been wiped out, others because the survivors had disowned them for a perceived lack of loyalty when they didn't return home to fight by their family's side. More than a few of these men couldn't return home now because of a bounty placed on their heads by their own surviving family members. All were itching for a chance to resume their lucrative careers. Renaldo took the opportunity to be selective in his recruiting, only bringing onboard the best and brightest of the remaining talent.

Renaldo had his network in place and operating long before the other families established themselves, most of them being stubborn and too entrenched in the old ways. They tried to work solely with their own people, too often limiting their resources and personnel to the point of stunting their ability to operate. The other families, one by one, changed their approach to mimic Renaldo's in order to try to duplicate his success. Most were able to survive and become established players, but none were able to bridge the gap created by his forward thinking. Because of Renaldo, the Rodriguez family enjoyed covert favor throughout the Colombian government, which still exists to this day.

From Javier on down to Hector, Alfonzo's father, the family had always lived by the two conditions laid out by Pablo. They never bit the hand that fed them—they stayed completely loyal to the Escobars right up till they ceased to exist. And after that, when the Colombian government came to them and established their partnership, the Rodriguez family had stayed equally as loyal. They maintained the second condition with equal conviction.

***

Never in the history of the Rodriguez cartel has anyone outside the family been in the position of command—not since Javier's first day in charge of his plantation up till now with Hector in charge and his body riddled with bone cancer. Hector is ready to pass the responsibility of leading to one of his two sons. The obvious choice is Alfonzo—he is the oldest, therefore next in line. He also possesses the strong leadership characteristics needed for the position. There is only one issue standing between Alfonzo and his rightful appointment: in order for a son to take over leadership, he has to have already given birth to his heir, thus always keeping the business firmly in the family. If the son has not conceived a child of his own, he will be passed over to the next in line; in this case, that would be Alfonzo's younger brother Julio. Julio stands firmly behind his brother and wouldn't dream of displacing Alfonzo. Though if called on by circumstance, he would dutifully fulfill his role.

That is the problem confronting Alfonzo as he looks over the paper at his less-than-cooperative stepson. He has not conceived any children because he cannot. Alfonzo is sterile. He grew suspicious as a young man when none of the girls he had spent time with ever turned up pregnant. It was not that he was trying purposely to impregnate them; just that he was not trying *not* to either. After so many partners over so many years, he could not understand how at least one of the women had not come forward with his child. The topic came up every now and again when Alfonzo went home. All his male cousins and both his younger brothers had children out of wedlock. To have children by multiple women, most considered a badge of honor that proved a man's sexual prowess. The other men often ribbed Alfonzo about his apparent lack of conquest over the opposite sex. His well-worn excuse was that it was his responsibility to his future as head of the family to not impregnate every woman he slept with, thus confusing the line of leadership when he passed it on. No one bothered to mention during these invariable talks that in order to validate his ascension, he had to impregnate at least one girl.

TWENTY-THREE

Soon after Alfonzo relocated to his Florida home, he thought he had finally sealed the deal. He had been seeing a girl he met while relaxing on the beach. He had noticed the way her attention lingered on him after he passed by and staked his place in the sand. She figured into his decision to come to a stop—well before his intended destination, down the beach to join a couple of his cousins who were already splashing in the surf. Who could blame him? This woman possessed all the physical attributes God could bestow.

Tall, toned and who cared if the tan looked sprayed on from a bottle? A natural blonde, not two weeks out of the cold of the twin cities of Minnesota and 19 years old, she had just dropped out of a cosmetology course at the local community college. With looks like she had, she did not really need the benefits of higher learning. Brandy was her name, and she had moved to Miami on a whim, knowing full well the path a girl had to walk to gain the life of wealth she craved. Brandy took one look at the handsome Latin man passing her by and decided she had to have him.

Alfonzo did not waste time pursuing the blonde, and she did not waste time playing hard to get. They dated for six months—the only six months Alfonzo ever spent with a woman when he did not stray. After the six months, Brandy told Alfonzo she was pregnant. She brought it up in a matter-of-fact way as the reason she needed a thousand dollars for an abortion. She was flabbergasted by his reaction. First he hugged her in elation and then he slapped her violently across the face, threatening to kill her for thinking abortion an option. Brandy felt scared and confused by the completely unexpected responses. After he explained who he was and what the baby meant to him, she became more settled and even decided to have the baby. Brandy accepted his proposal without hesitation; being married to the extremely wealthy leader of a Colombian drug cartel was way more than she had ever dreamed could happen.

Everything went great for the duration of the pregnancy and the couple plotted and schemed about their future. While you would not call what they had love, you could call it intense. The day the baby arrived started with great promise. Alfonzo rushed his bride-to-be to the hospital like many expectant fathers before him. He pulled to a stop in front of the emergency room and jumped from the vehicle, running around the car and helping Brandy out just as a nurse with a wheelchair met them. While the nurse cleared the way, Alfonzo pushed Brandy through the door into the busy hospital. The nurse led them to the elevators and they ascended to the maternity floor. As they entered the floor, assaulted by severe labor pains, Brandy let out a scream. She let the obscenities fly when the pain engulfed her. A doctor scurried over to intercept the couple. He motioned for an orderly to take control of the chair. The orderly politely wheeled Brandy from the lobby. Alfonzo stood there watching the nurse and doctor follow the retreating wheelchair. He started out in pursuit before being intercepted expertly at the nurses' station. The head nurse performed the task of spousal interference several times a day. She took Alfonzo firmly by the arm and led him toward the waiting room.

"Mr. Rodriguez, the doctor has to run a few standard tests and procedures, then you can rejoin your wife for the delivery if you would like."

"Uh, we're not married yet."

The nurse nodded automatically. She knew from experience expectant fathers will say the strangest things.

"Engaged then?"

"Yeah."

***

Alfonzo never rejoined Brandy for what turned out to be a very tough delivery. The umbilical cord had managed to wrap itself around the baby's neck. With a commendable effort from the doctor and his staff, baby and mother both made it through the delivery with their lives, though both would have to spend several days in the hospital. Alfonzo tried his best to pace a hole in the floor while he waited to hear from the doctor. Pacing, he had time to contemplate everything he felt within. He experienced a moment of clarity and openly admitted to himself he actually loved Brandy. He made a silent vow to never let anyone or anything harm her. It would not take him long to test that vow to its absolute limits.

A different doctor finally came into the waiting room; he looked around for a moment, seeing only Alfonzo, then turned to leave. Alfonzo stopped pacing as the doctor entered, then lunged after him, grabbing his arm and spinning him in his tracks.

"Doc, I still haven't heard about my fiancée and baby! It's been three hours!"

The doctor looked over Alfonzo skeptically.

"You are referring to Ms. Jenkins?"

"Yeah, Brandy Jenkins! How is she?"

"She pulled through okay, but the delivery was very difficult for her; she will need her rest. I'm sorry, but you won't be able to visit her till she has had a chance to sleep."

Alfonzo nodded, showing his relief.

The doctor watched with dawning comprehension. "Mr. Rodriguez, isn't it?"

"Yeah."

"The baby is much better than the mother; if you would like, I could take you to see him."

Alfonzo smiled broadly and smacked the doctor good-naturedly on the shoulder.

"That would be great, doc. Lead the way."

"If you'll give me one moment, Mr. Rodriguez, I'll be right back to escort you to the nursery."

The doctor left. Then, true to his word, he returned with a large male nurse in tow. The three of them made their way to the nursery in silence. Approaching the nursery for the first time, Alfonzo could barely contain his excitement. He couldn't help but notice the three nurses already inside—one female and two males. As the two male nurses looked over her shoulder, the female nurse removed a baby from its resting manger. The doctor slowed to a halt outside the nursery door and motioned for them to stop as well.

"The nurse will bring your son to you."

"Do you always keep the nursery so heavily staffed?"

The doctor and accompanying nurse exchanged a glance. "When we feel it's necessary. They're bringing your son now."

With excitement and anticipation, Alfonzo watched the woman and two men escort his baby out. They pushed the rolling bassinet to a stop. Alfonzo peered into it and carefully removed the warming blanket. The male nurses quietly crowded around. Alfonzo reached forward and stopped frozen in mid-reach at the surprise of what he saw. At first he thought there had been a mistake, but as he slowly stood, he realized why the nursery was so stocked with staff. Swallowing the profound pain and devastation of the truth of the moment, he looked the doctor in the eye. "The bouncers weren't necessary; you could have just told me."

The doctor dropped his guarded disposition and replaced it with sympathy for Alfonzo's pain.

"I'm sorry, Mr. Rodriguez, but we've found from previous experience that this is the best way, and unfortunately the orderlies have too often proven to be necessary in the past.

Profoundly hurt by what Brandy had done, Alfonzo left the nursery without another word. In all honestly, his first thought was to kill her . . . or have it done. As he considered it, he could think of several reasons why that would be a bad idea. But the one that struck him truest was the realization that he actually loved the girl, and he wanted to keep the vow he made to protect her. So he chose the high road. He had to see her one more time. There were a couple questions he needed answers to, as well as a couple things he had to make clear to her. So Alfonzo went back to the hospital the next day.

Brandy was awake when he entered her room. A nurse sat with her as she flipped casually through the TV channels. Brandy perked up when she saw Alfonzo enter the room.

"Hey, babe! I pulled through."

The nurse eyed Alfonzo warily. "Mr. Rodriguez, maybe you shouldn't be here."

Brandy looked confused when Alfonzo threw the nurse a withering glare.

"I don't really think it's any of your business. I'm here to talk to my fiancée in private, so if you'll excuse us, I'll let you know when we're finished."

The nurse bristled at the dismissive tone. She jumped to her feet and stomped triumphantly toward the room phone. "I'll just call the doctor, and he'll let security know you're up here causing problems like we knew you would!"

Brandy looked more confused than ever. She was just about to tear into the nurse for her absurd behavior when the doctor entered the room and cut the nurse off.

"That's enough, Ms. Jefferson. We all don't share your opinion, so please don't pretend to represent more than yourself when you express it. Mr. Rodriguez has already spoken to me and is well within his rights to be here. Now if you will come with me, we can give the couple the privacy they need."

"Thank you, doctor," Alfonzo said. Storming from the room, the nurse fumed in anger. Alfonzo stared at Brandy.

"What the hell was that about?" she asked.

"They haven't told you anything, have they?"

"About what?"

Alfonzo nodded his head in understanding. He took a moment, then reverted to his truer form and confronted Brandy with her child's appearance and her infidelity. Alfonzo asked the most important question on his mind. "How often have you cheated on me?"

Brandy chose to be self-righteous. "I did not feel like it was cheating; our relationship had not seemed that serious."

Alfonzo dismissed that as unimportant. "I simply want to know the number of times you were with other men around the time you conceived."

"Very low. Only one other man."

It had obviously been a black man, given the baby's ethnicity. And it had only been a couple of times. The guy was some athlete she met at a nightclub. He had been in town playing a game. The dude was too fly to pass up!

Alfonzo chose to ignore all the personal slights the woman had just dealt his pride. He did get an immense amount of pleasure from explaining to her in great detail what would happen to her and her family, including her parents and newborn son, if she ever mentioned anything to anyone about what she knew about him and his family's secrets. He left her with a very real fear for what he was capable of, as well as a fair sum of money to stabilize her life if she so chose.

***

Brandy watched Alfonzo go with some regret; she had looked forward to the lifestyle he would have afforded her. She couldn't believe the bad luck she had suffered. She must have had sex with Alfonzo fifty times without using protection, and then she hooked up with this other guy twice and bam, baby in the oven. Speaking of baby, it was time for Brandy to meet hers.

A nurse entered the room, carrying the little troublemaker. Brandy couldn't help but think, *At least adoption is still an option.* Brandy reluctantly took the tiny bundle from the nurse's outstretched arms. She awkwardly brought him into her body like she had seen other mothers do. The new mother looked down and froze in place. Time stopped for a moment. She was staggered by the most beautiful little eyes she had ever seen. Engulfed by the emotions of love and possession, her tears began to flow freely. She explored her little baby with an affection she didn't know she possessed. Old dreams fell away, as nobler ones filled with a child's future took hold in her heart and soul. From that moment forward, Brandy was now the second most important person in her life—next to this incredible gift that was her son. Nobel searched for his mommy's nipple as he instinctively nuzzled his way into her bosom, securely latching himself to her, for now, forever and always. Brandy fell asleep dreaming of a new tomorrow.

***

The debacle that had occurred with Brandy left Alfonzo in a quandary. A simple test confirmed his fear of being sterile. Although not an insurmountable obstacle, what made things more difficult was the fact that he had jumped the gun a little and hinted to his father back in Colombia his childless days were numbered. This had come as a relief to his aging father, who wanted no controversy when he relinquished control of the family. Alfonzo's lack of offspring had been becoming a larger and larger concern with passing years. He had already gone childless longer than any previous heir to the family business. Alfonzo could not bring himself to admit to his father that he still had not reproduced. He decided to explain his son's failure to appear on an over-protective mother, who would not allow her son to leave the country. When Hector offered to make the trip, Alfonzo easily convinced him otherwise, based on several warrants for his father's arrest out on him in the States.

Alfonzo had to be very selective in choosing his future wife. It was important for him to find a woman with a son the proper age and also of Spanish-American descent. Alfonzo had been very close to running out of time when he had first met Kim at the club he had just joined. He had seen her in passing with her son in tow and had done a double-take because she was a real beauty. He had dismissed her when he had first seen the boy, thinking she was his babysitter because of the vast difference in looks. But he had stopped and looked again when he heard the boy call out to his mother and she turned and answered. Alfonzo prayed that she was single or at least in an unhappy relationship. He had hired a private investigator, and he couldn't believe his luck when he found out the details of her life. The only hitch: a slight age difference of about two years between the two children's births, that and the child's unbelievable blond hair.

***

Alfonzo drops the newspaper, letting it flop carelessly on the veranda table. The sound breaks the spell both men had been under, each lost in their separate struggles to gain control of potentially hopeless situations. Paul stretches, stifling a yawn. He looks over his now-thoroughly-watered-down drink and decides he does not want it.

"Did the paper have any news worth reading?"

"I haven't been reading the paper."

Checking his watch, Paul looks surprised and a little annoyed. "Well, what have you been doing?"

"Same thing you have: thinking about how to improve my situation."

The two men stare at each other in silence. Alfonzo breaks the silence as he refills his orange juice from the iced pitcher. "I want you with me on the next shipment exchange."

Paul stiffens at the request he has feared would come. "When is it?"

"Thanksgiving weekend, down in the Keys."

Paul shakes his head negatively. "Can't be there. I'm supposed to be out of town."

"Well, you'll have to change your plans. It's high time you took an active role in the family business."

Paul raises his voice in anger. "Peddling cocaine is *your* family business, not mine. You're not my father, and I don't have to do what you tell me to anymore!"

Alfonzo keeps his cool demeanor; he knows the outcome of this disagreement will eventually lead to his desired results. "First of all, I don't consider moving five hundred kilos 'peddling,' and second, I may not be your biological father, but I've raised you since you were 10. And I'm the one who pays all the bills and provides all those pretty cars and unlimited credit cards."

"It's dirty money!"

"Call it what you want, but you'll be at that delivery, because you don't have a choice."

Alfonzo nods to a bodyguard on the veranda who has materialized seemingly out of nowhere. He is one of several Alfonzo keeps around him at all times. Paul follows the gaze to the bodyguard, and his resolve softens at the implied threat.

"I see we understand each other," Alfonzo said.

The two sit staring at each other. Alfonzo's very attractive personal trainer comes onto the veranda. She brushes by Paul as she rounds the table and massages Alfonzo's neck warmly. "And what are you two men discussing?"

Alfonzo continues to stare at his stepson. "Just conducting a little business."

The personal trainer turns her attention completely toward Alfonzo, ignoring the grimace Paul aims her way. She begins caressing him seductively, then pulls away from him slowly and heads back inside. "Come on, Mr. Rodriguez, let me help you relax before you have to go," she says over her shoulder.

Alfonzo waves away the woman, disregarding her attempts to seduce him. He can have the woman anytime he wants, but now he has more important matters to deal with.

His father, Hector, has informed him of his plan to announce a successor by the beginning of next year. Hector will gladly make his choice Alfonzo as long as he brings his son down to Colombia where his family can really get to know him and judge his leadership potential. Otherwise, his father is prepared to pass Alfonzo over and name Julio his successor.

Alfonzo finds himself at a crossroads. He has no intention of ever letting Paul take over the family, but he needs his potential in order to secure his own position. His ultimate plan involves the untimely death of his wife and son in some unfortunate accident. At this moment, he finds himself having to show more of his cards than he would like to his troublesome stepson.

Paul still sits fuming from the trainer's blatant advances.

Alfonzo attempts to bridge the gap between the two. "You shouldn't have to deal with such disrespect; she will be escorted from the grounds today."

"You'll just have her replaced."

"Maybe so, but I would never replace your mother."

Paul throws his hands up in frustration. "I don't understand your repeated attempts to incorporate me into your drug trade. I believe I have made it clear how I feel about doing those things."

Alfonzo sits back in exasperation from Paul's remarks. "I don't understand your hesitation. I'm offering you the world at your fingertips and you refuse. Are you worried about being arrested? Going to jail? We got every cop paid off from here to West Palm! We're untouchable. The cops are more criminal than we are."

Paul speaks his convictions. "My father would not have approved. He always worked hard to make an honest living, and I consider his values my values. I don't think my mother would want me doing the things you've got planned for my future."

Alfonzo contemplates Paul's words in silence. He tires of the boy's innocent blathering but must tread carefully in order to convince him to go along with his plans. Alfonzo refrains from telling Paul just how culpable his mother really is. True, she does not know the day-to-day operations of Alfonzo's outfit, but only a complete fool could live surrounded by the drug trade without having some idea about it. "Here's the deal, Paul. I understand your feelings, and I respect them. I really do. The problem I face is that I don't have a choice. My family has made itself very clear in this matter. You must come on board fully, assuming all the responsibilities being my son entails—"

"But I'm not your son!" Paul interrupts.

"As far as my family is concerned, you are, and if they ever found out otherwise you would be dead! Make no mistake about it. They would never allow an outsider with the knowledge you possess to live. And in case you're wondering, there's no way your mother could divorce me without a similar outcome."

Paul gasps in horror.

"It's about time you knew the score. I've coddled and protected you and your mother as long as I can. My people can never know that I'm not your real father. You will start immediately to take an active role in the business without complaints. You will never show your true feelings, and, in January, you will accompany me to my Colombian home to meet the rest of our outfit."

Alfonzo sits in silence for a moment, allowing Paul to fully grasp all that he's said.

Paul struggles slightly with his emotions but regains his composure. "I really *don't* have a choice, do I?"

Alfonzo rises from his seat. "Neither of us do."

Alfonzo leaves the veranda to Paul and his troubled thoughts.

TWENTY-FOUR

YAWNING, PHILLIP GRABS his briefcase and heads toward the exit of the first class section of the plane. He nods with a smile to the stewardess's repeated questioning if the flight was satisfactory. Phillip does not really know about the flight itself, but the nap that had lasted the majority of the time in the air was quite satisfactory. He had not been getting much sleep lately, last night no exception, a good deal of it spent booking the flight and making proper arrangements for his unexpected trip. He also did not know how long he would be gone, so that had complicated matters somewhat. He had packed for three days, and figured if he stayed longer than that, he could call Millie, his housekeeper, and she would do what had to be done.

He exits the plane, having to cover his eyes from the glaring desert sun. Phillip has visited the senator several times before, but no matter how he tries, he can never fully prepare for the stifling heat and dryness of the climate. He quickly descends the rollaway staircase and heads purposefully toward the waiting limo. He ignores the stares from the other passengers, loitering around the plane, hoping to see a departing celebrity. They disappointedly resume their journey toward the air-conditioned terminal after the lone man disappears from view behind the darkly tinted windows of the idling car.

The driver dutifully shuts the door behind Phillip, then quickly jumps into the driver's seat and accelerates away.

Phillip has not even had time to get comfortable in the seat before the limo slows to a halt outside the huge bay of a private hangar. He looks around with some confusion at his surroundings as his driver opens his door. He can't help but notice the running helicopter with its waiting pilot.

"The senator sends his apologies for the inconvenience; there's been a change of plans. He was not able to make it to the city."

Phillip grabs his briefcase and exits the car. He looks from the driver to the chopper.

"I've only been to his downtown offices."

"Then you're in for quite a treat, sir. The ranch has stellar views, and the trip there offers its own attributes."

Phillip motions to the chopper. "I guess that's my ride."

The driver nods his agreement. "For most of the trip." He does not conceal his amusement.

Phillip shakes his head warily at the driver's cryptic words. "I don't even want to know. I assume my luggage will be taken care of."

The driver acknowledges as much. Then Phillip turns and takes off toward the chopper.

Phillip joins the pilot in the cockpit without showing the apprehension he feels.

***

Years before, Phillip had been on a manhunt in his first days in the bureau. He had been a spotter in one of the search choppers. Well after midnight, they closed in on the suspect. The man had been on the short list of the FBI's most wanted. A very dangerous man, he had no intentions of spending the rest of his life behind bars, and he also proved to be well armed. The spotlight on the chopper was too inviting a target for the fleeing man. The pick-up truck they were pursuing had a covered camper top. The pilot didn't use good judgment when he came to a hovering stop, not forty yards from the idling vehicle. The man jumped from the truck and quickly reached into the side door of the camper. There were quite a few expletives uttered in the helicopter when the perpetrator pulled out a "freaking rocket launcher for Christ's sake," as the copilot very nervously put it. The pilot jerked the stick at the same time that the man fired. The missile screamed at the wildly turning helicopter.

Phillip grabbed hold of the overhead support, narrowly avoiding being thrown from the gyrating craft. The missile just clipped the tail, causing the pilot to lose control. Phillip's mind spewed a constant stream of prayers all the way to the improbable landing of the badly damaged aircraft. Everyone on board survived unscathed. The same could not be said for the suspect. He lost a short but intense gun battle not more than an hour after his unsuccessful attempt to destroy the helicopter.

***

This is not the first time Phillip has had to endure a ride since the accident. His job invariably requires it on occasion, though he never enjoys it.

The pilot glances over with amusement while Phillip fumbles with his seat belt. As Phillip succeeds in latching it, the pilot motions to the set of headphones. Phillip places the headset firmly on his head. The pilot expertly lifts the craft from the ground.

"How are you, Mr. Stevens?"

"I'm good. How long will the flight take?"

The pilot levels off and they head out over the desert.

"Flying make you nervous?"

Phillip nods. "Yeah, but I've learned to cope."

"Well, no need to worry; we'll be in the air about forty-five minutes, and it should be a pretty smooth ride."

Phillip does not answer. He looks out over the desert flowing by below.

TWENTY-FIVE

Senator Anthony Higgins leans casually against a decked-out dune buggy. Silently, he watches the helicopter come to a dusty landing a safe distance away. Phillip thanks the pilot for the lift, then quickly jumps from the chopper. He ducks under the still-spinning rotors and jogs to the waiting senator. Anthony smiles warmly and extends his hand to Phillip, who finishes covering the distance between the two very different vehicles.

"Phillip, it's good to see you. I hope the flight out wasn't too nerve-racking."

Phillip returns the smile as he completes the handshake.

"It's good to see you too, senator. And as for the flights, both were pleasantly uneventful."

"I share your relief. I want to thank you for making the trip on such short notice."

Phillip eyes the senator warily. "No problem. It sounds important."

"I wouldn't have had you fly out here if it wasn't, but that can wait for a while. First things first."

Anthony turns and throws his arm over Phillip's shoulder as both men check out the menacing-sounding dune buggy. It idles roughly as if waiting to tear off into the unsuspecting desert. Anthony's look of excitement is contrasted by Phillip's perturbed grimace.

"It doesn't look like I've arrived quite yet."

"Not yet."

Anthony pats Phillip heartily on the back, then jumps into the driver's seat. "Get in."

Phillip stalks around the buggy and climbs into the passenger's seat with nervous resignation.

"The chopper couldn't land within walking distance of your ranch?"

"We're not going to my ranch."

Phillip shows his confusion. "Where are we going?"

"It's a surprise!"

The senator releases the brake and throws the buggy into gear. Phillip quickly grabs the seat belt and hurriedly puts it on.

Anthony looks over and smiles. "Good idea."

"Just don't kill me."

"Don't worry. If I do, it will be an accident."

Phillip is not reassured and just shakes his head at the senator's flippant remark. "Good grief."

Phillip manages to relax somewhat, realizing Anthony handles the buggy with a familiar expertise. He loses himself in the beauty of the rapidly passing scenery. He hangs on loosely as the buggy slips and slides around the sharp turns and up and down steep hills, slinging dust high into the air in its wake. Phillip sits through a moment of terror when the buggy passes closely by the edge of a sheer cliff drop-off.

"That was close!"

The senator looks over and shrugs.

"I've been closer."

Phillip turns his head and eyes the quickly receding drop-off.

"Any closer than that and you wouldn't have all four wheels on the ground!"

"I know; it was close, but there was enough."

Phillip looks at Anthony with disbelief. The senator gives him a smile, then continues on in silence.

Phillip renews his grasp on the handholds, otherwise known as the "oh shit handles" as Anthony steers the buggy to the right of a fork onto a more rugged trail heading steeply up a rocky mountainside.

Anthony swings the dune buggy smoothly through the final turn of a series of switchbacks. He pulls the buggy to a sliding stop onto a plateau several feet back from the edge of a cliff hundreds of feet high, overlooking a 360-degree view of incredible rock formations in the seemingly endless desert. Phillip sits in awed silence, sharing the view with the equally appreciative senator. Both men exit the buggy silently.

"It's amazing!"

"I get goose bumps every time I come here!"

"I can see why."

They walk slowly forward, coming to a stop a couple feet from the cliff's edge. Anthony points out a peregrine falcon soaring through the air a couple hundred feet below.

"I see him! He's incredible!"

"It's moments like this that make everything we do, all the struggles and seemingly insurmountable challenges, worth it."

Phillip continues to watch the falcon fading to a speck on the horizon below. "We've got a problem?"

Higgins looks away from the stellar view. His mood now somber, he turns to his friend. "Yes, we do. We have a snoop."

Phillip focuses his attention on the senator and his words. "Hacker?"

"Not that simple. Apparently someone high up in the system has run a very passive search for the N.D.E.C."

"That type of query should go right to our people."

"It does. I'm not worried about the information they're looking for—that's secure. It's the fact that someone is searching that bothers me."

"I understand."

The senator eyes Phillip questioningly. "Do you?"

Philip looks at Higgins with slight confusion. "What's that supposed to mean?"

Higgins stares at Phillip for a long moment. "I think it's time you told me more about this noted public figure."

Phillip's mood darkens. "I can't do that."

"Bullshit! You know as well as I do that whoever this guy is he's got connections and he's trying to find out about N.D.E.C."

"He won't be able to."

Anthony becomes agitated by the argument. "Well, what happens after his review? If this guy chooses to come after you, how are you going to stop him?"

"That's never happened before. Besides, there are contingency plans."

"Listen, Phillip. Now, I know we've had past inquiries, even to the point of forced reintegration. But there is a ceiling on that type of operation. And anyone capable of running this type of search is bound to be above it! You need to tell me if this guy can hurt us!"

Phillip puts his hands in his pockets. "Anthony, I'm following protocol."

The senator turns away, struggling to control his anger. He throws his hands up and laughs sarcastically. "Protocol!" He turns back to Phillip, animated with frustration. "You know what I learned about protocol from my years working with the Special Forces?"

Philip stands there in silence.

"Protocol gets you killed. You need to learn to be more flexible. Adaptation in times of danger is what helps a soldier survive!"

"This isn't a war, and I'm not a soldier."

"I wouldn't be so sure."

Higgins turns away from Phillip again to try to collect himself. The helicopter comes into view in the distance. Phillip stands resolutely, refusing to be swayed by his mentor's argument. Wind from the approaching chopper mixed with flying dirt momentarily stops the heated debate. Both men turn their attention to the craft flying over their heads and watch it land on the plateau. Anthony realizes the younger man will not relent on his position of nondisclosure. Though it has proven a real detriment to their present situation, Phillip's impeccable moral standards were one of the main qualities Anthony had in mind when he made him director of the N.D.E.C.

Anthony decides to let the subject rest for the moment, his main objective having been met, to inform Phillip of their situation; trying to convince him to change his tactics was a long shot from the beginning. Anthony has known Phillip long enough to know how stubborn he can be.

"Look, Phillip, this is your baby and ultimately your risk. It's your ass if this goes wrong."

"I know. I'm doing the best I can."

Anthony closes the gap between them and places a hand on his friend's shoulder reassuringly. "I know you are. I wouldn't expect anything less. I just hope you'll know when to ask for help." Anthony breaks the contact and motions over his shoulder toward the waiting helicopter. "I figured you would be too busy to stay very long, so I arranged a ride back to Flagstaff. You're scheduled to fly out first thing tomorrow morning. You can stay at my apartment in the city—everything's already been taken care of."

Phillip nods his head in agreement and understanding. He hates disappointing the old man; he just does not feel he has a choice. Phillip shakes the senator's hand and says his goodbyes. "Thanks. I guess I'll see you back in Washington."

He leaves the senator standing amid the view and heads for his ride.

Anthony watches him go then calls out to his friend. "Phillip!"

Phillip turns at the sound of his name.

"You know you're like a son to me, and if there is anything you need, all you have to do is ask!"

"I know. I'll keep you posted."

Anthony watches Phillip reach the chopper and get in. He still stands in the same spot when the chopper takes off and flies back the way it came. After the helicopter is well out over the desert, the senator jumps in the dune buggy and starts back down the mountain.

TWENTY-SIX

S ANDRA ST. CLAIR sits at her desk, wearing a headset and microphone, occasionally typing a few words on the keyboard of her computer. She reads the incoming message with a frown on her face. She has dreaded receiving this message for a while, knowing it was only a matter of time before it came.

On the computer screen:

> The problem still exists. I was not able to alter course.

> Unfortunately, I'm not surprised. What are our options?

> Finish setting up the alternate-reality program and move forward with subject containment. Or permanent removal from the corporation; the choice is yours.

> That seems extreme! I would like to see the outcome of the reloop before considering removal.

I will trust your judgment. I would like to see nothing more than a successful reloop and integration. But if the program fails to provide immediate course deviation, you are to proceed directly to permanent removal. The situation warrants nothing less.

I understand. I'll move forward and prepare the subject for the reloop sequence.

Keep me posted.

END OF COMMUNICATION.
ALL FILES AND LINKS ERASED.

Sandra stares at the screen with worry in her eyes. She wonders how far she will have to go in order to maintain the company's security. She has already gone further than she ever thought she would. She has known of the potential problem for years—it has been one of her primary duties to apply preventive maintenance to avoid the scenario they now face. She has learned some people just couldn't be swayed, and when that is the case, she has to be willing to use other methods. She has been up to the task so far. She has never consciously thought they would ever have to use the removal option; now here they stand on the brink of that very thing. It is her job to use any means necessary to avoid drastic measures and situations, and God knows she has tried, but to no avail. As she sits there, she cannot shake her sense of frustration and failure.

When Anthony had approached her after her first year with the company and offered her the position of head of internal security, she did not know how to react. Of course she had wanted the job, she just could not figure out why Anthony considered her. She could identify several of her colleagues who had more experience and better qualifications. Sandra went to the interview with the notion she would not get the job. By the end of the interview, not only did she have it, she also left with the knowledge and understanding of the importance and secrecy of her new position. Her job had nothing to do with security in the traditional sense. Her duties were to look for potential problems within the day-to-day operations of the N.D.E.C. and to try to guide the company smoothly around the potential disasters. She had been very successful in her post over the years, using a soft touch and subtle suggestions to great effect. She now found herself in foreign territory, not used to being rebuffed so easily. It was time to earn her pay.

TWENTY-SEVEN

PHILLIP WALKS INTO his office to find Sandra sitting comfortably in his chair behind his desk. She looks up and smiles at her returning boss.

"How was the trip?"

Phillip takes off his jacket and throws it carelessly onto the sofa.

"Exhausting, but quick and informative."

"The senator tell you about the snoopers trying to infiltrate the company?"

Phillip is momentarily frozen in shock by Sandra's statement. He stops in mid-stride.

Sandra begins to laugh at his distress.

"You're not supposed to know about that yet!"

Sandra continues to laugh as Phillip finishes crossing the room.

He comes to a troubled and confused stop across from his hysterical colleague. "There's nothing funny about a breach in our security . . ." Phillip's attention strays from Sandra to a gun lying within easy reach of either one of them on his desk. "What are you doing with a gun?"

Sandra looks at the gun, then at Phillip coyly. "I figured to be fair about it this time, if you can beat me to the draw, you can shoot me!"

Phillip stands there totally bewildered by the situation.

Sandra nods to the gun, then speaks with a low, husky quality that in another circumstance a man would find very alluring. "Go for it, Phillip. It's you or me."

"This is nuts!" Phillip quickly reaches out to grab the gun; he has no intention of shooting Sandra, but he does not want to be shot either. As he lunges for the gun, his body slows down. The closer his hand gets to the weapon, the slower his hand moves, until it finally comes to a stop a bare inch from where the gun rests on the desk.

Sandra watches the vain attempt with malicious amusement. She leans slowly forward to within inches of the now suspended man in front of her. Phillip stands completely immobile, leaning forward precariously over the desk. The only things he can move are his eyes and mouth. His voice betrays the many emotions now assailing his mind.

"What the hell is going on?"

Sandra whispers into his frozen ear. "Not fast enough on the draw. Too bad." She takes the gun from under his outstretched hand and aims it at his chest.

"Why are you doing this?"

"Come on, Phillip, you're a bright boy; put the puzzle pieces together."

"I don't understand!"

Sandra shrugs nonchalantly. "That's too bad." She pulls the trigger. The bullet strikes Phillip, breaking his suspension and flinging him backward where he lands lifelessly on his office's marble floor.

TWENTY-EIGHT

THE STEWARDESS LOOKS over the moaning man with concern. He is obviously suffering from a nightmare. She reaches forward and gently nudges him on the shoulder. At her contact, the man bursts into consciousness and grabs the extended arm of the stewardess tightly by the wrist. He jerks the frightened woman into his lap and grabs her tightly around the waist.

"Not this time!"

"Sir! Sir, you're suffering from a nightmare! Please let me go!"

Phillip sees the woman he holds for the first time. He takes a quick look around the sparsely occupied plane to find the few passengers either sleeping or staring at him. Phillip recognizes the stewardess for who she is and releases his grip on her. "I'm so sorry, I was having a horrible dream where someone was attempting to do me harm."

The stewardess extracts herself from the handsome man's lap. She cannot help but think that under different circumstances, finding herself in the man's grasp would be quite agreeable. Seeing her supervisor approach to find out what the commotion is about, she smooths out her uniform.

"There's no need to apologize, sir. From the looks of it, you were suffering a substantially horrible dream."

The supervisor comes to a stop with a suspicious look plastered on her face. "What seems to be the problem here?"

The stewardess comes to Phillip's rescue before he can incriminate himself with too detailed an explanation. "There's no problem. He was suffering from a nightmare so I chose to wake him up. It took him a moment to orient himself."

The supervisor looks at Phillip with concern. "Are you all right, sir? If you feel sick or hurt, we can call ahead and have medical personnel standing by."

Phillip waves the idea off. "Ma'am, that won't be necessary; it was just a bad dream. I'm fine now. Thanks for your concern."

The supervisor nods, then leaves the two alone and heads farther down the aisle.

The stewardess eyes Phillip with a little more than concern and is reluctant to leave the man's side. "Is there anything else I can get you?"

Phillip chalks her attention up to duty, not realizing its true nature. "No, I'm fine, really. If you could just tell me how long till we land."

"We'll be landing in forty-five minutes. If you think of anything else you need, sir, don't hesitate to let me know."

"I should be fine, and thanks again for waking me up."

The stewardess looks the man over. She decides to take the straight-forward approach, not wanting to miss an opportunity to spend the evening with someone other than herself. She just started flying the D.C. route and does not have anyone in the city yet to spend her layovers with. "I would enjoy the chance to do it all over again, in a more intimate setting."

Phillip looks at her with confusion. "I can't imagine how that would happen; I usually don't suffer from nightmares."

The stewardess rolls her eyes. *This guy is either really clueless, or he's gay and doesn't want to hurt my feelings.* "That's too bad." She turns and leaves.

Phillip watches her go before his mind returns to the nightmare. He leans his head against the window while he goes over the dream, wondering about the significance of the recurring theme. This is the second time he has dreamed of being shot by Sandra. Phillip has never been a superstitious man, so it is hard for him to think there could be some kind of message to be received from his dreaming. This is an utterly new thing for him. Truthfully, in all his life he has never remembered his dreams, and to start now with the same dream, or at least a very similar one, he can't help but feel a little uneasy. His rational mind fights against the idea that there is hidden meaning to be sought, while his emotional self compels him to look for it.

Phillip's train of thought is interrupted by an announcement from the intercom, stating the need for passengers to put their seat belts on.

Phillip looks down at his watch with surprise. *It's already time to land! Where did the time go?* Fastening his seat belt, he speaks aloud, "I must be losing my mind."

TWENTY-NINE

PHILLIP ENTERS HIS office, half expecting to see Sandra sitting behind his desk. He scolds himself for the relief he feels at finding the room empty. He took the early flight, so it would have been with some surprise if he had found anyone but the nighttime security crew up and about. It's just after 6 a.m. and the sofa is too inviting to pass up. He takes off his jacket and lies out on the couch, thinking of resting for just a few moments.

Phillip wakes with a start when he hears a knock. He looks up in time to see Sandra peeking around the door. He waves her in before slumping back down on the couch. Sandra enters the office, shutting the door behind her. She covers the distance to the sofa in the company of two cups of steaming coffee and the click of her heels.

"Hey there, sleepyhead. The front desk told me you showed up at like 6 a.m., so I took the liberty of bringing you a cup of java."

Phillip sits up, repositioning himself to allow Sandra to join him on the sofa. "Thanks, you're the best. This is exactly what I need."

Sandra hands him one of the cardboard cups before she takes her seat. Phillip immediately begins to sip on the hot liquid. "Don't mention it. Jesus, Phillip, was the trip that rough? You look like hell!"

Phillip sips more of his coffee before he answers the question. "The trip wasn't pleasant, but the flight home was horrible."

"Really? What happened? Did the plane almost crash or something? I know how much you hate flying."

Phillip shakes his head between sips. "No, it wasn't anything like that. I was booked for the 6 a.m. flight back, but I couldn't sleep, so I called the airline on a whim just to see if they had an earlier flight about midnight. Turns out they had one leaving a few minutes after one. I got to the airport just before take-off and caught the flight."

Sandra listens to the story while sipping on her coffee. "Well, if the plane didn't almost crash, what happened?" She gasps, spilling a little of her coffee. "Don't tell me someone tried to hijack the plane!"

Phillip stares at her. "Have you lost your mind? No one tried to hijack the plane!"

"Then tell me what happened."

"If you'll give me a chance, I will. It's really no big deal, anyway. Apparently I fell asleep and had a nightmare. The stewardess had to wake me, and I damn near attacked her!"

Sandra puts her mug down as she stands to try to wipe off the coffee she spilled on herself. "Wow, another one. What was this one about?"

Phillip puts his own coffee down and retrieves a handkerchief from his jacket, handing it to Sandra.

"Thanks."

"It was actually similar to the one I had before."

Sandra looks up from her setting stain with surprise. "You mean I shot you again?"

Phillip grabs his coffee from the floor and heads to his desk. Sandra's gaze follows him. "I don't really want to get into it, but, yeah, you definitely busted a cap in me."

Sandra lays off the stain, grabs her cup and follows him to the desk. "I wonder what it means."

"It doesn't mean anything. Enough chitchat. Let's get down to business."

Sandra shrugs and returns her attention to her coffee stain. "You're the boss. Damn, I just bought this blouse. I don't suppose you have anything that will remove coffee."

Phillip opens the bottom drawer on his desk and pulls out a stain-remover pen. He tosses it to a surprised but grateful Sandra. "Here you go. This should take it right out."

"You're so prepared—such a boy scout."

Phillip takes a seat at his desk and pushes his computer "on" button. "Not really, I've just been the victim of untimely spilt coffee and have learned to keep one of those on hand."

Sandra applies the stain remover to her blouse, and the stain instantly begins to fade. She smiles with satisfaction and hands the pen back. "Good as new! I wouldn't bother trying to log into the network right now."

"Why not?"

"It's Wednesday. The I.T. guys always run search and cleansing programs. The network won't come online till after 9 a.m."

Phillip sits back from the computer. He tosses the stain-remover pen back in the bottom drawer.

"How did the meeting go with the senator?"

Phillip frowns at the mention of the senator. "Not as well as I would have liked; seems someone has been trying to dig up some info on us."

"I'm not surprised, considering who it is we're dealing with."

"Neither am I, but Anthony was, and he doesn't like it."

Sandra nods in understanding. She cannot help but share similar feelings with the senator. "I can't blame him. I take it you didn't tell him the subject's identity."

"Of course not."

"I figured as much. I've already finalized the meeting and secured the neutral site. That way if anything does go wrong, our location won't be compromised."

Phillip sits forward and runs his hands through his hair before he takes his quickly cooling cup of coffee and finishes it with a gulp. "I knew I could count on you."

"We also have a case commit for Thanksgiving weekend."

"Excellent. If we can just get through this month, things will slow down for a while."

Sandra smiles in agreement and takes the empty cup from the desk. "Phillip, I've got a few tasks to complete this morning. Why don't you get cleaned up, and we'll meet for lunch and go over the rest of the week?"

Phillip stretches, then gets to his feet. "Sounds like a plan. If something comes up, I'll be in the shower."

The now departing Sandra looks playfully over her shoulder. "Is that an invitation?"

THIRTY

Daniel Moore sits in silence by the crackling fire in his study. He patiently watches Warren, one of the many White House servants, expertly pour him one of his favorite drinks. Most presidents in the past would be partaking in some exotic liqueur from some foreign part of the globe, with a price tag equal to a lot of their constituents' weekly or even monthly income. But not Daniel Moore. One of the first things he had done as president was to go through his new home and have all the foreign beverages replaced with an American counterpart. Some uproar arose from a few overseas politicians, claiming the act counterproductive to foreign relations. Daniel simply stated that any man, no matter his station in life, has the right to choose his own drink. He had grown up on fine Kentucky bourbon and was not about to change now. The waiter leaves the bottle, then silently departs the room.

Daniel swirls his drink around in the glass, eyeing it expectantly before taking a sip of the fiery liquid. He then swishes it around in his mouth, letting the slightly syrupy liquor coat the inside of his throat completely before finally swallowing. Daniel got into this habit as a young man when he mimicked his grandfather, who never failed to savor every drop of his own special brew.

When a young boy, Daniel had looked up to his grandfather as an absolute authority. Robert Lee Moore took him under his wing and worked to mold Daniel in his own image. His grandfather was a proud man of a proud lineage who falsely claimed to be direct descendants from the great Southern general. Daniel's family, very clannish and loyal to their beliefs in racial purity, taught him from a young age the superiority of his race. Robert Lee, the leader of the local chapter of the clan, started taking Daniel with him when he felt the boy old enough. Daniel eagerly absorbed everything like most children would. He molded his beliefs to match those of his grandfather. Daniel wanted nothing more than to grow up and be just like the proud old man. And so he did.

As Daniel got older, he continued down the path he had been set on, growing into the narrow-minded, yet extremely intelligent young man with a tremendous amount of promise. Robert had taught him the necessity of hiding his true feelings and opinions from the ignorant masses, and only revealing himself to a select few who through time proved themselves to be of like mind. Daniel had learned his lessons well. The local chapter assumed, within their tight circle, that Daniel would take over leadership duties when his aging grandfather could no longer carry the torch. Everything went smoothly until Daniel met Emily.

A family of out-of-towners had bought the farm neighboring the Moore property. Concern arose as to the secrecy of the meetings being jeopardized since the actual meeting place, an old cabin on the Moore land, bordered the other farm. Old Man Jones, who had owned the land for as far back as anyone could remember, had died with a large lien left on the property. The bank had quickly resold the land to the new owners before any of the local families could put together the money to buy it themselves. Daniel had been sent to meet the new neighbors in order to determine the severity of the problem.

Daniel knocked on the door with a fresh baked apple pie, the standard welcome to the neighborhood. He expected anything but the green-eyed beauty who answered the door. Plain and simple, he had never seen anything like her. She was tall, a scooch under six feet, with dark brown hair falling just off her shoulders. She looked absolutely stunning in a pair of jeans cut off a couple inches above her knees and a white tank top. Daniel just stood there mesmerized.

Emily answered the door without speaking, eyeing the well-built local who appeared about her age. She smiled as she glanced from him to the pie and back again. She could tell right away he was attracted to her, and by the look of him, not a bad thing as far as she was concerned.

"Did you bake that yourself?"

The spell Daniel found himself under was broken by the playful words. He tried to recover, not quite hiding his embarrassment at being left momentarily speechless.

"Uh, no, my mom did." Daniel pushed the apple pie awkwardly forward. "It's a housewarming gift from my

148

folks. They figured it would be proper, us being neighbors and all."

Emily took the pie. "I'm sure my parents will love it. They're not here right now or I would introduce them to you."

Daniel still seemed a little disoriented. "Yeah, mine aren't either."

Emily smiled knowingly at the ridiculous statement.

Daniel shook his head as he realized he made himself out to be a lot clumsier and unsure of himself than he actually was. "Well, that sounded just plain stupid."

Emily nodded in agreement. "Not too smooth."

"I think I would like a do-over if I could, Miss . . ."

"My name's Emily. Emily Hopkins."

"Well, Emily Hopkins, my name is Daniel Moore, and I'm your neighbor." Daniel stepped to the edge of the porch and pointed out over the fields toward the woods to where his family's farm sat hidden from view. "We live not more than a mile straight through those woods."

Emily, still holding the pie, joined him on the porch and looked to where he pointed. "I'll keep that in mind when we return your pie tin."

Daniel waved off the idea. "Don't worry about returning that old tin. Mom's got plenty of them. But if you had another reason to stop by, I would recommend using the road. We're just the next drive down."

"I can't think of any other reason I would need to visit."

Daniel looked Emily right in the eye and responded matter-of-factly, "I wouldn't worry about that; you'll have plenty of reasons to stop by once we're going steady."

Emily returned the look with her own intensity. "That, Daniel, was much smoother."

Daniel nodded in agreement. "Yeah, that's more my style. You're just so damn pretty it took me off guard."

It was Emily's turn to blush and feel awkward. She couldn't help but like Daniel's straightforward approach. "Thank you."

Daniel left Emily standing on the porch and headed to his parked truck. He turned when he reached his driver's side door. "You be ready to go about eight on Friday, and I'll be here to pick you up."

Emily looked slightly confused. "For what?"

"Our first date, of course."

***

Daniel had spent a very nervous three days, hoping that when he showed up, Emily would be willing to go with him. He drove up to her house with mixed emotions. His initial responsibility was to the clan, and, for the first time in his life, he had kept something from his grandfather. He was not at all sure Robert would be okay with him taking out the daughter of the new neighbors before they figured out whether or not they sympathized with the cause. Daniel told himself it was okay because he was doing research on the new neighbors. He justified his actions as necessary for finding out what they needed to know.

When Daniel knocked on the door, Emily answered in a casual but nice outfit. He did not know how it was possible, but she seemed even more beautiful than he remembered. Emily posed for him with a little uncertainty. "You didn't tell me where you were taking me, so I was not sure how to dress. I hope this is okay."

Daniel looked her over with awe and satisfaction. "You look incredible. Come on, let's go!"

By the end of that first date Daniel knew he was in deep trouble. He had stuck to his guns and asked many questions about Emily and her family. He had been taught from an early age the art of information gathering that allowed a person to establish a very accurate picture of another's beliefs on pertinent subjects without ever directly asking about them. He carefully broached touchy subjects in a round-about way and quickly discovered his beliefs and hers were worlds apart. He knew that he should break off relations with Emily immediately. The only problem was that by the time he dropped her off, he had become painfully aware they shared an affection he desperately tried to deny was love.

Daniel and Emily fell and fell hard; he knew he couldn't be without her and he knew his family would never accept the union. Daniel had been brought up to be loyal to his family, so he tried in vain to ride the fence.

He figured after they were married, he could change her views to match his own and then integrate her into his family. Daniel moved away with Emily long enough to marry her, and when they moved back, he had managed to keep a wrap on his true values and beliefs to the point that she never suspected his true nature. Emily had told him she was pregnant, and they both considered it a blessing. He had used his family's overbearing ways as a reason to move away. And he had used the need to raise their future child among kin as a reason to move back. His family, as expected, vehemently opposed the marriage, knowing from previous experience these things were bound to fail.

***

The knock at the door pulls Daniel from the memories of his past, yanking him back to the study. He had been so deep in thought, he is now momentarily disoriented. He looks blankly from the now empty glass to the slowly opening door. Josh Weedy enters the room, and Daniel's present life comes flooding back into his consciousness.

"You wanted to see me."

Daniel, now fully recovered, motions to the chair across from him. Josh nods and takes the seat beside his friend.

"Let me pour you a drink."

Josh eyes the bottle with some trepidation—he knows from experience it packs a powerful punch. Daniel smiles at Josh's obvious reluctance to partake in the strong drink. He shows his understanding by grabbing a second bottle from the bottom shelf of the small table. He pours two drinks from the smoother and much weaker liquor. Josh takes a glass with relief. The two men sit in comfortable silence, slowly sipping their beverages.

"So you weren't able to find anything."

"Nothing. Everything I sent out came back negative. I could do more, but at the risk of letting whoever this is know we're looking."

Daniel waves him off. "No, that won't be necessary. To tell you the truth, I'm not really surprised. What about the hardware?"

"I got everything you asked for. Totally state of the art, and completely undetectable!"

"Great! I expected nothing less."

Josh finishes his drink and puts the glass back down a little harder than he had intended.

Daniel raises his eyebrows at the movement; he looks to Josh expectantly. "What's on your mind, Josh?"

Josh feels compelled to express his anxiety over the upcoming meeting he knows Daniel is planning to attend. "Listen, Daniel, the idea of you attending this review, or whatever the hell it is, has me really concerned. I must stress the security risks involved are immense; we don't know anything about this outfit. What if they plan on taking you out?"

Daniel listens to Josh's comments patiently. "Have you considered the fact that these people were successful in placing a memo on my secretary's desk that was a perfect match to my handwriting?"

Josh shows surprise and disbelief.

Daniel nods in agreement. "I had the memo looked at, and it checked out a hundred percent accurate! If these people wanted to kill me, I have no doubt I would be dead right now."

"I just don't feel good about this."

"Josh, I'll have our two best men with me at all times; that will have to do."

Josh holds his tongue. He recognizes the finality of Daniel's statement.

Daniel holds up his near empty glass and begins to slowly swish the liquid around. He senses his mind being pulled back to the past yet again. He stares past the drink into the softly crackling fire.

Josh studies Daniel closely when the conversation lags. He cannot help but notice the distance in his friend's eyes. He is looking at a changed man, and he is not at all sure it is for the better. Josh glances at his watch and sighs. Further inspection into his troubled friend's mind will have to wait. Josh gets to his feet. Daniel throws back the last of the drink and follows suit. "Well, if that's all,

I better be going," Josh announces, "I'm already an hour late for dinner, and Julie is going to kill me."

Daniel pats Josh on the back as he shakes his hand. "Tell her it was a matter of national security."

"I've already worn that one out. I better come up with something more important!"

Both men laugh as they walk to the door.

THIRTY-ONE

PHILLIP WALKS WITH Sandra briskly through the center of an empty warehouse. He looks over his surroundings with a critical eye.

"This looks good. What's our window?"

"The building is secure until the start of next week."

Phillip nods with satisfaction. "No chance of personnel overlap. What about the perimeter? I would hate to have a bum or homeless person breach the meeting."

"We have completed a full sweep; the building is clean. All units have checked in and the perimeter is secure. In fact, the only people currently out of position are us."

Phillip raises his hands in mock surrender. "Well, if that's the case then lead the way."

Sandra smiles and sets off at a hip-swaying pace toward a door on the far side of the large room.

Phillip follows quickly behind her.

Sandra leads the way into a room laid out in a perfect copy of the meeting room back at the N.D.E.C. The room consists of two chairs on the side of a table, facing the door they just entered. A lone chair sits on the opposite side of the table. The room is otherwise completely empty except for a door on each side. The door on the left wall has an observation window alongside it.

Phillip takes an approving look around. "This is perfect. How long will it take to break everything down and be out of here?"

"We ran three drills to iron out any kinks in the process. The final drill had us gone in under two hours."

Phillip smiles at the timeline with a real sense of relief. He looks around the room a final time then checks his watch. "Is Emily here?"

Sandra nods in affirmation. "She's sitting in the observation room."

"You deserve a raise."

***

Mark enters the room with Chad right behind him. Phillip and Sandra eye the two men expectantly. Mark puts his finger to the communication unit in his right ear and listens for a moment. "Sir, we have visual confirmation of a black SUV approaching the outside of the warehouse."

"Do we have ID verification?"

Mark listens into the earpiece again. "Tech support confirms the license plate comes from the White House motorcade."

Phillip nods and crosses his arms, with a grim determination enveloping his facial features. "Have the bay door raised so they can enter the warehouse before exiting their vehicle."

Mark speaks into his microphone as he and Chad take up positions on each side of the entrance. Phillip moves to his chair, and Sandra follows suit. Phillip turns to Sandra and takes her hands in his own with a rare show of feeling.

Sandra is taken a little off guard by the move. "What's up, Phillip?"

"I want you in the observation room on this one. I don't want both of our identities compromised."

"Do you really think that's necessary?"

Phillip shrugs. "Who knows?"

Sandra walks to a second door and disappears inside.

***

Daniel Moore sits in the backseat of the SUV, looking out the window, studying the slowly passing scenery of the deserted industrial complex. The driver pulls to a slow stop at the end of the cul-de-sac. The second agent in the passenger seat looks at the map on the screen of his laptop.

"Sir, this is the location of the GPS quadrants you gave me."

All three men look around warily at the isolated complex.

The driver looks into the rearview mirror at Daniel. "Sir, I don't like the look of this place; I feel like we're being watched."

"I'm sure we are."

A large bay door begins to slowly open in front of the idling vehicle. The two agents look from the door to each other with obvious trepidation. Trent folds up the laptop and slides it into a slot next to his leg, then quickly pulls a handgun from the breast of his jacket. "Sir, I think we should depart from here immediately!"

Daniel, dismissing the request, continues to eye the now fully raised bay. "Trent, it's your job to be worried, and I appreciate the concern. But you can put the gun away. It's not going to be needed. Now, Barry, if you would go ahead and pull into that building, I've got a meeting to attend."

Barry shakes his head. He puts the vehicle in gear and slowly pulls forward into the warehouse. Even before the SUV is fully inside, the door begins to lower.

***

Sandra stands beside Emily in the observation room. The two women look each other over with open curiosity. Both recognize the similarities of strength, beauty and confidence they share. Neither feels intimidated by or inferior to the other. A mutual respect and understanding blossoms without words between the two.

Sandra chooses to break the inquisitive silence. "Daniel's just arrived. He'll be here any moment."

Emily nods with some apprehension. "It's been a very long wait."

Emily eyes Sandra. "Ms. St. Clair, I have a few questions I'm just dying to ask, and I was thinking my flight out isn't until tomorrow morning—"

Sandra stops Emily with the touch of her hand. "I have a few of my own. How about dinner tonight?"

Emily smiles in acceptance. "Sounds good."

Both women turn their attention to the observation window and wait for Daniel Moore to walk through the unopened door.

***

Phillip sits in his chair flipping through a file, trying to exude casualness. Mark fingers his earpiece, listening intently. He turns to Chad and gives a slight nod.

"Mr. Stevens, the subject has arrived."

Phillip looks up and nods. He lays the file onto the table in front of his chair, then straightens his suit.

"Send him in."

Mark nods and talks quietly into his microphone.

***

Barry pulls the SUV to a stop in the middle of the mostly empty warehouse a safe distance from where a man stands in a suit very similar to his own. Barry and Trent look the room over carefully, noticing two more identically dressed men flanking a door on the far side of the room. Daniel eyes the door on the far wall.

"Barry, I want you to stand by with the vehicle, and, Trent, I want you to escort me to the door, then stand by and wait for my orders."

Both men look over their shoulders at Daniel.

"Sir, I must insist on one of us accompanying you."

Daniel shakes his head, denying the request.

"Gentlemen, you have your orders. Now, let's go."

Barry and Trent exit the vehicle. Barry takes up his position outside the front of the SUV. Trent opens the back door and Daniel steps out. Daniel takes a final look around then sets off at a brisk pace with Trent in step slightly behind him. The lone man in the dark suit extends his hand to Daniel as they approach.

"Thank you for coming, Mr. President."

Daniel ignores the man completely, passing him by without a second glance.

The man quickly recovers and speaks into his microphone, then begins to jog back to the door, reaching it at the same time as Daniel and Trent. Daniel motions for Trent to stand to the side, then casually looks over the two men guarding the door.

"I believe I'm expected."

The man from the rear nods to the men at the door. The one on the left opens the door and steps aside. Daniel steps boldly through without hesitation.

***

Phillip stands as Daniel approaches him.

"Mr. President, my name is Phillip Stevens, and I'm sure you're wondering what this is all about."

Daniel ignores Phillip for a moment, looking all around, noticing the observation room as well as the two agents by the door. After examining his surroundings completely, he finally turns to Phillip.

"Well, Mr. Stevens, please explain."

Phillip motions to one of two chairs opposite him. Daniel takes one and waits for Phillip to start.

***

Sandra and Emily turn their attention fully to the room. They both watch with apprehension. Phillip is explaining to Daniel why he's there.

"Are you as nervous as I am?" Sandra asks.

"You have no idea. I mean, Christ, it's been 20 years!"

"How bad was he?"

Emily remains silent, contemplating the question. Sandra can't help feeling she has overstepped her bounds.

"I'm sorry, that's none of my business."

Emily waves away the apology.

"Don't be. I just had to think about it. He was as horrible as he is great now."

"Well, the program certainly gets results."

"Kat's death is going to crush him."

"He looks like he's handling this better than most."

"I know. That's what worries me."

Sandra looks from the room to Emily. She sees the worry in her face and feels compelled to comfort her.

"You don't have to face him."

Emily smiles in appreciation of Sandra's sympathy.

"Yes, I do. He deserves that much at least."

Phillip looks toward the observation room window and signals for Emily to join them at the table. Sandra gives Emily a quick hug.

"Well, wish me luck."

"You're not going to need it. I'll call you after we're done here and set up dinner."

Emily nods.

"Everything will be fine. You'll see."

Emily gives a little laugh, then opens the door and leaves Sandra alone in the room.

***

Daniel begins to stand to greet Emily then changes his mind as she enters the room. He feels himself being enveloped by a tidal wave of conflicting emotions. The information he has just become privy to has shaken him to his core. He never in a million years would have guessed the nature of the deception of which he has been a victim.

Time seemed to slow down for him when his long-dead wife walked through the door, as alive and beautiful as he ever could have imagined. Twenty years had done nothing to diminish the looks of his Emily. He feels the love he always had for her push its way to the forefront of his mind, threatening to break his resolve and send him pleading for her to return to his side. Just as his will is about to crumble, he remembers the person absent from this obscure family reunion: Katy. And in a flash, the love is crushed by an incredible feeling of betrayal.

Time resumes its natural flow after Daniel consciously pushes all his emotions to the back of his mind, leaving only calculating awareness in its place. Above all else he must not betray his true feelings to these people; that would not serve his purpose at all.

"Hello, Emily. Mr. Stevens has filled me in on the details. I guess you feel you did what you had to do."

Overcome with emotion, Emily moves to Daniel.

"I'm so sorry, Daniel. Don't hate me. When Kat got sick I wanted to contact you so badly! But you were running for election, and we were afraid to . . ."

Emily's voice cracks, tears replacing unspoken words.

Daniel stares from Emily to Phillip to Emily again. "I don't hate you. It's been made clear to me that after your initial request, you lost control of the situation—"

Phillip interrupts Daniel with a needed explanation. "It's necessary for the integrity of the process."

Daniel ignores Phillip and keeps his attention squarely on Emily.

"Indeed. Mr. Stevens has informed me that you have a new identity, and that you wish to remain hidden from me."

"I just didn't know how you would handle it. You know if Kat were still alive, I wouldn't have kept her from you!"

"At least you wouldn't keep her from me anymore!"

"Mr. President, no one could foresee your daughter's untimely death." Phillip interjected.

Daniel continues to ignore Phillip.

"Daniel, can you ever forgive me?"

"You're right, Emily. I think it's best for you to keep your new identity. We both have different lives now."

Daniel stands, signaling the end of the meeting. "Well, if that's it, I have a country to run."

Phillip stands as well. "Mr. President, I would strongly encourage you to participate in our review-awareness counseling program. Most everyone that chooses full revival goes through it, and all agree it benefits them greatly."

"That won't be necessary, Mr. Stevens. Now if you will excuse me."

Daniel turns to Emily. The two share a moment of silence. Emily wants nothing more than to comfort her ex-husband—she just cannot figure out how to bridge the gap that time and events have created between them.

"Goodbye, Emily." Daniel turns and leaves the room.

Phillip and Emily watch him go. "That could have been worse," Phillip said.

Emily lets a single tear fall from the corner of one eye. Choosing not to wipe it away, she looks at Phillip and shrugs. "I guess."

***

Daniel sits silently in the backseat of the slowly moving SUV. Barry and Trent exchange a glance. Barry steers the vehicle out of the warehouse. All three men sit in troubled silence while Barry accelerates through the industrial complex and back toward the main highway.

Daniel looks out the window, lost in his troubled thoughts.

Daniel has always been definitive in his decision-making; once a path is chosen, he believes in seeing it through. He realizes the choice he makes now has the potential of unforeseen consequences. But does not every decision a president makes? The problem is, he just cannot see a clear enough picture to estimate the outcome. There is a point when what may benefit an individual may be detrimental to too many other people to justify his actions. *This might be one of those times,* Daniel worries. At the same time, he has no way of knowing for sure one way or the other. When all else fails, Daniel likes to flip his mental coin.

"Barry, pick a number between one and ten."

Barry and Trent look up with surprise.

"Excuse me, sir?"

"Pick a number between one and ten."

"Uh, seven."

"Now Trent you pick a separate number."

"Four, sir."

Daniel smiles with satisfaction.

"Good work, men. You just assisted me in an important decision."

Both agents share a look of confusion. Trent looks over his shoulder at his satisfied employer. "Is there anything else we can do, sir?"

Daniel nods. "Yes, there is. You can get me Josh Weedy on the phone."

"Now, sir?"

"Now, Trent."

Trent turns back and grabs the phone hooked to the console. "Get me Josh Weedy."

THIRTY-TWO

Emily sips her wine slowly and allows the waiter to take her dessert plate away. With curiosity she studies Sandra who is speaking mutedly into her cell phone. Sandra puts the phone away.

"Sorry about that. With my job, work follows me everywhere."

Emily sets her glass on the table. "I can imagine."

Sandra grins. "Yeah, I guess you can. So you said you had questions."

Emily grabs the bottle of wine from the ice and pours them both another glass. "Just a couple. I'm wondering how you and Phillip can do what you do without it giving you . . . I don't know . . . a God complex."

Sandra raises her eyebrows at the question, then takes a drink from her glass. "Nice ice-breaker."

"No sense beating around the bush."

"Well, as far as what we do giving us a God complex, all you have to do is keep tabs on submitters like yourself.

It's a constant struggle in a lot of cases just to keep them from making contact with the subjects. Too often, as time passes, they will experience extreme feelings of guilt and regret. If left without surveillance, they would make contact, and that could cause all kinds of trouble."

Emily cannot hide her surprise. "That's happened?"

"I'm probably not supposed to be telling you this, but, yeah, once or twice in the early days. From what the files state, there were some real disasters."

"How did they fix it?"

"I'm sure I can't tell you that. I *will* tell you that's why we require at least five hundred miles between submitter and subject."

Emily smiles, enjoying the remnants of another glass of wine. "Makes sense."

"So what else do you want to know?"

"Is it worth it?"

Sandra sits thinking for a minute. It is a question she has often asked herself. "I think that's a question better answered by you than me."

Emily considers the question as carefully as Sandra before her. "Yeah, it's worth it. When I think about the road Daniel was forcing me down, I can't imagine surviving. Had Kat lived and been brought up in the environment Daniel wanted, it would have been more than I could handle."

Emily breaks off her conversation when the waiter approaches.

"Would you ladies like another bottle of wine?"

Sandra shrugs her indifference, letting Emily make the decision.

Emily looks at Sandra and shakes her head. "I think I'm good on the wine. How about we get out of here and take a walk? I could use some air."

"Sounds great."

The waiter nods his understanding. "Would you ladies like me to split the check?"

Sandra interjects before Emily can. "That won't be necessary, the meal's on me."

"Very well. I'll be back in a moment." The waiter leaves the table and ladies behind.

"You don't have to do that," Emily protests.

Sandra waves her off. "It's nothing, really. Besides, you can leave the tip."

"Deal." Emily stands from her chair. "I think I'll visit the restroom before our walk."

"Don't try ducking out before I get to ask *my* questions." Sandra playfully responds.

"I look forward to the inquisition."

Sandra laughs as Emily heads toward the bathroom.

***

The two ladies walk side by side down the sidewalk. They wear similar ankle-length coats to protect them from the stiff breeze rolling off the sluggishly flowing river parallel to their route. It's a chilly October evening, but not so cold as to keep the locals indoors. The ladies keep pace with the rest of the foot traffic before angling toward the rail of an observation deck overlooking a bend in the river.

Emily stands in silence alongside Sandra. They watch a couple of geese swim slowly past. Sandra grimaces at the large birds swimming eagerly over to where an old man farther down the rail throws bread into the water. "Talk about your ugly ducklings!"

"I don't know, I've always kind of liked them."

Sandra eyes her companion with open disbelief. "Are you serious?"

"They remind me of the farm, back when we first bought it. Daniel met me in the middle of those woods that separated our farms, and we walked down to the river that flowed through the back of our property. We sat and talked for hours about everything and just watched the geese and ducks float and fly by."

Emily watches the old man feed the geese, and Sandra watches her.

"I wouldn't think you would have too many fond memories from your farm."

Emily smiles before she answers. "You kidding me? The early days were heaven. I wasn't at all happy about the move when I first found out about it. I mean, I was leaving behind all my friends. I had just graduated high school, and I wasn't ready for college. My parents had talked for years about buying a farm and leaving the city. They knew I wanted to finish school in Boston, so they waited until my senior year to start looking."

Sandra listens intently in silence, allowing Emily's story to unfold. "My mom and dad found a great deal on a perfect piece of property in Kentucky, so just like that, two weeks after graduation, I'm standing on my new front porch talking to Daniel."

"What was he like?"

"Handsome, and country as could be, but smart and confident too. He was also very calculating and clever, as I found out after we were married and I was pregnant with Kat."

"How did you guys start dating?"

"He asked me out the very first time we met. I didn't have to say yes—he just assumed I would. After our first date I knew there would be no one else for me."

Sandra cannot help but be surprised by Emily's pronouncement. "Wow! There must have been some real chemistry between the two of you."

"I'm not sure what you would call it—chemistry, an aligning of the stars, soul mates." Emily laughs at an undisclosed joke, while Sandra looks on quizzically.

"What's so funny?"

Emily's mood sobers significantly. "I was just remembering what I used to call it."

"What's that?"

"'Serendipity' . . . and I couldn't have been farther from the truth."

"Maybe not, if you look at the long view. I mean, look what a profound difference that chance meeting has made in the entire world. Most people consider Daniel our greatest president."

Emily stretches from the guardrail, mulling over Sandra's words.

"There is just too much pain for me to call Daniel's and my past serendipity."

"How about 'fate' then?"

Emily nods in agreement. "I can live with that. Hey, you want to walk?"

Sandra pushes from the rail and points further up the walkway. "Sure. There's a little coffee shop a couple blocks up. We can get a cup and warm up before we call you a cab."

Emily glances down at her watch. "Sounds good."

The ladies start out for the coffee shop.

"So is there anything specific you wish to know about Daniel or myself?"

"Not really. You know this whole process has been very difficult to handle. The farther up the political ladder Daniel rose, the more complicated the review became for us."

"I can imagine."

"Well, you can also imagine the amount of time I've spent dwelling on the problem. I often wondered the type of woman you were. And after meeting you, I can't come to terms with someone of your caliber allowing someone else to control you."

"Love is a powerful force, and in the beginning, I freely went where it took me. And in the years after, when Daniel disclosed the ugly truth of who he really was, fear became just as powerful as love. You have to remember he didn't reveal himself until after Kat was born, and he made it very clear after my initial disgust and rebellion against his family's ways that there would be severe consequences to dissenters."

Sandra pulls up short. "I read in your file that he openly threatened you."

"Not only me, but my parents too, who never knew anything about Daniel's family. And as the worst-case scenario, he explained that if I didn't reform my ways to match his, then I could rest assured that not only would I be permanently dealt with, but my family would be killed as well, and Kat would be raised up by him and his family without interference. For the sake of my daughter, I couldn't allow that."

Sandra takes Emily's hand and pulls her forward, resuming their walk. "I don't know how you survived."

"In some ways, I didn't. If it weren't for the intervention of your people, I'm afraid I wouldn't have lasted much longer. I had become very depressed and had lost a lot of weight; I often thought of ending it all.

You know you're close to the edge when a bullet seems like your only friend."

"But you don't feel that way anymore."

"Certainly not. After we got away from Daniel and his family, I promised myself I would never return to those dark thoughts. When Kat got sick it really tested my resolve, but she was always such a beautiful soul. She refused to let her illness take away her spirit or mine. She was positive right up until the end, and, honestly, she kept me sane."

"You make her sound so wonderful."

"She was."

"Did she ever know about Daniel?"

"When I realized she was not going to recover, I decided to tell her about him. We would lie side by side scrunched up in the hospital bed, and she would ask all kinds of questions about him, and I would tell her whatever she wanted to know."

Sandra stops in front of the small coffee shop. She is so involved in Emily's story she hesitates to interrupt her and enter the shop. "How did she handle what you told her?"

Emily looks at Sandra with a tear in her eye, then smiles and wipes it away.

Sandra frowns, thinking she again overstepped her bounds with questions that might be too personal. "I'm sorry. I shouldn't be so inconsiderate; this is probably something too personal to share."

Emily pulls out a tissue from her coat pocket and delicately blows her nose before putting the tissue back in her pocket. "Don't apologize. This is the first time I've ever been able to tell anyone about all this, and it feels like a huge weight has been lifted from my shoulders."

"Then you don't feel like I'm intruding?"

"Not yet."

Sandra nods in understanding at the gentle warning.

"Kat handled the story of her father like she handled everything in life—with grace, acceptance, understanding and empathy," Emily continued. "She never blamed her father and said I shouldn't either. She said he could not help what he was bred to be."

"She really was amazing, wasn't she?"

Emily looks over Sandra's shoulder to the open coffee shop. "She was the purest soul I've ever met. And now I'm all talked out and could really use a cup of coffee."

Sandra accepts the end of their conversation without complaint. "Well, follow me in because I have led us to the best coffee shop in the city."

THIRTY-THREE

Daniel sits behind his desk with Josh sitting across from him. They are finishing listening to a recording of the meeting he had with Phillip and Emily.

Daniel, with hands clasped in front of him, is deep in thought.

Josh listens with a look of extreme disbelief and anger. The recording comes to an end, and Josh jumps to his feet and starts pacing around the room. Daniel turns off the recorder, then takes it from his desk and slides it into a drawer. He pulls a bottle of bourbon with two shot glasses from the same drawer.

"Unbelievable! I don't even know what to say. You must be losing your mind right now."

Daniel nods in agreement. "I've adjusted to the situation." He pours two double shots and slides one across the desk. "Here—have a drink."

Josh takes the shot glass, raises it to his lips and slugs it down, then resumes his pacing. "Jesus, Daniel,

I've never heard of anything like this. These people are monsters. What kind of demented sickos would do something like this?"

Daniel gulps down his shot, grimacing through the burn of the liquid going down his throat. "That's what I want you to find out."

Josh stops pacing and grips the desk with animated determination. "Just give me the word, and we'll burn these bastards down!"

Daniel pours two more shots then puts the bottle back in the desk. "That would be getting ahead of ourselves. We can't do anything until we figure out who we're dealing with." He motions to the second glass while he turns up the other.

Josh takes the glass and follows suit. He puts the glass down then wipes his mouth with his sleeve. "I'll call Langley and see what they have."

"I already have." Daniel takes the two glasses and puts them back in the drawer. "They don't have anything on the N.D.E.C. Said they have never even heard of it."

"NSA?"

"Struck out there, too."

Josh moves back to his chair and slumps down into it. Both men sit in their silence, contemplating their next move.

"I think we should start at the meeting point. I'll send in Bo Simmons' team to go over it with a fine tooth comb. If they made any mistakes, he'll find it."

Daniel raises his eyebrows in surprise. "I thought Bo was in Brazil."

"He was, but they finished up early. They got back stateside two days ago."

"Excellent. Also have a sketch artist brought in. We can get an image of this Mr. Stevens and run him through our database, see if we can turn up a match."

"Daniel, you think they're connected with our government?"

"I'm almost positive of it. This whole deal reeks of black ops!"

Josh looks up at Daniel with trepidation. "There's no way this could be some kind of elaborate hoax is there?"

"Explain."

Josh squirms a little under Daniel's gaze. "I don't know, like, maybe someone is playing a trick on you."

"Who do you know that would be able to bring my wife back to life after being dead for 20 years? You're right. That would be hilarious."

Josh wilts and backpedals under Daniel's angry sarcasm. "I'm sorry, that was very callous of me. I was just trying to explore every possible scenario."

Daniel calms down. "It's okay. There's no need to apologize. It's your job to do exactly that."

Both men visibly relax.

"What else?" Daniel asks.

"We should have someone research what really happened to you at that park 20 years ago. There could be some clues there."

"Make it happen."

Josh perks up with an idea. "What about Emily? If we can locate her and bring her in, I'm sure she has some information that would be helpful."

The two men sit in silence, thinking about Josh's idea. "Have her located, but don't bring her in. I don't want these people alerted to our investigation."

"No problem."

"How do you think they're funded?"

Josh smiles at the question. "There's got to be a money trail! We just have to find it."

"Listen, Josh, this is your highest priority, but make no moves unless I authorize it. If this got out, there could be huge political fallout."

Josh stands and gathers himself to leave. "I got this, Daniel. Don't worry; we're going to get these bastards!"

Daniel nods in approval. "Josh, send in Angie as you go."

Josh nods, then turns and leaves the room.

***

Josh stops in front of Angie's desk, watching her type away at her computer. He thinks about the recording and the revelations it revealed. He has never been so blindsided before in his life. Josh stares off into space, the implications of the knowledge he possesses overwhelming him. In the course of an hour, he has learned more about his friend than he had learned in the past fifteen years. He found the origins of Daniel's life to be nothing less than astounding. And the deception that he had operated under all these years, simply incomprehensible.

Angie eyes Josh curiously. *There has to be some reason for him to be standing there lost in thought.* She can't help but wonder what has the man so obviously confounded.

"Hey, Josh, what's up?"

Josh looks at Angie with confusion, shaking off his mental wanderings. "What's that you said, Angie?"

"I said what's going on with you? I couldn't help but notice you seem a little distant. You got something on your mind?"

"It's that apparent is it?"

Angie smiles with amusement. "Uh, yeah. You were, like, lost in space there for a moment!"

Josh blushes with embarrassment. "Well, I've returned from orbit to inform you that the boss wants to see you."

"And when I see him will I be launched as far into the atmosphere as you were?"

"If he chooses to launch you, then I'm sure you'll be launched."

Angie rises from her seat, and moves around her desk. "Sounds exciting!"

"More like overwhelming."

"Do tell."

"I've already said more than I should have. You caught me in a moment of weakness." Having said all he is willing to, Josh turns and continues on his way.

Angie watches him go, more intrigued than ever. She closes the distance to Daniel's office quickly.

***

Daniel busies himself organizing his desk when he sees Angie enter the room. With curiosity in her eyes, she scurries over to where he sits. "You needed to see me?"

Daniel looks from his desk to her. He immediately notices the mood she is in.

"Exactly what did Josh tell you?"

"He just told me you needed to see me, though I must admit by the look of him you must have dropped a real bombshell on him."

Daniel taps his fingers on the desk. His air of contemplation leaves Angie feeling she might have betrayed more of Josh's confidence than she should have.

177

"Well, I certainly put a lot on his plate," Daniel says. "I guess I'll have to overlook his mistake."

Angie frowns at Daniel's remark. "I wouldn't think anything he said to me would be betraying your confidence, Daniel."

Daniel chooses not to respond. He waves away the subject. "That's not why I called you in here."

"Well, why did you?"

"I need you to clear some substantial space on my calendar. I've got some personal business that could take some time."

Angie nods in understanding. "I'm sure I can shuffle some things around. How much time do you need? A day or two?"

"More like a week or two."

Angie stares at him dumbfounded. "Daniel, you've got so much going on right now! There's the gifted children's silent auction." She frantically flips through a planner. "You have the trip to see the prime minister in London, plus a stopover in Geneva after that. Not to mention your upcoming speech on foreign affairs . . ."

Daniel looks back at Angie. "Reschedule everything, or cancel it. I really don't care which."

"What am I supposed to tell all these people?" Angie stands there stunned.

Daniel rises from his chair and starts collecting his belongings in order to leave. "I don't know—make something up."

"Daniel, what's going on with you? This is so unlike you. You would never miss the children's auction."

He finishes gathering his stuff and meets Angie at the door. He gently takes her by the arm. "Just do it, okay? I'm going to be out of the office the rest of the afternoon."

In complete confusion and consternation, Angie offers no further protest when Daniel brushes past her and leaves the room.

THIRTY-FOUR

PHILLIP SITS IN a black leather recliner with a book in his hand. He casually flips to the next page of the Charles Dickens' novel *Great Expectations*. He has always enjoyed the classics, and whenever he finds the time, he spends the evening rereading one of the many he owns. He takes a sip from the drink resting on the lamp table to the left of the chair.

His living room is as stark as his office. The furniture consists of two chairs, a couch he rarely uses and a deserted coffee table. An entertainment center along a far wall contains a flat screen TV, used as often as the couch, and a stereo that currently plays soothing music at a low volume. At the wall facing the couch, a bookcase displays the many books Phillip has collected over the years. There is nothing remarkable about them to Phillip other than their value as good reads. On the end table—other than the lamp providing just enough light to read and the keys to the various locks, ignitions and whatever else a man's keys go to—there is a cell phone, which at this moment is choosing to interrupt Phillip's reading with its persistent ringing. Phillip looks at the clock on the otherwise bare wall, currently boasting the time to be slightly past ten in the evening.

Phillip checks the caller ID and recognizes the number. He taps the phone open and positions it next to his ear. "Phillip speaking."

The voice of Mark fills the receiver. "Sir, we have a code blue."

"I'm on my way."

Phillip ends the phone call, grabs his keys and heads for the door.

***

Phillip briskly enters the N.D.E.C. headquarters control room and finds Sandra already there along with Mark. Sandra nods to Phillip who takes up a post alongside her. Both look over Mark's shoulders, watching him make adjustments in the map displayed on the overhead monitor.

"What's the current situation?" Phillip asks.

Mark clicks a command that brings up a couple of pulsating blips on the map. One is stationary while the other moves steadily toward it.

"What's the location of the stationary?"

Mark hits another command, pulling up the address of the location. "The Rose Bowl?"

Sandra chooses to speak. "It's a college football game. USC is playing Nebraska."

Mark nods his approval. "It's a big game with playoff implications: whoever wins this game is guaranteed a top-four seed and a first-round bye! I'm pulling for USC."

"I'm glad you approve." Phillip sarcastically responds. "Now, if you don't mind, maybe we can get back to the impending disaster we're trying to divert."

Mark refocuses on the screen, hiding his sheepish look from his superiors. "Sorry, sir."

"Have we run background yet?"

Sandra reaches for a file lying on the control counter and hands it to Phillip. As Phillip begins to read it, Sandra gives him an oral overview "Our stationary is the submitter and currently dwells in Southern California. We've made audio contact. He is attending the game as a chaperone for his 12 year-old-son's Boy Scout troop."

"So extraction is a last case scenario," Phillip responds while continuing to read. "What about our other blip?"

"Has lived in Nebraska since being submitted. We have every reason to believe he plans on attending the game."

Phillip looks up from the file. "How were the distance alarms bypassed?"

Mark types frantically at his keyboard, pulling up a travel itinerary. "Sir, low-level alarms were tripped three days ago and checked out. We looked into the flight plan and deferred action because the subject was flying into Seattle. There was a second alarm when he took another flight into San Francisco. We then investigated further, finding a return flight to Seattle scheduled for tomorrow night. There were no further travel accommodations of any kind."

"So what's he doing in San Francisco?"

"Looks like he's visiting a friend from college. They both went to Nebraska."

"With our cross-referencing program, this still shouldn't have happened."

Sandra takes another printout from the control counter. "I thought the same thing and did a diagnostic check. The mistake was made when the team programmed-in Seattle as the travel destination point. The computer never cross-referenced Nebraska and California."

Phillip tosses the file back on the table. "So the game never showed up!"

"Nope."

Phillip runs his hands through his hair and weighs their options. "Tell me we have an agent en route."

Mark continues to update the map. He types a command and a third blip appears on the screen. "We have one on the way; he's an officer with the Los Angeles Police Department."

The three of them follow the two blips converging toward the third. Sandra taps Mark on the shoulder. "Can we compare tickets?" Mark begins to type quickly.

Phillip reaches for a set of headphones and puts them on. "Get our agent on the line."

Sandra slides in beside Mark and quickly punches in the sequence of numbers on the communication console. Mark pulls up the two sets of seats on the computer screen. "Sir, you're not going to like this."

Phillip looks at the screen with apprehension. "Damn! This is unbelievable! They're practically sitting on top of each other! There is no way we can risk contact."

"Phillip, I've got the agent on audio," Sandra says.

"Great . . . put him through to me."

"This is agent Dan Grover speaking"

Phillip responds into the headphones. "Agent Grover, this is Director Stevens. I need to know your current operational situation."

"Sir, I'm currently on duty in my patrol car. I have just established visual contact with a vehicle matching the information your team has relayed to me."

"That's good news, agent Grover. Please continue to follow the subject."

Phillip moves the mic away from his mouth and eyes Sandra intensely. "What are our options here?"

Sandra responds with introspection. "We have to figure out a way to separate the contacts without submittal removal or submitted awareness."

Mark looks up from his console. "I could upgrade their seats."

Phillip and Sandra eye the subordinate hopefully. "Can you do that?"

"Certainly. It will just take a little time."

"How much time?"

Mark frenetically types commands into his keyboard. "About twenty minutes."

Sandra updates the map. "That's too much time—they're only about five minutes from the stadium."

Phillip looks at the screen with frustration. "We need to stall them!"

Sandra taps her fingers as she searches for a solution and then snaps her fingers as one comes to her. "Just pull them over."

Phillip looks at her, confused. "But they haven't done anything wrong!"

Sandra rolls her eyes and Mark looks briefly up at Phillip's ridiculous statement. "Phillip you are such a boy scout. You should be at that game with the rest of the troop. Just tell Grover to pull them over so you can stall them."

Phillip replaces the mic and speaks hurriedly into it. "Agent Grover, I need you to do something . . . uh, unethical."

"You want me to pull them over, sir. No problem. I can run them in on some trumped up charge."

Phillip shows his surprise. "No, that won't be necessary. Just stop them, and don't let them leave till I tell you." Phillip shakes his head and again displaces the mic. He looks at Sandra. "I must have been the only honest cop in America!"

Sandra laughs. "Just think in shades of gray."

"Whatever."

"Sir, the subject has been stopped."

Phillip looks at the screen with approval. Sandra leaves her seat and joins him.

"How are the tickets coming?" Phillip asks.

"Be another few minutes, sir. I've found a pair reserved for unexpected celebrities, located on the opposite side of the field, right near the fifty-yard line. I'm actually very jealous."

"Just don't get any ideas for the future."

"I wouldn't dream of it, sir."

Sandra nudges Phillip with her shoulder. "Have you thought about how these guys are going to find out about the upgrade?"

Phillip shakes his head. "I haven't got that far yet. Have you?"

"As a matter of fact, I have!"

"Let's hear it."

"Well, we have Agent Grover put these guys through the ringer, talking about how they match the description of some criminal or another. He keeps them a few minutes into the game before 'discovering' their innocence. Having asked their destination, he offers to make a call to a friend of his who might have some good seats. You know, as a friendly gesture for the inconvenience he has caused them."

Phillip smiles, picking up on the idea. "I get it. He calls us and we tell him where to direct them to retrieve their tickets!"

"You got it."

Phillip flips the mic back down and begins speaking with Agent Grover.

Having finished explaining the plan to Grover, he removes the headset and places it on the control counter. Mark types a final key then nods to Phillip. "All done."

"Good. You can relay the rest of the information to Grover."

Sandra shares a relieved smile with Phillip then motions to the door. "Why don't you get out of here? It's my turn to stay over, and I think between Mark and Grover and me, we can keep the situation in check."

"I think I will. Just be sure to add systems diagnostics to our next meeting. We need to reevaluate the processes to eliminate whatever loophole got us here."

"Consider it done."

Phillip nods to Mark and waves at Sandra. "Good job guys. And be sure to let Grover know how much we appreciate his efforts."

Phillip turns and quickly exits the control room.

THIRTY-FIVE

PHILLIP LUNGES FORWARD, swinging his racket and hitting the small compact ball powerfully. The ball flies toward the far wall and careens off its lower portion at an angle that is impossible to return. The ball bounces once, then twice, then several more times before Chad scoops it up from the floor. Phillip raises his hands in triumph. His much younger adversary smiles, acknowledging the shot.

"Yes! You're mine now, Chad!"

"Nice shot, boss. It's my serve now."

Chad assumes his serving stance and Phillip prepares his return—body square, knees bent, swaying slightly from side to side in anticipation.

"What's the score, boss? Oh, yeah—it's nine to two, my way."

"Just serve the ball already."

Chad smiles then rips a mean serve off, sending the ball screaming at the wall and back so fast Phillip has only enough time to make an obviously futile attempt, diving forward, racket flailing wildly. The ball passes by untouched. Phillip picks himself up quickly from the floor, ignoring Chad's smug look.

"Nice serve. Seems like you put a little more English on it than usual."

"Maybe."

"If I'm not mistaken, didn't you win the city championship a few years ago?"

Chad picks up the racket ball from where it has come to a rest and returns to the serving line.

"The under-25 age group, three years in a row."

Phillip stretches out a couple of kinks from the fall before he acknowledges the impressive feat. "Wow. That's considered the toughest age group. What happened the fourth year?"

"I turned 25."

Phillip nods his understanding, then resumes his position. "Well, try to keep in mind I'm damn near fifty!"

Chad smiles and calls out the score. "Ten serving two."

Chad lets loose with a somewhat gentler serve and Phillip returns it smoothly. They volley back and forth, each hitting quality shots that challenge the other's return game. While the two men continue to compete, Sandra approaches the glass and watches the contest with interest. The point is finally decided in Phillip's favor. Sandra taps the glass, getting his attention. Phillip motions for her to wait for him. He takes his position for a final point. "Looks like I got to go, Chad. How about next point wins?"

Chad just shakes his head with a smile, preparing to serve one last time. "Sure, boss. Whatever you say."

Chad serves and Phillip returns the ball. The two men exchange volleys. Phillip hits a hard shot trying to end the point, but Chad makes a great save, and Phillip isn't able to reach the return. Phillip throws his hands up in defeat. The two men shake hands.

"Better luck next time, boss."

"Yeah, right. Winner gets to put away the equipment."

Chad laughs as Phillip leaves the court and joins Sandra waiting outside. She hands him a towel from the rack. He towels off his soaked head and face.

"How did you do?"

"The man's unbeatable!"

"Keep trying. I'm sure you'll get him."

"Or have a heart attack trying."

The two walk away together, heading toward the locker rooms.

"So what's up?"

"We just got this update." Sandra hands Phillip a piece of paper, and he looks it over.

"Seems pretty straightforward. Are all the facts verified?"

"Yes, but the contacts want immediate action."

"I don't see anything here that would make that a problem. I mean, we pretty much knew this one was ready for processing. That's why we already have a team in place."

"One of us will have to go to Vegas."

"You go. I took the last trip, and you could use the chance to get away."

"I'll be on a plane tonight."

Sandra looks at Phillip with a little apprehension. "Have you spoken with the senator?"

"Spoke with him a couple of hours ago. He hasn't heard anything yet."

"I'm keeping my fingers crossed."

"If you think you need to." Phillip returns the document. "I'll see you in a couple days." He turns and enters the men's locker room.

THIRTY-SIX

JESSICA QUICKLY APPLIES her favorite shade of lipstick: cherry red. She has worn it daily since discovering the alluring qualities of beauty-enhancing cosmetics and revealing outfits. She loves the way the color accents her dark red, shoulder-length hair. She looks in the mirror critically and overall approves of what she sees. A beauty. Everything about her exudes sensuous sexuality, and that's the way she likes it.

Now, though, the wear and tear of her chosen lifestyle is starting to show its effects. The bags under her eyes never used to be there, and they are accompanied by a few wrinkles that are becoming harder and harder to cover up. Her drug habit keeps her weight down, so at least excess fat is not a problem. But the physical defects that arise with long-term heavy drug use are beginning to show. Pasty, pale skin along with facial and body blemishes, are an ever-increasing problem. Not to mention for the first time in her life she is suffering from moderate tooth pain. Jessica does steady business with one of the local dentists who tries his best to maintain her beautiful smile, but he is slowly losing the battle. She looks in the mirror and doesn't deny what she sees; she just chalks it up to a lifestyle she enjoys too much to walk away from. In a nutshell, lots of drugs, accompanied by as many sexual partners as it takes to maintain her habits, is what she likes. Hell, most guys are willing to pay her extremely good money to do things she otherwise would do for free.

***

Jessica learned at a young age the influence she possessed over the opposite sex. By age 14 she had already developed physically into the woman she was to become. Everywhere she went, men never failed to notice her. This became an ever-increasing problem at home, along with what would become a developing drug habit. Jessica came from a very strict background, and her parents tried to no avail to control their rebellious daughter. They would ground her when they found out she smoked at school.

Jessica didn't care, she just continued to smoke. So when her parents found a bag of pot in her book bag in the eighth grade, they overreacted.

They decided to send her to rehab, hoping it would help cure her supposed illness. Jessica didn't want to go. Once she arrived she found herself to be the youngest patient in a ward full of addicts participating in a program they wanted nothing to do with. Barely 15when she entered that facility, she was still a virgin in more ways than one. Every guy in that place damn near broke his neck staring at her when she walked in.

It took her all of an hour to get turned on to her first experience with cocaine. Brandi, her roommate, looked her over and pegged her as a lost cause right away. She offered Jessica her first line. After Jessica readily did it, Brandi took her by the arm and led her to the door of their dorm-style dwellings. Brandi asked her if she liked the cocaine and wanted more. Jessica said "yes" to both. Brandi simply pointed down the hall to all the doors identical to theirs.

"Behind those doors is as much dope as two girls like us could ever hope to do. All you have to do is go get it and bring half of it back to me."

Jessica couldn't hide her confusion. "How? They're not just going to give it to me."

"Try the doors on the left side of the hall. Those are the ones with guys behind them."

"You're telling me that if I knock on them doors, the guys inside will just give me drugs?"

"Go knock and find out."

With that, Brandi had pushed Jessica through their own door and shut it between them. An hour later Jessica had come back with two grams of coke. Brandi just smiled when she received her cut.

"They weren't too rough on you were they?"

"You crazy? They weren't rough enough. I'm going back in a couple hours."

Brandi looked at Jessica with a little surprise. "So you've done this before?"

"No, I was a virgin."

Brandi's look had changed from surprise to pure shock. She almost spilled her small bag of coke. "You telling me that was your first time?"

Jessica mimicked Brandi's handling of the dope, but without the near spillage. "Yes, but it won't be the last!"

Brandi returned to the task of chopping her stash into fine even lines with Jessica doing a fair job of imitating the girl. "I knew it as soon as I laid eyes on you—you're insane."

Jessica continued to expand her deviant activities over the course of her stay at the rehab center.

***

The center, needless to say, was not very competently run. Most of the staff were recovering addicts themselves, with more than one of them in various stages of relapse.

At the time of Jessica's arrival, Jordan Cummings, the director of the center, spent the majority of his day holed up in his office, fielding phone calls from various government agencies concerning the operational defaults of the center. There were also inquiries into rumored embezzlement of donated funds. While the rumors were fresh and few people had heard them, Jordan felt positive it would not take long before word got out and the authorities came calling. He based this assumption solely on the fact that the rumors were true. He had funneled a fair sum of the center's money into his personal accounts.

Jordan, a recovering drug addict and also a very bad gambler, managed to gain control over his habits after a particularly scary situation involving people he owed money to back in his early thirties. He had then rededicated his life to helping others. The directorship of the center became the culmination of twenty-five years of clean living.

Power, the downfall of so many, added Jordan to its list of victims. He did well for the first five years, but as is often the case, one bad decision led to another.

An old friend of Jordan had come into town. They had enjoyed dinner together, and, in the course of conversation, the old friend had spoken of an upcoming boxing match about which he had inside information on the outcome. By the end of dinner, the two men decided a bet would be placed on the fight with a substantial amount of Jordan's money. The inside information turned out to be wrong. Jordan lost the bet and found himself owing twenty-five grand he didn't have. Things only got worse from there. Like a true gambling addict, he tried to make his money back.

Jordan now owed a little over a hundred grand, and that after the hundred he had taken from the center's operating budget. Jordan got rid of the highly paid professional counselors at the center and replaced most of them with low-paid recovered addicts and volunteers. The thing with counselors in recovery is they're hit or miss. The best drug counselors in the world are recovering addicts who have the ability to relate in a manner that others can't duplicate. The worst counselors are also recovering addicts who backslide, often taking their patients with them.

Jordan had several of the latter on his staff. So as he sat holed up in his office, rediscovering his own forgotten demons of gambling and, more recently, heroin, the wolves of authority and accountability slowly circled their prey. Unfortunately, they would not be in time to save Jessica from the center's own wolves of drug abuse and prostitution, for these were much quicker in pouncing on their prey.

The end came when Jordan was found dead in his office of a heroin overdose. He had been dead for two days. The center quickly shut down with all the troubled teens being sent back to unsuspecting parents.

***

Jessica arrived home in a drug-induced haze. Her parents were concerned and tried to reach out to her. Jessica rebuffed their attempts; she just wanted to be left alone. She refused to go back to school and spent most of her time in her room. She had managed to bring home a fairly substantial amount of powder. The boys at the center had been more than willing to pay whatever she demanded for the chance to spend an hour alone with the fiery-headed beauty.

As Jessica steadily depleted her stash, her thoughts dwelled on how to get more. She wasn't worried about the method—sex to her young mind seemed a fine way to attain what she wanted. Opportunity was the issue. She knew in no way would she be able to live the lifestyle she longed for under her parents' roof. She also realized if she stayed close to home, her parents would eventually find out about her. And if they were willing to send her away over a bag of pot, she could only imagine what they would do about her new habits.

Jessica decided there was only one thing to do: she would run away. *Where do I go? How do I get there?* she asked herself. She jumped on the Internet and typed in travel destinations. Near the top of the list of cities her answer stood out before her with crystal clarity. Las Vegas. Where else would a girl like her go? Once she knew her destination, she looked around the web until she found a local travel blog full of people willing to pick up passengers in order to lower their trip expense. Jessica made plans to hitch a ride with a van full of frat brothers driving to Vegas for two weeks.

***

Clint and Bonnie Henderson worried about their daughter. She had been rebellious before her stay in rehab, but since she had returned home, she seemed more docile and withdrawn, almost to the point of depression. She stayed locked in her room almost all day; then they would hear her rummaging around into the early hours of the morning. They would take turns going upstairs to inquire about her well-being. She always said, "I'm tired and want to be left alone." They both agreed that in the few glances they got of her, she seemed wide awake and very fidgety. They knew they had made a big mistake by sending her away, but they didn't know the magnitude of the mistake until the morning they woke up and found her gone. She had left a note that simply read,

> *I took the bank card. I will mail*
> *it back to you after I withdraw*
> *five hundred dollars. I'm not*
> *coming back. Don't try to find me*
> *because you won't be able to.*

That's all the note had said. Clint and Bonnie had been distraught. They contacted all the local authorities, but, true to Jessica's word, she could not be found. Several years elapsed before a private detective tracked her down in Vegas. By then Jessica was 20, and her parents did not have the power to make her come home.

Bonnie had written her daughter at the address the detective had given her, begging her to contact them. Jessica, after some time and thought, wrote her parents to let them know how she was, and though unwilling to return home, she gave them permission to come and visit her on occasion. Clint and Bonnie quickly made plans to see their daughter.

In Vegas, their eyes were opened to what Jessica had so willingly become.

"Please come home," her mother begged. "You don't have to live this way."

Jessica simply refused. "I understand your concerns, but I'm happy with my life." The last five years had consisted of her parents frequently visiting Vegas, helpless as they watched their only child slowly kill herself.

***

Jessica thinks about her parents' pleas with contempt. They have never been able to come to terms with her chosen life. Bonnie and Clint have just left her apartment, her mother in tears as usual. Jessica often thinks inviting them to come see her is a mistake. They make the trip out more and more frequently. At first she had been genuinely glad to see them. She had also experienced a perverse feeling of joy at her parents' distress over her lifestyle. All that became old, as almost every visit ended the same—with her ignoring their pleas and wishing they would just leave and them breaking down in tears and finally leaving with a vow to never return.

Jessica looks at the clock on her bedroom wall. Half past ten. She jumps up in a flourish and heads for her front door. Her parents have made her late, and it ticks her off considerably. She knows from experience that the choicest marks will all be taken by other girls by now. She should have been in position at her spot thirty minutes ago!

"Damn it!" She detours just long enough to do a quick line then sprints from the apartment. She takes the back stairs down to the parking lot and finds Buddy her driver waiting patiently by his car. She covers the distance in a rush. Buddy opens the passenger door for her, and she slides in.

"Sorry I'm late, Buddy."

Buddy smiles broadly. "You ain't never late. I would wait for you till the end o' time."

Jessica looks in the visor mirror and wipes away the remnants of the line. "That's sweet of you to say, Buddy, but if we don't get in gear I'm going to miss the rush at the casinos."

Buddy moves smoothly around the car and takes the driver's seat. He has the car in motion and out of the parking lot with surprising speed.

THIRTY-SEVEN

A BEAUTIFUL WOMAN dressed in a mini skirt and high heels walks through the busy casino. She passes by all the games being played, makes her way to the bar and takes a seat. The bartender notices her familiar face as he approaches her.

"Jessica, you know Vinny isn't going to like it if he catches you here. Not after that commotion your mom made in here the other night."

"Well, if you don't tell him, I won't either."

The bartender shrugs in resignation. "Don't say I didn't warn you. You want the usual?"

A man walks up and sits down next to Jessica while she responds to the bartender. "You know it. Crown and Coke, hold the Coke."

The bartender shakes his head and turns his attention to the man. "What can I get you?"

The man looks from the bartender to Jessica with a grin. "I'll have what the lady is having."

The bartender watches Jessica and the man exchange glances and smiles.

The stranger hands the bartender a hundred-dollar bill. "Put the lady's drink on me, and keep the change."

"Whatever you say, mister." The bartender turns to the glass-walled counter behind him and begins to make the drinks. He can't help but smile to himself. This guy is in for a wild night. Jessica is known as one of the best tricks in all Vegas, definitely willing to go the distance. This guy better be willing to pay though—she is anything but cheap.

The stranger positions himself closer to Jessica. She takes out a cigarette. He takes a book of matches smoothly from his pocket and lights her smoke for her. "Those things will kill ya, you know."

Jessica takes a deep drag and exhales the smoke slowly. "So will a lot of things . . . eventually."

The stranger smiles in agreement. "My name's Trent by the way."

The bartender places the two matching drinks on the counter. "If you guys need anything else just let me know."

"Thanks, Don."

Don shrugs then heads farther down the bar in order to serve other thirsty patrons.

Trent takes his glass and holds it out to Jessica in order to toast.

Jessica rolls her eyes as she grabs her own drink. "And what is it we're toasting?"

"New places and new friends."

Jessica laughs obnoxiously and holds up her own drink.

Trent looks slightly confused, not understanding what is so funny. "What are you laughing at?"

Jessica punches him playfully on the arm. "You, ya big weenie. Allow me to set the proper mood for the evening."

"All right, maybe my toast was a bit hokey. Let's see you do better."

Jessica holds up her glass and Trent follows suit. "To drugs, sex and sound effects. To getting laid and paid in the sun or the shade. And all of this we must do as soon as possible, and as much as possible." Jessica turns her drink up and gulps it down then slams the glass onto the counter. Trent watches with surprise mixed with anticipation.

"How was that?"

He takes a much smaller swig from his own glass and sits it on the counter next to hers. "Perfect."

Jessica stands from her seat and pulls Trent from his. "You have a room here?"

"I do."

She takes his drink and finishes it off, then turns back to her newfound friend. "Lead the way, Trent. I wasn't kidding. It's time to party!"

***

Jessica and Trent burst through his hotel suite door in a passionate embrace. They almost fall to the floor after the door gives way. Jessica covers Trent in kisses before she pulls away and twirls around the room checking it all out.

Trent takes off his jacket and slings it on a chair. He moves to a mini bar along the wall and makes two drinks. "I'm sorry I don't have any Crown. I hope Jack will do."

Jessica moves to the bar and strokes his shoulder seductively. Then she takes one of the drinks. "Jack is just fine."

"So, how much is this going to cost me?"

She smiles over her glass. "Five hundred for an hour of pleasure, but a thousand gets you the whole night of anything you want."

Trent looks at her intrigued. "Anything?"

Jessica nods her head approvingly. "Anything you want, Trent. I like it all!"

***

Jessica lies tied to the bed in nothing but her bra and panties. She pulls slightly on her bindings while she waits for Trent to join her. "What are you doing in there? Come on! I'm ready to play!"

Trent comes out of the bathroom carrying a small case. Jessica cannot help but notice he is also fully dressed. Jessica looks at him with curiosity.

"I thought you were taking a shower."

"There's been a change in plans."

Trent sits on the bed beside her and lays the case on the nightstand. He then leans over and strokes Jessica's face and hair. She looks at him with widened, shifting eyes.

"What do you mean, Trent? You're scaring me!"

"Don't be scared, Jessica. We're still going to play."

Trent pulls open the nightstand drawer and pulls out a roll of duct tape. He then opens the case, revealing a large needle with a vial of some liquid. Jessica sees this and looks on with interest.

"What you got there? I hope you're going to share!"

Trent begins to prepare the needle. "This isn't going to get you high."

Jessica looks at the needle and duct tape with fear and anticipation. She does not like the way Trent's mood has changed, and the tape and needle frighten her. But damn if she isn't aroused by the whole situation. "Then what's it for?"

Trent finishes with the needle, then lays it to the side and picks up the tape. He pulls off a large piece and grabs it with both hands. He looks down at her with murder in his eyes. Jessica realizes far too late Trent has more planned for her than a good time.

"It's for killing your slutty little ass!"

Jessica struggles and screams jerking her head from side to side in an effort to keep the tape from covering her mouth. Trent roughly tries to tape her mouth shut.

"Someone help m—"

Trent clamps his hand down over her mouth to muffle her screams. Continuing to struggle, Jessica bites him fiercely. He pulls his hand away in pain.

"OW! You little bitch, you bit me!"

"Help! Someone—"

Trent punches her hard in the face. Jessica collapses, knocked out cold.

Trent looks at the piece of duct tape and shrugs. "Don't guess I need this anymore." He takes the needle from the table and injects it in Jessica's inert body.

Suddenly the door opens from another room, and Sandra walks in with a couple of other men. She looks at Jessica's body. Trent finishes with the needle, then repacks it in the carrying case.

"Got kind of rough with her didn't you, Trent?"

Trent looks at his bleeding hand. "She's lucky I didn't strangle her feisty little ass."

Sandra rolls her eyes and smirks. "Just get the body ready and clean this place up."

She turns and walks back toward the door she came through.

Trent watches her go. "What? No thanks or appreciation for a job well done?"

Ignoring the comment, Sandra doesn't turn as she leaves the room.

THIRTY-EIGHT

JESSICA LIES IN a drug-induced coma on a hospital bed in a room that looks very similar to an operating room. She is connected to various machines that monitor her vital signs. Phillip and Sandra stand with Clint and Bonnie, talking and observing the unconscious girl.

"She looks so helpless and frail. Are you sure she's all right?"

Sandra answers with the sympathy she always feels toward submitters. "Bonnie, she's fine. Basically, she is in a deep sleep that will last until we bring her out of it."

Clint takes his wife by the hand trying to comfort her troubled heart. "Will we be able to talk to her?"

"I'm afraid not." Phillip answers the question with little emotion. He always fields the questions with negative answers, allowing Sandra to field the ones with a brighter conclusion. They have operated like this for years; it just seems to work. "Submitting clients aren't allowed to have any contact with those they have submitted."

Bonnie struggles with her tears at the dispassionate statement. "Why not?"

"Because there is a very good chance you would compromise her thought pattern accidentally, or intentionally. It's likely you will have feelings of guilt and regret."

"Clint, we should never have done this to her!"

Clint takes his wife by the shoulders and looks her in the eyes. "If we didn't, you know she wouldn't have stopped the drugs and hooking till it killed her. Is that what you want?"

"No! I just feel so terrible." Succumbing to her anguish and guilt, she drops her head to his chest.

Clint wraps his arms lovingly around his grieving wife, holding her tightly. Sandra and Phillip guide the couple from the operating room. Sandra walks side by side with Bonnie, wanting nothing more than to alleviate the woman's suffering.

"Don't worry, Mrs. Henderson. We will provide you with regular progress reports so you can see how well she is doing."

Bonnie and Clint nod appreciatively.

Phillip steps forward with a business card in hand, offering it to Clint. "Mr. Henderson, I also recommend both of you participate in our submitting clients counseling program. You can meet with others who have had to follow the same course you have, as well as talk to counselors to help you through your adjustment period. On this card is a number you can call. Just present your case number when you call, and the operator will set up everything you need."

Clint takes the card, then shakes Phillip's hand thankfully. "Mr. Stevens, I want to thank you and Ms. St.

Clair here for what you've done. If it wasn't for your help, I don't think Jessica would have made it to see thirty."

"We do what we can, Mr. Henderson."

***

Clint steers his car through traffic. He looks worriedly over at his crying wife. "Bonnie, I know you feel bad about what we did—hell, I do too. But it was the only choice we had. You go on crying as much as you need to, but when we get home, I don't want to see you crying no more!"

Bonnie takes a tissue from her purse and blows her nose. "Clint, I just can't help thinking this is that rehab center all over again."

Clint grips the steering wheel tightly, knuckles whitening with anger. "That damn rehab center is what ruined her! And if that damn Cummings wouldn't have killed himself, I would have liked to have done it for him. Whoever heard of a rehab director dying of a drug overdose?"

Bonnie looks at her husband with love in her eyes. He has always been her rock through all the trouble they had with Jessica. She knows he blames himself for her behavior. He always second-guessed himself, often saying he should have been less strict and more flexible in his ways. Bonnie sometimes thought the same thing, but deep down she knew better. Clint was a good man and a good father. Some children just can't be tamed, and Jessica was worse than most.

The rehab was, in hindsight, probably overkill. But the effect that place had on their daughter was just plain bad luck. If they had sent her to any other facility around, she would not have been exposed to her degraded way of life.

"Don't blame yourself, honey. You did the best you knew how, and that would have been more than enough for most."

Clint relaxes somewhat, enjoying the feel of the steering wheel in his hand. He pilots the car onto the freeway. "I know, Bonnie, but sometimes it's hard not to. But don't you worry about this N.D.E.C. They're the real deal if ever there was one. They'll fix our little girl and put her on a better track!"

Bonnie adjusts herself more comfortably in her seat. They have a long trip ahead of them. "I hope you're right, Clint."

THIRTY-NINE

PHILLIP GATHERS HIS keys and a few other necessities, preparing to leave. He leans over to shut down his computer just as Sandra enters the room. He finishes the process quickly and meets her in the middle of the large office.

"What's up?"

She looks at him pleadingly. "I need a favor."

Phillip eyes her warily. "Uh oh. Who do I have to kill?"

"It's not quite that serious. My car's in the shop, and I need a ride home."

"I thought you had a ride worked out with Karen."

"I did, but something came up, and she's not heading home till much later."

Phillip's eyebrows rise in speculation. "More like *someone* came up."

"Entirely possible. Now how about that ride? Can you do it, or do I have to hitchhike home?"

"I think I can squeeze you in."

"Thanks, you're the best." Sandra kisses Phillip quickly on the cheek, then turns and heads toward the office door.

Phillip watches her go then calls out to her retreating form. "Hey, I was just about to leave. You are ready to go, aren't you?"

Sandra stops at the door and peeks back over her shoulder with a wave. "I'll be ready in a cinch. I just have to grab a couple of things from my desk."

Phillip shrugs in resignation after Sandra disappears from view. He looks down at his watch, not liking what he sees. *Oh well. I should still be home in time for the start of the second half.*

***

Phillip drives the car through the city with Sandra in the passenger seat. He really does not mind taking her home from work. They talk casually as they leave the city on the freeway and move closer to the suburbs. Sandra cannot help dwelling on the Henderson couple.

"That poor old lady was so sad."

"They always are."

"I know. Sometimes I just wish there was a way to take away all the pain and hurt these people go through."

"That's exactly what we do."

Sandra looks at Phillip with doubt. "I'm not talking about the counseling and therapy. I know it helps, but it can take years to fully bring some of these people out of their depression."

Phillip looks over to Sandra for a moment before returning his attention to the road ahead of him. "I'm not talking about the therapy either. I mean, think about it. If we weren't here doing what we do, then where would those people be?"

He stops talking long enough to guide the car onto the proper exit, then continues his point. "How many of them would have gone on in their same horrible cycles till the inevitable happened? And either they lose their loved one completely, or, even worse, they're killed and then everybody loses. So if you think about it, we're really doing the most good possible."

Sandra sighs in concession. "I guess."

After driving along in a few moments of silence, they approach a gated community and pull up to the guardhouse. The guard comes out and looks in the window at Phillip then Sandra.

Sandra leans toward the guard, talking over Phillip. "Is there a problem?"

He smiles in recognition. "Good evening, Ms. St. Clair. Sorry I didn't recognize the vehicle. Sir, you can go on through."

***

Phillip drives down a lane filled with identical two-story houses on both sides of the road. The only perceivable difference in the dwellings seems to be the color schemes of the homes and the cars in front of them. He slowly passes several houses before turning into the proper driveway and pulling to a stop. He turns the ignition off and the two sit for a moment, thinking of very different things. Breaking the silence, Phillip betrays his tunnel vision of focus on work. "Everything set on the Key's case?"

Sandra eyes Phillip with a little disappointment he fails to notice. She diverts her thoughts from a much more personal subject to match his. "The team is already in place, and we can fly down on Friday."

"Sounds good. Do you need me to pick you up in the morning?"

"No, I can get a ride from Karen."

"You sure?"

"Yeah. Worst-case scenario, she doesn't come home; then I'll just take a taxi." Phillip nods while Sandra opens the door and exits the car. She turns back to talk to Phillip and looks him over. "You could come in for a night cap if you would like."

"I better not. I have to drive home."

Sandra looks at him coyly. "Do you? You could stay if you want."

Phillip grimaces, not understanding Sandra's meaning. "No thanks. Your couch is hard as a rock."

"Who said anything about the couch?" Sandra turns and hip checks the car door shut, then walks to her door.

Phillip sits there allowing the proposition to finally hit him. *Did she just hit on me?* He shakes the idea off as something to think about later.

Sandra walks to her front stoop. After a moment, the car cranks and reverses out of the driveway. She unlocks the door with resignation and speaks to herself. "I'm not going to wait forever, Phillip."

FORTY

JOSH WEEDY LEANS against a shelf filled with spare parts for computers as well as boxes of printer paper and anything else a small surveillance and research room might need. He looks over his team with satisfaction. Kelly works diligently at her computer, scrolling through long lists of highly classified material, searching for anything that could possibly be related to the N.D.E.C. She has been looking for several days now with no luck. Josh is not surprised by this, considering the sheer volume of data she has to pick through. He feels sure if anything does exist, she will find it.

Kelly has been a part of Josh's research and surveillance team for a little over two years. She came to him on recommendation from an old professor he had in college. Josh gave her a try as a favor and has yet to regret his decision. She is pretty in her own way. A brunette with a few extra pounds, she has a smile unmatched in its sincerity and enthusiasm. She also has a great personality that lights up the room. Josh thinks fondly of her.

Tim, his other staff member, is the reason he finds himself cramped in this small closet of a room. Josh came right down after he had received a much anticipated phone call. It seems Tim thinks he has found something and is eager to show Josh what it is.

Tim is the classic nerd—clumsy and awkward with huge Coke-bottle glasses. He also is as smart as they come and pretty damn funny too. Tim's task has been to sneak his way undetected through the witness protection agency in order to locate Emily and her new identity. Tim is sure he has achieved his goal. Josh leans over the young man's shoulder to get a look at his computer screen. "What makes you so sure this is Emily?"

"Well, there are only four subjects in the database that completely match the criteria that you gave me. And of those, this is the only one that's been active recently."

"How can we verify?"

Tim clicks around on his screen until a picture appears. "If you have someone who has seen her, you can have her visually identified."

Josh pats Tim affectionately on the shoulder. "Great work. Get me a printout of all this."

"No problem, boss."

Kelly waves to Josh. "I think I've found something!"

Josh looks up from where the report is coming out of the printer and joins Kelly at her computer screen.

On the computer screen:

> Crisis intervention think-tank established 2030
> Sponsored by Senator Anthony Higgins
> Financial report 2047

Budget 100 million dollars—est. surplus:
19 million dollars

Josh reads the screen with a higher pitch than usual in his voice.

"Crisis intervention think-tank! One hundred million a year budget! What kind of think-tank needs that kind of money?"

"When you see numbers like this," Kelly says, "it usually means the think-tank's primary focus has become a working operation."

"How did you find this?"

"I got to thinking there must be a link between the N.D.E.C. and the witness protection agency. I cross-referenced the two agencies and this is what came up."

"Anything on the N.D.E.C.?"

"No, nothing. I think the only reason we found this is a leak on the part of the witness protection end."

Josh and his team share a moment of silent contemplation. "They're supposed to be one of our most secure agencies."

Kelly smiles. "Apparently they're not as secure as this N.D.E.C., boss."

"Can you get me a location on this think-tank?"

"Give me a minute." Kelly returns to her keyboard and retrieves the address from the depths of her computer. "Here we go."

"Get me a printout of everything you got."

"Already did. It's coming out in your office right now."

Josh gives Kelly the same pat on the shoulder he gave Tim, then he grabs the printouts that Tim has prepared and runs out the door. "Great work, guys!" Josh leaves them smiling to each other over a job well done.

Kelly eyes Tim smugly. "Ha! You thought you beat me."

Tim returns the look of superiority. "I did beat you—you had to use a cross-reference on my work in order to make your discovery."

"Maybe so, but my task was harder, and I think my pat on the back was given with more sincerity."

Pointing to his chest, Tim turns to fully face Kelly. "No way. When he patted me on the shoulder, he let his hand slide down to brush up against my man boob!

Kelly bursts into laughter and leaves her computer console. "You are such a liar!"

Tim joins her at the door. "Maybe, maybe not."

***

Josh enters his office and snatches the printout from the printer. He quickly scans it, then grabs the phone off his desk and pushes zero. He holds the receiver to his mouth, eagerly waiting for the White House switch operator to come online. After what seems like a much longer time than has actually passed, he hears the operator's voice.

"This is the switchboard. How can I be of service, Mr. Weedy?"

"Get me the president."

"Right away, sir."

Josh waits a moment. The line clicks over and begins to ring.

"Hello?"

"Hi, Dan, it's Josh here, and I have some news."

"What is it?"

"I've got an address. I think we should send in our team to set up the works."

"Do it as discreetly as possible. No leaks."

"No leaks heard. I've also got a line on Emily, but I need you to give a positive ID.

"Send me everything you got."

Josh hangs up the phone after the line goes dead, looks over the printouts and contemplates his next move. He picks the phone back up and punches in a number very few people have and waits for the phone to ring. The line is picked up on the second ring.

"Bo speaking."

Josh smiles to himself at the sound of a good friend's voice. "Hi, Bo. It's Josh over here at the House."

"Hey, Josh. This is a surprise. I didn't expect to hear from you until our meeting next week."

"I know, Bo, but something has come up, and it needs immediate attention."

"Hold on a sec, I need to secure this line before we go any further."

Josh listens patiently while his friend makes the proper adjustments to his encrypted receiver. Josh feels a weight lift from his shoulders. It has been a frustrating week of inaction up to this point, and damn if it does not feel good to be making some moves.

Bo's voice fills the receiver, signaling the reconnected line. "We're good now, Josh. What do you have for me?"

"Bo, I need you to infiltrate a high-security area and set up the works for surveillance."

"Where are we going?"

"Well, that's the good news. You don't have to leave the city."

Bo remains silent, surprised by the proximity of the job. It takes him less than a second to conclude whatever his target, it's an internal probe.

"What's the bad news, boss?"

"We need this done yesterday, and with complete discretion."

"I had a feeling this was going to be tricky. I'll call the boys in, and we'll be ready by 0500 tomorrow."

Josh flips through to the address in the files he has. "I'll have the coordinates emailed over directly."

"You'll be up and running in thirty-six hours."

"I knew I could count on you, Bo."

FORTY-ONE

Bo Simmons looks over the building with a critical eye. The structure looks like so many others in the city. Ten stories tall, made mostly of glass walls from the second floor up. The top floor has a wrap-around balcony, and from the building's schematics, he knows there is a helicopter landing pad on the roof. The front of the building has a well-kept lawn separating the parking lot from the main entrance.

Bo is a little surprised by the apparent lack of pedestrians. Very few people have entered or exited in the two hours he has been studying the premises. Several members of his team have staked out positions at various points around the building. Bo will soon call his guys in. He needs information, but he does not like . their lack of cover. There are just not enough people for them to blend in with. He will wait until James, his man currently inside, has resurfaced. Bo sighs with relief when he sees James finally appear and return to his vehicle. He speaks into his comlink. "All right, guys, let's pack it up."

Bo and his team work in the rare comfort of their headquarters, reviewing all the information they have collected over the course of the morning and afternoon. The data is quite substantial, considering the resources his team is able to draw from. Working directly for the White House definitely has its advantages—virtually unlimited security clearance and the freshest technology available, to name a couple.

Even with these advantages, though, Bo does not feel as comfortable as he would like. The operational timeline could not be worse. All the information they have gathered so far points to an extremely well-run organization with an unlimited budget. Whoever these people are, they are bound to have all kinds of passive security, and linking into their systems without detection is going to be a nightmare. The only good news he has received so far is the fact that the night-shift security team is light, with only two men patrolling the whole building. The human factor in an operation like this is huge. If the security team had been much larger, their chances for success would drop considerably.

***

Bo's team consists of fifteen of the toughest, smartest, most highly trained men on the planet. In order to prove worthy, a man must go through over two years of vigorous training of every sort imaginable. And that is after passing several levels of situational testing where the individual is placed in desperate situations with zero resources except his own ingenuity. If the man passes these tests, which he is not even aware he is involved in, only then is he approached and extended an invitation to participate in the training program. Only one in twenty passes situational testing, and of those, only one in ten makes it through. No one ever quits in training. But for some, their bodies or minds literally fail them, and they are excused from the program with high honors, knowing they functioned to the very best of their abilities. And who could find shame in that?

Bo looks over his team with pride. He knows every man here would gladly take a bullet for any other man. They have proven themselves time and again in the most hostile of environments—bullets flying; bombs exploding, sending shrapnel screaming in all directions; targets being eliminated well behind enemy lines. They have experienced it all.

But he can look into each man's eyes and see the unasked questions. For the first time his guys are working outside their very broad comfort zone. The suddenness of the mission combined with the unheard of proximity to home has his men on edge. No one here likes the fact that most of the team lives within twenty miles of their target. The whole unit shares a feeling of their two very separate worlds coming precariously close together. Bo never in his illustrious career imagined for a moment he would find himself on a mission he would rather have turned down. The soldier in him requires unwavering dedication. Today, as he gathers his team for the final debriefing, he grimly acknowledges the profound distaste he feels for this mission.

"Listen up. I'm not going to pretend for a moment that I like this deal any more than you do."

The gathered soldiers give their commander their full attention. This is the man they respect above all others. They may not like it, but whatever Bo says, goes. If he told them to parachute into hell, not one of them would hesitate long enough to grab a glass of water before jumping out of the plane.

"Be that as it may, we've been given a job, and we're damn well going to do it. Each one of you has been briefed on his assignments. I have no doubt that every man here will perform his duty to the best of his ability. Time is short. Separate into your five-man teams and address and solve any issues that need attention. Spend two hours on this, then get some rest. We move out at 0200."

***

Bo takes a seat in the back of his mobile command post—a cargo truck painted to look identical to one used by the city power company. He puts on a headset in order to listen in on the communications of his two field teams. James commands the primary team, currently en route to their target with the main objective of bug placement. Marcus commands the advance team; their main objective is infiltrating the building and neutralizing all alarm systems while also keeping tabs on the security guards in order for James' team to work unmolested. Bo himself commands the third team. His primary job is perimeter surveillance as well as backing up both teams in whatever capacity is needed. Bo watches through mobile cameras attached to his unit leader's gear. He gets a lead view of Marcus working quickly and expertly to disarm the security system.

Bo splits his attention between Marcus's progress and the now arriving primary team. "How we doing, Marcus?"

"The system is good, but not unmanageable. There we go. All systems have been disarmed. Primary team is good to go."

"Excellent. Now get inside and locate those guards."

"On my way."

Bo watches Marcus and his team enter the building from the loading dock. Bo peers over at the schematics of the internal layout of the building, which his team hacked from the public works department.

"Marcus, the security desk will be through the door at the end of the loading zone in the main lobby."

"Roger that. We're at the door now. Infrared is showing two heat sources in the area of the security desk. Deploying the Bee now."

Bo nods to himself in satisfaction.

The Bee is a motion/sound-activated, remote airborne-surveillance device the size of a honeybee. It could be programmed to follow any source of movement or sound from a point of contact to a distance of a linear mile. The Bee will also alert any team member of its approach by sending out an electric impulse every five seconds to a vibrating wrist band.

"All right, James, the alarm has been neutralized. You may proceed with bug placement."

"Roger that."

Bo focuses his attention on the screen showing James' team moving methodically through the various types of rooms within, placing their surveillance devices in every nook and cranny. Bo knows there is no need to place bugs on the communication devices since they are able to plant an information-gathering unit on the master processor in the building's IT room. He cannot help but feel the whole operation is running too smoothly when James interrupts his thoughts of success.

"Sir, we have a problem."

Bo refocuses on the mission, silently berating himself for his unusual mental slip.

"What's up, James?"

"Sir, we have encountered a hidden vault."

"What do you mean?"

"Well, sir, from the plans we have of this building, there seems to be a large space in the middle with no access."

Bo looks at his own schematics and studies the area in question.

"There should be a door right in front of you."

"I know, sir, but there isn't one. I'm facing what appears to be a solid concrete wall."

Bo looks through the view afforded him and frowns, seeing the obstruction.

"Have you passed any other walls similar to this one?"

"No, sir. That's what makes it stand out. It's almost as if it's on purpose. Even if we didn't have the plans for the building, this wall is in contrast to the design of this place."

"I agree, sergeant. Can you get a reading from any of your equipment?"

"No, sir. Nothing from anything."

Bo examines the wall while he thinks. He does not like the idea of this building being so easily penetrated up to this point. He has no doubt there is something behind that wall, and if his team can't get through it, then it can't be done.

"Okay, James, set up everything you can around your location, then pull out of there. I think we have been here long enough."

The uneasy feeling in the pit of Bo's stomach has only grown. He watches his men exit the building. James and his team are closely followed by Marcus and his unit. Bo gives both groups a five-minute head start before he finally allows his driver to depart and follow suit. He feels only slightly relieved by the apparent success of the mission. The hidden area in the building bothers him. Bo pushes his unease to the back of his mind and prepares to contact Josh.

Contemplating the not-quite-completed mission, he punches in the number of Josh's surveillance center.

FORTY-TWO

Josh watches Kelly and Tim man their computers and bring the surveillance equipment online. All three look to the phone beeping in on the secure line linked directly to Bo's mobile command post. Kelly reaches over and punches the button that connects the line.

"This is base. Go ahead, Alpha team leader."

"All systems are in place and should be fully operational."

"Roger that, Alpha, please stand by."

The two computer jocks type away vigorously as they watch their monitors begin to upload the various images from the well-placed cameras and listening devices. Josh is overwhelmed by the many camera views quickly flashing onto the screens, then disappearing to be replaced by another. "How do we expect to monitor all those cameras at the same time?"

Tim briefly looks over his shoulder before answering Josh's question.

"We won't, sir. All the monitors are motion/sound activated. So whenever one detects movement, it will automatically record and be displayed."

"Nice."

Kelly points out the system check-off list.

"We're bringing everything online now . . . all systems are a go. Good work, Alpha team leader."

Bo responds to the praise with his usual lack of outward emotion.

"Alpha out."

Tim turns to address Josh.

"They won't be able to take a leak without us knowing how many times they shake it when they're done!"

Josh nods approvingly and leaves the room.

Kelly waits until the door closes before rolling her eyes with disdain.

"Nice analogy, Timmy."

Tim responds with a smug smile, "I thought you'd like that."

The two coworkers focus steadily on the computers, going through the system, checking for glitches and ironing them out. They continue in silence until Kelly tries to bring the cameras pointed at the concrete wall into proper focus.

"Uh oh!"

Tim looks up from his computer. "What's 'uh oh'?"

Kelly types a few commands into her computer, trying without success to clear up the pictures coming from the cameras.

"Have you tried a system restore?"

"Of course! I'm not an idiot!" Keely barked.

Tim throws up his hands in surrender. He has seen the few times Kelly has been stumped by a problem and knows from experience she can turn into quite a terror. Tim slides over to her console and looks at the images on her computer. He pats her on the shoulder and returns to his work.

"Don't beat yourself up, babe. There's nothing you can do to fix that."

Kelly allows her frustration to control her response.

"Oh, but I bet Mr. Super Genius can. Is that it?"

Tim quickly slides back over to Kelly and clamps a hand roughly over her mouth, stifling the insult that is sure to follow.

"Before you say something really mean but true about my failures with the opposite sex, let me explain. The problem with the picture is signal interference on the other end. Somewhere around that wall is a device programmed to distort sounds and images from potential bugs."

Tim slowly takes his hand from Kelly's now sheepish face. She looks at him with please-forgive-me puppy dog eyes. Tim shrugs and returns to his console.

"I'm sorry, Timmy, will you forgive me?"

"Don't worry about it, babe; I know you don't mean it."

Kelly returns to her computer and concentrates on the unfocused images.

"Don't you think it's strange that the only place with interference is a dead-end hallway?"

"Alpha seems to think there is a hidden area behind that wall." Tim brings the building schematics up on the computer. He types in a few commands and waits for the results.

Kelly slides next to him to look over his shoulder. "What are you doing?"

"I'm finding out how large the hidden area of the building is."

Kelly lays her head on Tim's shoulder. Tim pretends not to notice.

"I'm sorry about getting angry."

"You already said that."

"I know. I just thought I should say it again."

Tim leans forward with a jerk, almost knocking the unsuspecting Kelly from her seat.

"Jeeze, Tim."

Tim looks over to Kelly and pulls her back beside him. "Sorry, didn't mean to, but look at this!"

They both crowd around his monitor.

"What is it?"

"Look at the square footage displacement! Twenty-five thousand square feet—that's huge."

Kelly can't relate to the size, but she knows from Tim's reaction it is a substantial amount of space. "How big an area is that?"

"Almost a full tenth of the building's total size."

Kelly registers her own disbelief. "You mean there is the equivalent of an entire floor missing from our surveillance grid!"

Tim nods his head in affirmation.

"Yep, and there's nothing we can do about it."

"Josh isn't going to like this."

FORTY-THREE

Senator Anthony Higgins sits behind his desk, looking over several pages from an open file lying before him. He murmurs to himself, hastily reading the troubling documents.

John Powers sits across from him with a permanent scowl etched on his face. He is intimately familiar with all the details contained in the file. In all his years in the senator's service, he has never had to relay such a dire report. He had spent last night scrutinizing every variable, looking for a brighter outcome. Zero success. Once the Kat variable is entered into the simulation, every outcome falls between bad and a lot worse. He had left out the President's daughter several times just to see, and the outcomes had been totally reversed. In all John's years doing the simulations, he had never seen one variable come anywhere as close to changing the outcomes so conclusively, and so drastically. Take into account the potential for rippling, and the negative consequence can't be measured. All this appeared in the conclusion of the report. The ripple worried him, which in this case would be better described as a tsunami. In a couple of his bleakest Kat scenarios, the simulation program had actually locked up. This had only happened previously when they had run a simulation of a Texas-size asteroid striking the Atlantic Ocean.

Anthony chances a glance at his longtime friend and colleague. Over the years, John's simulation reports have always proved incredibly accurate. Anthony can tell by the look on John's face that he fully believes in the accuracy of this one.

"This reads pretty bad."

"All signs indicate worst-case scenario. We've been fully compromised."

Anthony nods his head, then looks out his window.

"Well, it looks like our predictions were correct."

"They usually are, sir."

"That's how we stay ahead in the game."

Anthony turns back to John from the window.

"Have St. Clair move ahead with the alternate reality and reloop program."

John nods in understanding.

"Yes, sir."

FORTY-FOUR

SANDRA WALKS SLOWLY around the hospital bed, dragging her fingers softly along the inert form of Phillip's body. Pausing at the head of the bed, she looks lovingly at her unconscious friend. She checks the monitor displaying brain activity with satisfaction. Sandra carefully inspects all the equipment connections that feed from Phillip's body to the many machines. This is a job normally delegated to one of the lab technicians, but with so much invested in her dear patient, she chooses to perform as many of the hands-on procedures as her busy schedule allows. Everything is as it should be, so after another moment of adoring inspection, she leaves the bedside.

Sandra crosses the floor slowly and enters the patient-observation room. There she joins Bill, senior lab technician, who is performing a complete system-diagnostics check, one of three run every day. Again this is not the normal procedure, but all involved agree that safety redundancy is paramount when so much is potentially at stake. Bill nods a greeting.

"How are we doing, Bill?"

"I'm just finishing the first screening." Bill smiles with satisfaction, having completed the task with no abnormalities. "Once again, everything checks out, Ms. St. Clair."

"Bill, I've told you a thousand times to call me Sandra."

"I know, old tricks and new dogs, or however the saying goes."

"Close enough, I guess."

The co-conspirators allow the silence of the mutual feelings of guilt and regret to fill the room as they look through the observation window at their boss, friend and now unwilling patient.

"Sandra, I can't help but feel like this is all wrong."

Sandra does not respond to Bill's statement. What is there to say? She agrees completely; she can't count how many times she has entertained similar thoughts and feelings. The problem is there is nothing to be done about them. She knows the deal, and she understands the lack of options available. Sandra does not allow her empathy to show; very few people understand the complexity of the situation, and she simply cannot allow her uncertainty of the outcome to become common knowledge.

"Bill, it's time to move forward with our patient agenda. I expect you to see to everything personally. Do not delegate anything. Do you understand?"

Bill hides his surprise and discomfort at the unemotional instructions he has received. This is a new Sandra he has not dealt with before. He chooses to respond with an equal lack of emotion.

"Yes, Ms. St. Clair, I will handle everything personally."

Sandra leaves Bill to his task without further comment. Bill watches her go with a hint of relief in his mind. Never one to procrastinate, he turns his attention fully to his patient and the work ahead of him. Bill begins to punch commands into the console, initiating a very complicated chain of events. He lets his attention rove between the various readouts and the inert form in the other room. Phillip's body begins to shake and convulse, straining against the well-placed restraints.

"Right on time."

FORTY-FIVE

THE PILOT GUIDES the Learjet smoothly toward the runway. Above him the sun shines brightly, illuminating the crystal clear blue sky. He chances a peek out the cockpit side window—not a cloud in sight, and that's just the way he likes it.

"Nice day to land a plane, huh, Bob?"

Bob nods to Tony his copilot, giving him a broad smile. "Nice day to do a lot of things."

Tony returns the smile and begins the landing sequence. "Itching to start that vacation?"

Bob lowers the landing gear and carefully checks his readouts. "Sure am. Brenda's been here since Wednesday, and as soon as we get this puppy on the ground, I'm meeting her at the gate and we're flying to Australia."

"That's quite a flight from Miami."

"We're not going to make the flight all at once. We plan on stopping a couple of times along the way and doing some sightseeing."

Bob stops talking while he lines the plane up for its final approach. He concentrates fully on the job at hand. He has landed more planes than he can count and in all kinds of weather, and he is considered a very good pilot. Bob has always believed that what made him so good at his craft were his attention to detail and his unwillingness to leave anything to chance.

Tony watches Bob work with a confident feeling within. Tony has been partnered with several pilots now, and while all of them were competent, none of the others applied the consistent care and effort that his current flying companion does.

***

The Learjet comes in to land smoothly. The wheels touch down with a screech. The jet rolls down the runway and slowly taxis toward a private hangar. The plane passes through the bay doors and comes to a gentle stop beside a large, black SUV. The exit door opens with the steps coming down. Phillip and Sandra exit the jet and head directly toward the waiting vehicle. Both hastily get inside. Chad, the driver, puts the motor in gear and quickly navigates away from the airport.

Phillip and Sandra share the spacious backseat. Phillip waits attentively while Sandra shuffles through the file of papers on her lap, organizing them into proper sequence. "We've got a boat chartered with our guys already in place as the crew. We'll take it down to the meeting spot in the Keys."

Phillip nods understanding. "How long'll that trip be?"

Sandra continues sifting through her notes. "The weather is supposed to be clear for the next several days.

So it should be smooth sailing. We will be there tomorrow night, a full day ahead of schedule."

***

Tim adjusts the color contrast on his computer monitor. He smiles with satisfaction after the view of Phillip and Sandra jumps into focus. Kelly ribs him for his rookie technique. "Nice work troubleshooting the hazy picture."

Tim shrugs off the sarcastic remark. "The simplest solutions are often the hardest to figure out." He freezes the feed while he tweaks the image.

Josh Weedy enters the surveillance room, momentarily interrupting the playful banter. He immediately concentrates on the incoming audio and video from the SUV. "What am I seeing here, guys?"

"Sorry, boss," Kelly says. "We were just ironing out some visual defects."

Tim raises his eyebrows with surprise at Kelly's forgiving assessment.

Josh disregards the apology. He has always tried to exude a deflated sense of power, so he did not mind the continued conversation Kelly and Tim were having. "No problem."

Tim restarts the feed, and all three listen intently to Sandra debriefing Phillip.

"Where are they?"

While Kelly takes the lead in answering Josh's inquiries, Tim brings up a map showing the progress of the bugged automobile. The map shows the state of Florida with the lower portion superimposed on the city of Miami.

"Miami."

Josh eyes the progress of the blip on the map with impressed surprise. "How did we get this?"

"We've downloaded their complete itinerary from their computers. We were able to send Bo Simmons' team to Miami two days ago. They were able to infiltrate their transportation network."

"Nice! What about their boat?"

"We already chartered our own. The team is just about finished with the surveillance modifications. They will be ready to leave dock when these guys do."

Josh allows the concern in his voice to show at the thought of his adversaries being tipped off to the fact that they are under surveillance. "They're going to follow from a safe distance, I hope. We absolutely can't allow these people to know we are onto them. I find the idea of a boat following them fairly obvious."

"Not to worry." Kelly assures him. "As long as our guys stay within five miles, we can see and hear everything they do from the satellite link. That will put them outside of their radar."

"Are we sure about this?"

Kelly nods confidently. "We are. Bo has been all over their boat and feels very confident there is nothing on board they could use to discover us."

"Excellent! I want you to patch everything you get through to the executive viewing conference room."

Tim types commands into his console, setting up the connection between the two monitoring stations. He completes the simple task and gives Kelly a slight nod. "Done. We have a link set up on seven-second delay."

Josh smiles broadly at the efficient work of his small team. He leans forward and shakes both Tim and Kelly affectionately by the shoulders. Tim has to catch his glasses to keep them from falling from his face.

"You guys are the best. Let me know when the action heats up so I can keep the president up to date."

Josh leaves the room in a rush. Tim replaces his glasses and watches Kelly rub her neck, massaging out the unintended pain from Josh's powerful grasp.

"Crap, he almost broke my freaking neck!"

Tim sighs with agreement. "What do you expect with those Popeye forearms."

***

Phillip and Sandra ride along in silence. Chad guides them toward the waterfront and the marina. Phillip tries not to dwell on the mission in front of them. He has discovered over the years that he has a tendency to do this. If he did not feel a negative effect of this, he honestly would not try to stop. Phillip has never minded his work dominating his life—in fact, he likes it. The problem is that the amount of built-up stress he is under has started to cause physical and mental symptoms. He has spent the better part of a year with a severe case of insomnia, which in turn is leading to memory loss and short bouts of confusion.

It did not take long for his symptoms to cause problems at the office. He had started missing meetings and would often lose his train of thought in the middle of discussions. Sandra, ever in tune with his moods and personality, had not waited long when the symptoms began. She immediately set him up an appointment with the company shrink. The doctor expertly diagnosed Phillip's stress issues and made it perfectly clear what he needed to do. Phillip took two weeks off while at the same time a mood-altering doctor on their staff taught him a litany of relaxation techniques. Phillip had secretly been relieved it wasn't something worse, like the brain cancer he had feared. Knowing that in order to function at his highest level he would have to learn to separate himself from his career on occasion, he learned the relaxing techniques and now practices them often. One of the simplest ways to break a ruminating cycle he currently finds himself in is to start an open-ended conversation about something unrelated. So he does.

"Looks like we'll have some time to kill."

Sandra smiles at the comment. She has been thinking the same thing along with some ideas about what she thinks would fill their spare time wonderfully.

"You know what I would like to do?"

"What's that?"

"Snorkeling. They've got some great spots we'll pass on the way down!"

Phillip looks at Sandra smiling; he has always enjoyed her unbridled enthusiasm when it comes to the simple joys of living. He never misses the chance to allow her to do something she wants when their duties do not interfere.

"Make it happen."

Sandra lights up with excitement and Phillip laughs. "Really? Oh, Phillip, it'll be so much fun. You know, they have an underwater statue of Christ outside of Key Largo!"

"Sounds like someone did a little research."

Sandra smiles playfully. "You will not regret it."

FORTY-SIX

MARCUS JONES SIPS his fruity drink from a straw; he eyes the yellow little umbrella with contempt. *Who in the hell thinks up this hokey shit?* Marcus will always be a Budweiser man when he does drink, which is fairly rare. It is not that he does not enjoy the buzz; it is just the fact that Bo expects his officers to set an example for the lower-rank men to follow. Marcus chooses to keep his body and mind in peak condition, and alcohol does not fit into the Marcus Jones work-out program.

He looks beyond his Virgin Long Island Iced Tea to the boat he has been ordered to follow, now docked three piers down. With a casual eye, he watches a man board with a knockout brunette in tow behind him. He would not be a man if he did not let his eyes linger on her; he would not be a soldier if he could not dismiss the distraction. Marcus turns from the mind-numbing beauty and peeks into the cabin where his two subordinates prepare the boat for departure.

242

"Lucas, how are we doing?"

Lucas glances at Marcus with a gum-smacking smile. "Right on schedule, sir. We'll be ready to head out in thirty minutes."

"Timetable has been moved forward; we leave in ten."

Lucas motions to the third man who has the mother board of a computer pulled apart and is currently soldering a loose component.

Looking Ben over, Marcus shakes his head in resignation. Ben loves being a soldier like they all do, and he loves dressing like one even more. Dressed in full combat fatigues, he sits crouched down in front of the torn-open hard drive. He wears a red headband in the same fashion as his childhood hero Rambo. Ben finishes off the look with face paint in the classic style of jungle warfare.

"Ben, can we do it?" Marcus asked.

Ben nods affirmation. He lays the soldering gun to the side and blows lightly on the still smoking repair.

"I've fixed the bad connection. Give this another five minutes and we can activate all the surveillance equipment." Ben quickly stands, leaving the computer in pieces, and heads toward the engine compartment.

Marcus eyes the computer warily. "Don't you need to finish with that?"

Ben stops next to Marcus and assumes a look of deep concentration as though he is contemplating some profound philosophical wonder. He bows his head while grasping his chin in the classic thinking-man's pose. Marcus waits patiently through the sarcastic performance.

"Well, I could put the computer back together now, but then I would have to wait to start the engine until I finished with the computer. That would put our departure time closer to twenty minutes than ten. As it stands now, even in its current state of disarray, the computer will in fact do the tasks required by our glorious heads of state and leaders of the free freaking world. Now on the other hand, while equally as capable of performing the duties delegated to them, our twin engines as of yet require the assistance of yours truly in order to—how shall I say—"

Marcus grabs Ben by the shoulders and shakes him vigorously. "I get it man! Just go start the damn boat!"

Ben smooths out his uniform and salutes Marcus, almost poking him in the face. "As you wish." He slips past Marcus and moves his way to the enclosed helm.

Marcus watches him go. "Oh yeah, smart guy? Well, guess what—you smeared your face-flauge with your stupid thinking pose!" He looks at Lucas who has been watching the entire exchange with amusement.

Lucas gives his commander a thumbs-up sign. "Face-flauge? I like it."

Marcus leaves Lucas in laughter, shakes his head and returns to the deck of the boat. He watches the other boat slowly leave the dock and head to the open sea. Grabbing the abandoned drink, Marcus attempts to take a sip but accidentally sticks the umbrella in his mouth and the straw in his left eye. He jerks back from the attacking straw, spilling most of the drink. "Are you kidding me?" he says out loud.

He looks up to find the brunette from the other boat, watching his comical error, holding her own drink. She pointedly removes the straw from her beverage before smiling, then sipping her drink successfully.

Marcus shrugs, laughing while he removes the umbrella and straw from his drink as well. He refills his drink from a pitcher on the table before parking his rear in the lounge chair beside it. He grabs a magazine from beside the pitcher and pretends to read it, casually watching the boat with the brunette smoothly glide down the line of piers toward the channel to the Atlantic Ocean. Lucas appears on deck, dressed in the costume of a vacationer on a deep sea fishing expedition. He joins Marcus and pours his own drink.

"I've stowed all our gear and brought the surveillance system online. We're ready to go." Both men pause as the boat's engines roar to life.

Marcus climbs from the chair and points to the ropes that secure the yacht to the pier. "Tell Ben to head for the channel. I'll be below as soon as I pull in the lines."

"Ben wants to know when he can come above deck."

"Anytime he wants after he gets out of that ridiculous outfit. Otherwise, not till we're out of visual range of the coast."

"Thought so." Lucas disappears below deck, leaving Marcus to bring in the tow lines.

FORTY-SEVEN

PHILLIP SLIDES HIS swimming trunks over his bare skin and ties a knot, securing them around his trim waist. He looks into the mirror and grimaces at his untanned skin. *I'm going to be cooked like a lobster in about twenty minutes.*

He looks through his travel bag and pulls out sunscreen promising ultimate protection from the damaging ultraviolet rays. He squirts a generous portion into his hand and rubs it onto and over as much of his bare skin as he can reach.

Sandra sashays into his cabin in a huff of impatience and excitement. Phillip does a double take, seeing the toned, tanned body of his coworker. Sandra smiles at the view of Phillip's eyes roving her scantily clothed figure. She strikes a playful pose, wiggling her hips from side to side.

"What do you think? I bought it just for this trip!" Phillip snaps out of his trance and sticks out the sunscreen for Sandra to take.

"I think you're the only person I know who has a perfect tan in November in D.C."

"Tanning beds can do wonders, but I asked about the bikini, silly."

Phillip looks Sandra over critically for a moment then turns his back to her. "I can't reach my back; will you give me a hand?"

Sandra squeezes out some more sunscreen and tries to hide the disappointment in her voice. "You didn't answer my question." She begins to apply the protecting lotion.

"Honestly, Sandra, I was afraid to."

Sandra finishes with the lotion. "Why?"

Phillip turns and takes the lotion from Sandra and motions for her to turn around. She turns and he begins to apply lotion to her unreachable spots.

"Because you might be the most attractive human I've ever seen and that damn bikini just sealed the deal. You're like the sun in that thing: if I stared too long I would go blind."

Sandra turns at the heartfelt compliment and jumps into Phillip's arm and kisses him firmly on the lips. "Oh, Phillip! That's the first time you've ever said you thought I was pretty!"

Phillip pries Sandra's arms from around his neck, disengaging from her grasp. "I never felt the need to state the obvious. Now, let's go look at some fish before you give me a heart attack!" Heading for the deck, Phillip pushes by the now disappointed but glowing Sandra.

Sandra joins Phillip on deck in time to watch him dive into the crystal clear blue water. She quickly dons her snorkeling gear and follows suit.

***

From his viewing monitor, Lucas also watches Phillip dive into the water. "Well, at least someone is having fun."

Marcus sits across the spacious cabin, reading a magazine dedicated to really big guns. He continues flipping the pages. "We are not here to have fun."

"Why is the company having us watch a couple on vacation anyway?"

Marcus looks up. "They're not on vacation. They're supposed to be here performing some type of black operation. We're here to observe and record whatever they do, and then send it upstairs."

Lucas types a command, and the picture on the screen switches to a different angle, showing a better view of Sandra putting on her snorkeling mask. "These guys part of the network?"

"Not our concern."

Lucas shrugs. "Different foot, same body."

Marcus puts the magazine down in resignation and stands to leave the cabin for a quieter spot on the boat. "Just keep an eye on them and keep me posted." Marcus turns and exits the cabin.

Sandra climbs to the edge of the boat, preparing to dive in. Lucas watches happily through the hidden camera, giving him a perfect view of her backside. "No problem."

FORTY-EIGHT

Paul stands at the stern of his stepfather's hundred-foot yacht, looking back toward the receding marina with a heavy heart and troubled mind. He cannot help but feel he is betraying his father's memory—a man he barely remembers, but longs to emulate.

He looks out at the vanishing shore, imagining his soul vanishing with it. He cannot shake the feeling of impending doom, dreading the meeting that will seal his fate. Paul never wanted to be involved in his stepfather's drug trade, but he sees now he never had a choice; he tried for years to avoid the inevitable. Alas, Alfonzo had hidden the trap too well to be sidestepped. After this weekend's deal goes down, Paul will be established as a player in the game, he will have responsibilities and duties to perform. He will also be held accountable for any mistakes he makes. Not performing is not an option; Alfonzo had made the consequences crystal clear. Anything less than complete compliance, and his mother's life will be forfeited. And that's the hook—if it concerned just his own life, he feels he could stand firmly by his principles, come what may. But like so many defiant souls who have been subdued by their enemies, everyone has a kryptonite and Paul's mother is his; so he will fall in line, he will play ball.

***

Alfonzo approaches his stepson from the main cabin of the yacht. He carries with him two drinks—one for each of them. He offers one to Paul who silently accepts. Both men stand side by side, watching the sun go down over the distant shore line. Alfonzo studies his stepson from the corner of his eye; he is pleased with what he sees. There is a determined resolve in the young man's manner that is crucial for his successful assimilation into Alfonzo's world. He is not the first to have to adapt to a life he would not choose, and he will not be the last. But anyone who does has to have the resolve to do so. Alfonzo places his arm affectionately across Paul's shoulders.

"I am proud of you, Paul. You have really shown me something these last couple of weeks."

"I've accepted my fate. I will not defy your wishes any longer."

Alfonzo pulls Paul toward him, forcing him to face him.

"I realize you are trying, son, and I commend you." Paul stiffens ever so slightly at the paternal implication. Alfonzo raises his eyebrows and points at Paul with the hand holding his drink.

"You see? We have further to go if we are to fool our adversaries. You must not bristle when I refer to you as my flesh and blood. And even more so, you must be able to interact with me affectionately as if we are truly father and son." Paul nods his head in understanding, not trusting himself to speak.

"In order to establish the proper familiarity between us, we need to start now. Do you agree, son?" Alfonzo stares in silence, waiting for Paul to reply.

Paul looks briefly back at the sunset— just in time to see the last of the sun disappear behind the endless horizon— and then looks at Alfonzo. A lone tear slips from his eye. "Yes, father, I agree."

Alfonzo smiles broadly and embraces his stepson warmly. Paul hesitates then returns the hug awkwardly. Alfonzo breaks the embrace then motions to Paul to turn up his drink. "We do not have a lot of time before our rendezvous day after tomorrow, so we must make positive memories together now. So drink, my son. This night we will drink together and be drunk. We will fondle women and yell at each other as a true family." Alfonzo turns up his drink and Paul follows suit. Alfonzo throws his empty glass into the swaying ocean, then grabs Paul and drags him affectionately toward the lounge and awaiting women.

***

Paul takes another drink, one that he should have left in the glass. The room sways from more than the movement of the ocean.

Candy, one of the four girls on board the yacht, straddles him and kisses his neck seductively. "When are you to take me to your cabin, Pauly? You want more than just a cracker don't you?"

Vanessa, the other girl sharing his side of the lounge, snorts a large line of coke from the mirror-surfaced coffee table. She hands Candy the straw and points to the two remaining lines. "I think this is what our handsome sailor needs to have some of, so that his mast will be in proper position when we get ready to board."

Candy slides off Paul's lap and guides him toward the coke. She expertly leads him through the process off snorting a line. The effects are instantaneous. Paul comes immediately back to life, and before he can react, Vanessa pulls him onto her and kisses him relentlessly.

As Candy snorts the last line, Alfonzo stands up from where he has been camped out with the other two girls and heads for his private cabin with them in tow. Alfonzo pauses by the scene being played out on the sofa. "I expect you ladies to take good care of my son. I look forward to hearing all the gory details tomorrow."

Vanessa breaks off the kiss. "Don't worry, Alfie; we are going to take real good care of Pauly."

Paul cackles, leaning up from the couch. "'Alfie!' That's golden! I think that'll be my new name for you."

Alfonzo smiles graciously. "For tonight you can call me Alfie."

Alfonzo resumes his lurching walk but pauses at the doorway, remembering an earlier phone call. The girls, half undressed, are already molesting him mercilessly.

"Pauly, I just remembered—your friend Sandra called right before we left port. She said she would be seeing you soon." With the message relayed, Alfonzo allows the women to pull him into the cabin, closing the door behind them.

Paul tries to assimilate Alfonzo's words; he struggles for a moment trying to understand. "Sandra?" Paul tries to sit up, and then understanding filters its way into his inebriated skull. "Holy crap . . ."

Candy straddles his torso while Vanessa straddles his chest, removing her bikini top and wiggling her goods playfully in front of his bulging eyes.

"Sorry, Pauly, Sandra will have to wait her turn. You're ours tonight."

And like a giant tidal wave, some forces simply cannot be denied.

FORTY-NINE

PHILLIP STICKS HIS head out the main cabin sliding glass door. Nodding, he looks down at his wristwatch. "Right on schedule." He moves through the door and joins Sandra on deck and watches the other boat motor up to their starboard side. "I'll secure the lines if you want to head inside and prepare the notes for the debriefing."

Sandra nods and quietly leaves the deck.

Chad throws a line from the now idling yacht to where Phillip stands ready to receive. Phillip yanks the line from the air and ties the two boats together. Chad leaps from his craft, landing smoothly onto Phillip's with a second tie-off line in hand; he moves to the opposite end of the boat, securing the second line. With no fear of the boats drifting apart in the night, the two men shake hands, warmly greeting each other.

"It's good to see you, Chad."

"You too, boss."

"Any problems on the way up?"

"Nope. We trailed our target out of Miami yesterday. From the intelligence we gathered, they're scheduled to meet the Colombians Sunday morning."

"Good, that gives us plenty of clean-up time." Phillip motions to the main cabin. "Have the rest of the guys join us in the lounge in ten minutes for a briefing session; I want the operation to go smoothly as possible."

"We'll be over in a jiff." Chad quickly reboards the other boat and disappears from sight. Phillip turns and heads for the lounge.

***

Phillip, Sandra, Chad and five agents sit around the cabin going over the details of the upcoming mission. Each person has a file they're looking over. The agents have various guns and other equipment they're checking as well.

Phillip eyes each man critically; this, to be honest, is his favorite part of his job. He has always experienced an intense flush of emotions during the hours leading up to a mission. It is the only time in his daily life when he is not able to wrangle in and subdue the influencing feelings with his analytical mind. Danger, excitement, fear, apprehension and the anticipation of success mixed with the intense pride of performing a service for the greater good make a potent cocktail too strong to suppress. Often Phillip will experience moments of intense clarity and purpose bordering on the spiritual awakenings he has often heard about, but in which he has never really believed. He has wondered more than once if Sandra or the others suffered similar emotional explosions. If so, it's miraculous any of them were able to perform their duties. At the same time, he has noticed that personally he functions at a much higher level when he suffers these emotional outbursts. Phillip clears his mind and refocuses on the briefing.

"Is everyone clear with the plan and what they're supposed to do?"

Chad raises his hand as he looks the file over. "What about the client? How do we identify him?"

"You don't. We want to neutralize everyone on board with initial contact. We can separate the client after the boat is secure, and then revive him." The agents nod in understanding, sharing glances of approval. They know from experience this is the wisest way to operate.

Phillip looks the men over expectantly, allowing them the opportunity to voice any concerns they might have. "Are there any other questions?"

The men remain silent, having nothing further to add. They are all trained ex-military wanting nothing more than to complete the mission at hand.

"All right, that's it." Phillip stands to leave, and Sandra follows suit. She moves around the group of commandos, retrieving the files from them. She will spend the next hour going over the documents, double checking to make sure every page is accounted for, and after doing so, she will destroy them, leaving no written record for anyone to find.

She gathers the last copy from Phillip, then looks the men over with a smile. "Everyone try to get some sleep. Four a.m. comes awfully early."

The men grunt and shrug and continue preparing their gear. Phillip and Sandra leave them to it.

FIFTY

Alfonzo lies in his king-size bed, comfortably trapped between the naked bodies of Wendy and Sherri. The large doses of Valium they have all consumed have had the desired effects. After a couple of hours of the kind of partying most men can only dream of, he finds himself on the edge of consciousness. His wavering thoughts mix between the satisfaction that Paul has finally come around and the erotic memories of his fun with the now sleeping girls. Alfonzo smiles with relief that the worries of so many years are finally lifted from his shoulders.

He begins to succumb to the effects of the Valium, eyes closing, drifting toward sleep. Just before he would be whisked away, movement catches his closing eyes. *What was that?* Alfonzo struggles to reopen his eyes, barely succeeding in time to see a masked man, dressed fully in black, level a gun at his inert body. *Why now?* He tries in vain to move, but the weight of the women combined with the effects of the drug make it impossible. Alfonzo never makes a sound; the cloaked figure pulls the trigger, once . . . twice . . . three time's the charm. Alfonzo's consciousness is swept into a much deeper oblivion.

***

A second man joins the first and looks over the scene with a touch of envy. "Lucky bastard!"

The first man shakes his head with disagreement. "Hardly . . . not by the time we get done with him."

"True that." They leave the cabin and reenter the hallway. They move stealthily down to the second cabin on the other end and each take up positions on opposite sides of the door. The man on the left carefully tries the door, opening it slowly. The two men creep into the room one after the other only to find the cabin deserted. The first man whispers into the tiny microphone attached to the night vision goggles he wears.

"Lead to Alpha. Cabin two is empty."

"Roger that, Lead. Continue with the sweep."

Both share a glance then move to the final door in the small hall. This door leads to a staircase that in turn leads to the lower deck and the crew quarters. There are four cabins for the crew, much smaller than the ones upstairs, with far less amenities, though each comfortably furnished with twin beds, a love seat and a small desk with a TV/ stereo on top.

Lead has time to notice all this while quietly passing through the first door on the right and dispatching the boat steward—the man responsible for piloting the vessel. The steward's cabin also has an alarm to notify him of weather alerts or position changes in case of anchor failure. As Lead exits the steward's quarters, his partner enters the first door on the left. Lead takes his position watching the hall and his partner's back just as the second door on the left opens, revealing a sleepy and startled man dressed in an unbuttoned chef's jacket. Both men are surprised by the presence of the other. The cook freezes in shock. Lead raises and fires his weapon in one fluid motion, hitting the man in the chest. Roughly falling to the floor, the heavy man makes more noise than Lead would have liked. Lead's partner enters the hallway, weapon raised in alarm, expertly assessing the situation. Lead shrugs then points to the final cabin.

***

Chad quietly climbs over the side of the boat. He lets his body slide to the deck, then slithers behind a small lifeboat that hides him from view of anyone who might be awake at this late hour. He is part of the second unit; his responsibility is to secure the upper levels of the large yacht. He listens to Lead's comment on the empty cabin while his partner Mark joins him behind the lifeboat. Chad now knows the upper floor is occupied. He signals Mark, and they move methodically over the open deck toward the doors of the main lounge. They leapfrog each other, one watching the other. They cover the entire deck, establishing there are no targets present. Both men reach the open doors without incident.

Chad motions his intent to enter. Mark gives him a thumbs-up and prepares to follow suit. One by one the two men slink into the lounge, the only lighted part of the upper deck. Chad moves into the main part of the room, finding Paul and Vanessa asleep, their unclothed bodies entwined on the sofa. He quickly fires tranquilizing darts into the bodies. Mark joins him, and they both give the room a critical inspection. Mark points to the two sets of high heel shoes kicked into the corner of the room. "We're missing a girl!"

They turn in unison at the sound of a toilet flushing. Both men raise their weapons to the opening door of the bathroom. A bikini-clad blonde exits. Candy takes two full steps into the lounge before she notices the two masked men. She looks them over with hopeful fear. "I don't guess there's anything I could do for you boys to keep you from shooting me, is there?"

"I'm sorry, miss." Chad shoots Candy without further comment.

Mark shakes his head in disappointment after she crumples to the floor. "Man, I hate shooting the hot ones!"

"Let's just finish the sweep. I don't want to find anyone else jumping through doors at us." They move rapidly through the rest of the upper deck.

FIFTY-ONE

PHILLIP WALKS BETWEEN the two rows of bodies, four on his left and five on his right. He stops at the feet of a young man, naked except for a towel they have laid over his waist. There are similar towels on the other naked bodies. He can't help but wonder if there are even any clothes kept on the boat. Of the nine bodies, five are completely bare, with a sixth in a very revealing bikini.

Sandra makes her way through the lounge and joins him on the opposite end of the young man. "Looks like we interrupted a hell of a party!"

Chad stands near the bar, awaiting orders. "More like an orgy if you ask me."

Phillip ignores the comments. He points to the young man. "Revive him; he's the client."

Chad moves forward quickly. He kneels next to Paul and removes a needle and serum from his mission supplies. Phillip and Sandra move to the rear of the lounge, allowing Chad to do his work while they discuss their next move.

Sandra speaks in a hushed voice, matching the somber mood that rooms full of unconscious people always exude. "We will meet the boats about 0300 and can be well up the coast by daybreak. Mark estimates he will need about ten hours to completely erase our footprint."

Phillip crosses his arms, calculating all the variables he has been presented, a habit that goes back as far as he can remember. "What about Chad?" They both look to where Chad administers to the slowly waking boy.

"He says he can have everyone fogged in half that time," Sandra responds.

"I want the girls fogged and dropped in a hotel room."

"Where?"

"We'll stop in Savannah. That should be far enough. We'll leave them with a couple grand apiece. That should insure their safe trip back to Miami."

"I'll set it up." Sandra says.

Phillip takes her by the arm and leads her back to where Chad is now standing and replacing the needle in his pack. "Come on. Let's go meet our client."

Phillip and Sandra watch Paul awaken. He groans, slowly opens his eyes and looks around the cabin in confusion. He sees the bodies and the soldier standing over him; he also sees Sandra and Phillip looking down at him from a few steps away. "What happened? Who are you people?"

Phillip steps forward to address the confused young man. "You were knocked out with a tranquilizing dart. And we are the people you called with your problem."

"I didn't think you guys were real." Paul looks at all the bodies then begins to cry. "You didn't have to kill him!"

Phillip pats him on the shoulder. "Calm down, Paul, they're not dead. They are all just asleep. We tranquilized them just like we did you."

Paul wipes away his tears. "I guess I should have known," he said.

"It's to be expected. Listen, Paul, I want you to go with Ms. St. Clair. She will fill you in on all the crazy details of what's happened here and tell you all about your new life. Phillip turns and begins to discuss with Chad what to do with all the bodies.

Sandra offers Paul a hand up. He accepts it and starts to struggle to his feet, then realizes he's clothed only with a towel. He freezes midmotion, trying unsuccessfully to keep the towel from falling to the floor.

Sandra lets go of his hand, allowing Paul to fall to the floor along with the towel, sparing him further embarrassment.

"Shit! This scene is heavy!"

Sandra smiles sympathetically. "So are you. Now wrap that towel around you and follow me."

FIFTY-TWO

DANIEL SITS ACROSS from Josh, watching a video screen
showing the unfolding events on a large yacht far from
the small-but-comfortable room hidden in the lower levels
of the White House. Daniel sips his drink while Josh leaves
his untouched. Josh is totally engrossed in the unbelievable
images flowing in seven-second delay from the tracking
boat to a satellite, then to the room they are in.

Daniel cannot help but be impressed with the still-
expanding scope of the N.D.E.C. operations. They
have managed to test the limits of even his boundless
imagination. From what he is now seeing, this outfit's
span of influence goes much farther than he originally
thought. If there was ever any doubt whether or not he
would shut them down, it is now removed. The idea that an
organization could grow so large and be so manipulative
while remaining completely hidden bothers Daniel to his
core. He is the President of the United States of America:
no one operated above his influence—outside of, maybe,

but never above. Some things are not to be tolerated! Continuing to watch his enemies at work, Daniel hides his growing anger.

Josh watches with incredulity. He grabs his drink and gulps it down without tearing his eyes from the screen. He is having trouble assimilating the information he is receiving. As Josh watches, his mind entertains thoughts that are completely new to him. *What is the true nature of these people? Are they in fact responsible for the current political state of the country?* Josh tries to dismiss the idea, but it will not fully leave his mind. From what Daniel previously shared with him, the actions taken by this N.D.E.C. changed the course of the president's life completely. *Would Daniel even be president? Would I be his chief of staff?* Josh shakes his head trying to dislodge the thoughts before they can lead him farther down a path he does not want to explore. He has invested way too much of himself into Daniel to question him now. Josh pushes the disloyal thoughts almost violently to the farthest depths of his consciousness. "Christ! These people are out there!"

Daniel just nods in agreement and continues to watch the screen. For a few more moments, the two men observe in silence the masked agents under Phillip's direction putting the bodies in bags and carry them from the lounge. One of the men grabs the still-unconscious cook, but Phillip stops him.

"Put him in the galley and then inject him with the memory eraser."

"Yes, sir." The unnamed soldier takes the head end while Chad comes into view and takes the legs. The two men lift the cook and carry him from the lounge.

"I think it's time we made our presence known," Daniel says.

Josh eyes him with surprise. "Do you want to hit them now?"

Daniel continues to watch the action with outward detachment, but with an inner rage. "No. Wait until they're back here in Washington. I want to get them in their own building while they're in operation. We still have pieces to this puzzle to discover. I am most interested in what goes on in the hidden area of the N.D.E.C. headquarters. I have a feeling our only chance of finding out what they're doing in there will be to catch them in action."

Josh nods in understanding and approval, the recent doubts of Daniel's credibility momentarily forgotten.

FIFTY-THREE

Three days later

SENATOR ANTHONY HIGGINS ascends the rocky path up the side of the treeless mountain with ease for a man on the wrong side of seventy. He covers the distance to the plateau above slowly but surely.

Taking a quick break, he wipes the sweat from his brow. He thinks whimsically back to the days when he did not have to rest or wipe sweat from his brow. He has been climbing this mountain since a small boy raised in the Arizona desert. He used to play with the children from the reservation to the west of his father's land. They had contests to see who could reach the top first, and try as he might, he never won. But he never quit, and he always made it to the top, usually battered and bruised from a spill he took on the way up, and always covered in dust and dirt being rained down from the reservation boys above him. Anthony always reached the top only to find the other boys already starting back down.

At first this had bothered him and he cried and begged for them to wait for him. This changed when on a particular day the race had started much later. All the boys had been in town trying to catch a glimpse of a big-time sports hero staying down at the hotel for a day before departing on some well-funded hiking trip. Anthony had tagged along. They waited around the hotel most of the day only to find out they had missed out on meeting the football legend; he had left out before they got there.

All the boys trekked the couple miles back in various states of disappointment and anger. Their path home took them right by the climbing mountain. The Navajo boys huddled together and quickly figured out a way to rid themselves of their disappointment. The boys all took off at once toward the mountain, and there little Anthony went running harder than ever, as fast as he could, after them. He made it to the top in record time, not far at all behind the last of the reservation boys, all older than he. As usual, though, they immediately started down the mountain. More than a little worn out and needing to rest, Anthony could not immediately follow.

He looked out at the distant sun and lost himself in the incredible beauty. He had never been at the top of the plateau at sunset before. The view was mesmerizing. Awed, Anthony watched the sun slowly disappear behind the distant mountain range. But the magical moment disappeared with the sun, instantly replaced with darkness and fear. Anthony's wonder turned to terror at the realization he could not leave the mountain. With the night fully on him, he could not see to navigate his way back down the steep trail. He began to cry after he found a place to huddle against a large rock. The cold of night soon set in, chilling him to the bone.

Anthony sat shivering uncontrollably, listening to the sounds of the desert night, which were beginning in earnest. First a coyote far away howled only to be answered by one much closer. Anthony tried to stay calm amid the howls that filled the night all around him. He eventually became somewhat used to the repetitive sounds. He fell into a fitful sleep soon to be awakened by the terrifying scream of a prowling mountain lion. Fears flew anew. His mind assaulted him with visions of death at the hands of the large desert cat. Again sleep took him. He managed to sleep undisturbed for a couple of hours.

***

Waking much later for no reason that he could discern, Anthony stared above him and was struck by the sheer magnitude of the now risen full moon. It seemed no more than an arm's length away, hovering directly overhead. He spent most of the rest of the night giving thanks to the God or gods—he did not know which at such a young age—who provided him such a personal gift. He watched the moon casually cross the sky, moving away from his perch on the mountain, slowly but surely. Again he slept, but with a newfound peace in his heart.

When next he woke, the night and moon had passed, leaving a growing, predawn light. Anthony stood and stretched from his bed of rocks and sand, feeling surprisingly refreshed. He walked slowly toward the still hidden rising sun. Just as he stopped, perched near the edge of the sheer cliff, looking outward toward the distant mountain range, the sun shattered the dawn with the first rays of the day. For the third time, the incredible beauty of a celestial nature astounded him. Anthony gave the sunrise his full attention and appreciation. He waited until the day was well established before making the trek back down the mountain trail.

Karl, his very worried father, met him halfway up the mountain. His dad had spent most of the night running around the neighboring reservation talking to the parents of the other children with whom Anthony had last been seen. His father, despite being the sheriff in the county, had no jurisdiction on the reservation. At first, he had no luck questioning the young Navajos; they had all claimed to know nothing about the whereabouts of his son. Joseph, the youngest of the boys and the closest to Anthony, had spoken to his parents after Karl had left. Joseph told how the boys had all climbed the mountain with Anthony trailing behind. Joseph's father quickly called Karl and relayed the story. Karl, only slightly relieved, knew his son had to spend the remainder of the night alone atop the mountain.

Anthony's father felt more than a little surprised to find his son in such a serene state of contentment. He questioned Anthony earnestly about his lonely night in the wilderness. Anthony remained vague and dismissive about the night, at a loss for words to explain how the experience, while scary at first, had turned into a spiritual awakening of sorts. Karl noticed quite a change in his son. Anthony stopped following the older boys around and became very independent. Over time Karl adjusted to his son's new wiser ways and decided whatever had occurred on the top of that mountain was a blessing. Deeply impressed by Anthony's change, he hesitated only slightly when Anthony announced his plans to annually return to the plateau on the full moon closest to the one-year anniversary of his first night on the mountain.

***

Anthony stands only slightly winded on his sixty-sixth trip up the mountain for a night of what he now considers a spiritual cleansing and recharging.

This is his sacred spot, and he is more than a little annoyed by the fact that a helicopter now sits atop his mountain, loudly idling, obviously waiting for him to crest the top in order to sweep him away. Anthony sets out to finish the last bit of the climb. He knows that whatever message waits for him, it cannot be good.

Anthony reaches the top of the trail and comes into view of the helicopter. The waiting figure of John Powers immediately starts jogging toward him. The two men meet near the middle of the small plateau. Anthony firmly shakes the extended hand of his assistant. They fall in step, walking steadily back toward the chopper.

"I'm sorry to be here, senator. You know I would not have come if it was not urgent."

"I know, John, so spill it already. What's the emergency?"

John hands the senator a sheet of paper. Anthony stops his stride long enough to read the document. "This just came in. It looks like the president has decided to move forward with full intent."

Anthony finishes reading the file. "It looks like he has activated the NSA and the FBI."

John nods in grim agreement. "Plus the Secret Service is on full alert."

"This is not too much more than what we expected."

"The problem is the timetable, senator. They're moving much faster than we anticipated!"

Anthony eyes John with worry and apprehension. "How much faster?"

"They have federal agents en route as we speak!"

"Shit! Have you warned Phillip?"

John's grim look tells Anthony all he needs to know. He roughly hands the file back to John, then reaches for his cell phone. Anthony looks down at the missing signal bars with frustration.

"Damn! No signal! Come on, we got to move!" Anthony heads to the chopper at a pace a 73-year-old man should not be able to achieve. John starts out after the senator with surprise; he cannot help but notice it is harder than it should be to catch the old man. Both men reach the chopper at the same time. They swiftly board and the helicopter takes off. For the first time in sixty-six years, the plateau will be deserted on the mid-fall full moon.

FIFTY-FOUR

WITH A CRITICAL eye, Sandra watches Bill Sluder and his two assistants prep the complex program about to be run on their patient. She nods with satisfaction when Bill relays their readiness to proceed.

"We are all set to initiate the alternate reality program."

"Good. We'll start as soon as our fearless leader joins us." Sandra looks over the state-of-the-art equipment with pride. Their computer has the ability to interface with the human brain from the inside. She looks around the room and through the observation window to where the subject lies in an artificial coma. They are about to run a sequence of programs that can be duplicated nowhere else on earth. Her thoughts are broken by Phillip's arrival. He enters the control room offering no apology for his tardiness.

"We are ready to start the illusional sequence." Sandra says.

Phillip takes the position reserved for him. "Have you finished the diagnostic checklist?"

Sandra ignores the slight irritation she feels from Phillip's question. "Affirmative."

"Did you check it twice?"

Sandra rolls her eyes at the implied incompetence. "We double checked it, and then we triple checked it. You know, this isn't my first rodeo."

Phillip dons a virtual reality helmet and headset. "Just following protocol." Sandra mimics Phillip's words, mouthing them as he speaks them.

The three technicians chuckle quietly at this.

Sandra motions to the still smiling technicians. "Gentlemen, you may proceed."

***

Alfonzo lounges comfortably beside Paul on the deck of his oversize yacht. The younger man pulls a random kilo of coke from a large case packed full with the potent drug. Alfonzo nods with approval, watching Paul sample the product. Across from him his Colombian business partner, Edgar Salazar, lounges in equal comfort. One of his bodyguards methodically counts a large amount of money and transfers it from one case into another. Paul inhales the drug deeply through his left nostril. The effects are instantaneous; the young man is momentarily frozen by the intense rush from the almost pure coke. Alfonzo smiles with satisfaction. Paul recovers enough to offer him a sample. Alfonzo tastes the product but does not inhale the line.

Edgar raises his eyebrow when Alfonzo refuses the high. "Do you not wish to test the product for yourself, my friend?"

Alfonzo nods at Edgar while Kim, his wife, delivers a tray of drinks and begins to hand them out to the men.

"I'm quite sure your coke is of the highest quality. As longtime friends I trust you completely. On the other hand, the businessman in me warns never to show too much eagerness for the product, lest the prices rise to meet the perceived demand."

Edgar winks, and with a sly smile, takes the offered drink. "You are a wise man." Alfonzo takes the last of the drinks from his as-of-yet-unnoticed wife. He slowly raises the drink to his lips before the realization of his wife's presence shatters his mirth. Alfonzo sits up with a jerk, spilling the drink all over his expensive Italian suit.

"Kim! What the hell are you doing here?" As Alfonzo berates his uninvited spouse, Edgar's bodyguard finishes counting the money and shakes his head in disapproval at his boss. "This is only half the amount."

Edgar grimaces, then motions to his men who until this moment had been standing casually in the background. The five men act as one, coming to attention and drawing their up-till-now concealed weapons. Alfonzo notices none of this, his anger, confusion and attention resting solely on his wife. Without emotion, Kim and Paul watch Alfonzo's rage escalate.

"Answer me, woman! Where have you been hiding?"

"Enough!"

Alfonzo is stunned by the unexpected shout from Edgar. It is unthinkable for one man to interfere in the domestic dispute of another in Colombia, and Alfonzo could do anything short of murdering his wife with no thought of intervention. Alfonzo turns in confusion to the now fuming Colombian.

"I believe you have bigger problems than your wife right now, Alfonzo."

Alfonzo eyes Edgar, then for the first time notices the drawn guns being held by the men.

"What is the problem? Why all the hostility?"

"You are two million dollars short."

"Edgar, that is impossible." Alfonzo pales in shock. "The price was supposed to be two million. That is what we agreed on!"

Edgar shakes his head in denial. "You are mistaken, Alfonzo. The price was four million, and I think you know this. It is too bad. You know the rules."

Alfonzo looks on in growing horror at the men raising their weapons. He pleads for his life. "Edgar, wait! I can get you the rest of the money!"

Edgar stands, pulling a handgun from a holster hidden within the breast of his jacket and shoots first Kim, hitting her squarely in the head. He then turns his aim to Paul and dispatches him with equal accuracy. Kim falls to the deck, and Paul simply slumps in his seat. Alfonzo looks from one to the other in terror.

Edgar brings the gun slowly to bear on Alfonzo. He looks with contempt on his old friend. "I'm not a greedy man. Two million plus all my coke will be fine, I think."

Alfonzo looks at his dead family with dread, then recovers and tries again to plead for his life. He slides from his seat, coming to rest on his knees and throwing his hands up in defeat. "Edgar! You are right. Take all the money and the coke. You already have my wife and son as payment. Please spare my life!"

Edgar lowers the weapon and paces back and forth, thinking over Alfonzo's words.

Alfonzo watches, clasping his hands in hopeful fear. "Hell, take the yacht too!"

Edgar stops pacing at this and stares at Alfonzo.

"Yes. Yes, I think I will." He raises the gun and shoots Alfonzo twice in the chest.

One of the watching gunmen hears a noise behind him and turns around to look over the sea. He sees a helicopter quickly approaching. The gunman turns and shouts an alarm.

"COAST GUARD!" All the men turn in unison to see the chopper.

Edgar quickly tosses the murder weapon overboard into the ocean. "Get to the speed boat. We can be back in Cuban waters in five minutes!" Edgar starts to leave the deck in a rush but comes up short at the voice of the alert gunman.

"What about the money and the bodies . . . and the coke, boss?"

"Grab the money and screw the coke. I've got plenty of that! Edgar looks down at Alfonzo struggling to breathe and laughs at the desperately wounded man. "Leave the bodies for the coast guard to clean up."

The Colombians quickly grab the case of cash and depart from the yacht into their waiting speedboat. They are already well away when the chopper comes to a hovering stop over the yacht.

A coastguardsman looks down at the deck and sees the bodies with Alfonzo still moving.

"Get me down there! One's still alive."

FIFTY-FIVE

ALFONZO SITS UNCONSCIOUS in a chair, alone in an otherwise barren gray room. He comes slowly to from a deep black sleep. Someone persistently calls his name.

"Alfonzo . . . Alfonzo, wake up."

Alfonzo wakes with a start and grabs at his chest. "My God, I've been shot!" He looks down at his chest, but sees nothing wrong. "What the fu—"

The voice returns with a deafening vengeance. "SILENCE!"

Alfonzo looks around frantically for the source of the voice. He tries to stand, but invisible bonds hold him in place. He looks down then all around, becoming even more terrified. Alfonzo continues to struggle with his bonds.

"You could struggle for all of eternity, and you would never break those bonds."

Alfonzo quits in frustration. "Who's there . . . are you God?"

The walls flicker in and out with the messenger's boisterous laughter. "You think you're worthy or important enough to stand in God's presence?"

***

Sandra and the technicians watch the monitors. Phillip watches also, speaking into his headset. The techs make various small adjustments to the console.

"How are our stress levels?" Sandra asks.

Bill quickly checks the stress monitor before responding.

"Keep an eye on them; we don't want a cardiac arrest." Sandra continuously scans from one monitor and readout to the next.

Phillip talks on to Alfonzo, "Well, do you?"

Sandra smiles, listening to the only side of the conversation she can hear. *He loves this part.*

A phone on the console rings. Everyone in the room looks at it in surprise, except for Phillip who is completely unaware of the interruption.

Sandra scowls at the beeping light indicating an incoming call. "Answer that, and get rid of them." Cody, one of the technicians, answers the phone. Sandra returns to the monitors with obvious anger.

"Jeeze, who would be stupid enough to call while we're in session?" Devon, the second technician mutters.

Bill answers the question with the only answer he can provide. "I don't know, but you can believe he'll be shopping his resume around tomorrow."

Sandra lets her extreme agitation show with a rare rebuke of her team. "If you two don't want to be joining him, you'll cut the chatter and do your jobs."

The two men look at each other sheepishly then return to their monitors. Cody, looks at Sandra with apprehension. "Ms. St. Clair, it's Senator Higgins, and he wants to speak with you . . . he says we have a Code Black emergency."

Sandra stares at Cody in utter astonishment. Bill frowns with grim awareness, ignoring the two assistants' looks of confusion.

"What's a Code Black?" Devon asks Bill quietly, hoping Sandra will not hear him.

Sandra springs into motion. She reaches for the phone and jerks it from Cody.

Bill shakes his head with mournful resignation. "It's the end of our world, son."

"Sandra speaking." Sandra listens into the phone. Her face shows growing fear and disbelief.

"My God . . . how long before they arrive?"

***

Alfonzo begins to weep, watching the messenger slowly materialize in front of him. The messenger clothed in his dark gray robe stands reaper-like in front of the whimpering man. "Have you figured out where you're at yet, Alfonzo?"

Alfonzo blurts out a blubbering response. "I'm in hell!"

The messenger shakes his head slowly, barely stirring the hood he wears. "Close, but not quite. You are in purgatory."

"You mean like limbo?"

"Close enough."

Alfonzo jerks his head around, craning his neck as far as it will go, trying to discover something to orient him to his surroundings. "But why?"

The messenger begins to slither back and forth in front of a very confused and terrified Alfonzo. "Well, as they say, every dog has his day. And today is your day, Alfonzo."

"But I'm dead!"

"If that's the road you choose, then so be it." The walls disappear showing the abyss of fire completely engulfing them. Alfonzo screams at the horrible flaming pit that now surrounds him. "Wait! I choose to live!"

The messenger ignores Alfonzo's pleas. He suddenly jerks his head up, causing the hood to fall backward revealing a blurry image Alfonzo cannot make out. "What? Now is not the time!"

While the messenger seems to be ignoring him, Alfonzo continues to plead for his life. "I said I want to live!"

Obviously listening to someone Alfonzo cannot hear, the blurry unidentifiable image waves Alfonzo off. "Not you, Alfonzo: be silent . . . that's impossible . . ."

Alfonzo watches the messenger with fascinated trepidation.

"How long before they arrive?"

Alfonzo does not want to imagine who the messenger is referring to, but he feels compelled to ask. "Wh— who's coming?"

The messenger manages to convey his disbelief through the thick robes. "Holy Christ!"

Alfonzo jerks his head around spastically looking for the Savior. "Really? Where?"

"Try to hold them off! And suspend animation for God's sake!" The messenger freezes in midframe, leaving Alfonzo alone with his fears.

"What's happening? Please don't let me burn in hell!" Alfonzo cries out in sorrowful terror, but no one hears him.

***

Marcus swings the large van through an almost 90-degree turn, causing Bo Simmons to hold tightly to the overhead handhold. The van careens into the parking lot of the headquarters of the until-now-unheard-of N.D.E.C. Bo is sure the two right wheels of the cargo van are well off the ground. He struggles through a moment of apprehension, wondering if they're going to flip before the wheels finally touch back down. Marcus guns the engine, barking the tires with a screech, accelerating over the remaining distance to the entrance of the building. He spins the steering wheel. The van goes into a power slide and comes to a violent stop directly in front of the doors to the lobby. Marcus looks up with a mischievous smile at Bo in time to see his boss pry his hands from the handhold.

Bo readjusts his now skewed headset and pats Marcus on the shoulder. "Great driving. Remind me to never let you do it again!" Bo ignores the look of indignant hurt from Marcus as both men jump from the van. Bo speaks orders into his microphone, and Marcus directs their crack team into position. "All right, men, you know the deal. We want this building locked down and secured yesterday!"

A second van pulls to a sliding halt with James jumping out, along with the rest of his team. He expertly gathers his unit. "We have the perimeter. Men, move out. Remember, no casualties. We meet at the concrete wall in three minutes. Now move!" James and two of his men march-run around the left of the building. At the same time, his other three men head off to the right, disappearing from view.

The crack-unit sprints through the doors into the building, two men following Bo while two follow Marcus.

Bo leads his team quickly through the building; he is in no way pleased by the lack of people wandering the halls. His men had only encountered two people in their sweep toward the hidden part of the building. One, a security guard, had been tranquilized and handcuffed; the other, a janitor, had met the same fate. He now stood beside Marcus, listening to a similar story. Marcus's team had met three security guards and subdued them. Five people in the entire building just didn't add up. Mulling over the empty building, Bo watches his explosives expert wire the wall. Their surveillance equipment had shown a building bustling with people and activity.

***

Phillip jerks the virtual reality helmet off and scrambles to his feet. He looks frantically around the control room in disbelief as everyone scrambles about the tasks of stabilizing their patient.

Phillip grabs Bill roughly by the shoulder and spins the man around. "Forget the patient. I'll handle him. I want you to flush the computers then get the hell out of here!" He turns to Sandra and the two technicians. "That goes for all of you! Evacuate the building immediately!"

***

Bo looks at Marcus backing a safe distance from the now armed wall. "They were tipped off!"

Marcus nods as they hunch down in cover. "I was thinking the same thing."

The charge explodes, throwing debris and dust everywhere while creating a large hole in the cement wall. Bo wipes the dust from his face, then creeps to the newly made gaping hole. As the dust settles, he catches the first glimpse of the hidden part of the building.

"Let's move, people."

***

Everyone in the room is momentarily halted by the sound of an explosion within the building. Sandra looks at Phillip with horror. "What about you, Phillip? They just blew through the barrier wall! The agents will be here any minute!"

"Don't worry about me! Just take the tunnel out and make sure the systems are flushed!"

Phillip tears open the door to the patient room, then looks back at his colleague who is standing frozen, looking at him. Phillip grabs Cody, the closest man to him, and pushes him violently toward the exit door. "What is wrong with you people? I gave a freaking order, and I expect it to be carried out! Now move!"

Bill and Cody, then Devon hurry from the room.

Sandra looks longingly at the man she loves, letting a tear fall. "Oh, Phillip, always so damn noble!" She turns and runs from the room.

Phillip spins and runs to Alfonzo's side. He looks frantically at several of the monitors connected to Alfonzo's body. He talks to himself while pushing buttons deactivating machines. "Hang with me, Alfonzo; I have a long way to bring you, in order to get you back." Phillip works feverishly to restore Alfonzo to a stable state of sleep. He finishes the process with a sigh of relief. He only has to inject the imagery eraser to ensure the recent events will not be remembered. Phillip pulls a needle from a tray.

FIFTY-SIX

ALFONZO SITS ALONE except for the still frozen image of the messenger. He weeps quietly to himself; he has given up hope of rescue or redemption. *Is this hell? It doesn't hurt like I thought it would, but Christ it will be about another twenty minutes before I go completely insane.* Alfonzo is swept along in a fresh wave of terror, watching the walls around him begin to disintegrate.

"Oh God, help me!" Alfonzo closes his eyes to the raging inferno behind the walls. He doesn't notice the flames begin to disintegrate, revealing Phillip, along with the room he now resides in and all the medical equipment that surrounds him.

With satisfaction, Phillip watches the remaining working monitors tell him his patient is now fully conscious. He calls out to the terrified man, "Alfonzo, open your eyes."

Alfonzo keeps his eyes squeezed tightly shut in fear. "Don't burn me, Satan!"

Phillip reaches out and shakes Alfonzo gently by the shoulder. "Open your eyes. I'm not Satan."

Alfonzo opens his left eye to take a quick peek. He sees Phillip peering down at him and opens his eyes further, overwhelmed with fear and extreme confusion. "Are you God?"

Preparing to inject the memory eraser, Phillip does not bother to answer.

"Halt! Don't move or you are a dead man!"

Phillip barely acknowledges the man behind him with the gun. "You don't understand. I need to administer this drug to stabilize his memory."

Bo moves quickly forward, motioning his men to spread out to his left and right.

"You're right, mister. I don't understand. But if you try to inject that man with that needle, you'll be dead before you can blink your eyes. Now slowly lower the needle to the floor and lie face down on the ground."

Phillip does what he's told with resignation; he slowly kneels to the floor and lays face down, putting his arms behind his back.

Alfonzo looks around in complete bewilderment, his eyes bulging. He tries to comprehend the incredible events unfolding in front of him. "Hey, what the hell is going on here? You can't bust God!"

Marcus moves quickly forward and handcuffs Phillip.

The rest of the men spread out. Bo walks forward and looks from Phillip to the confused man strapped to the hospital bed. "Brother, I don't know who this guy is, but I'm reasonably sure he ain't God."

FIFTY-SEVEN

Brandon Carter looks around, impressed by his surroundings. He stands in the middle of the "laboratory" of the N.D.E.C. The joining rooms seem to be a hybrid of the latest computer technology organically spliced with the most advanced neurology equipment found anywhere on earth. Brandon, the NSA's leading medical scientist, has been examining the various drugs in the lab safe for almost two hours now. There are three he has not seen before and has no idea what they do.

Brandon has worked within the biochemical development program for ten years without ever hearing a peep about the existence of the N.D.E.C. Now head of the department, Brandon has the job of figuring out not only what these people do, but how they do it. A task easier said than done. From what the preliminary reports have told him, they were able to flush their computers, erasing all records and data from the mainframe. A remarkable feat, considering the speed and efficiency of the surprise raid. Not only that, all the personnel within the hidden lab had made a successful escape except for two men, one more confused than Brandon himself. Through the observation window, Brandon eyes the other captive, handcuffed and guarded, who, when caught, was in the process of administering one of the unidentifiable drugs.

The man who calls himself Phillip Stevens looks up when Brandon's partner Darren enters the room, carrying a small file. Darren hands over the file with a look of impressed disbelief. "This is everything we were able to retrieve from the mainframe."

Brandon frowns at the tiny file. "There's nothing here."

"We were lucky to get this; apparently the file was in a state of suspended animation that kept it from being flushed with everything else."

As Brandon rapidly scans the three sheets of paper, Phillip continues to watch the agents, wondering what is in the file they are currently reading.

Brandon finishes the file. He looks at his partner then to the patient being examined by an NSA doctor. He takes Darren by the arm and leads him out of earshot of the dazed man. "This is some crazy shit. These people really know how to screw with someone's head."

Brandon turns his attention to Alfonzo. "Make a couple more copies of this and be ready to debrief the confused Mr. Rodriguez."

Darren retakes the file. "What are you going to do?"

Brandon motions toward Phillip who is now staring back at him. "When you've finished making the copies, join me with Mr. Stevens. I think it's time we tried to crack this nut."

***

Phillip sits handcuffed in the observation room with Brandon and Darren. They look through the window into the lab and see Alfonzo approached by a third agent holding a freshly made copy of the recovered documents.

"If you let that man go, you'll be putting his family in grave danger!" Phillip warns.

"You keep saying that, Mr. Stevens, but you refuse to tell us why."

"I've told you already—it's classified."

Brandon throws a form down on the table in front of Phillip. "And I've shown you a release form signed by the president allowing full disclosure!"

Phillip looks at the form and shrugs. "It doesn't apply."

Brandon throws his hands up in frustration. "Yeah? And why is that?"

"Conflict of interest."

Brandon's curiosity is piqued by what his instincts tell him is probably the truth. Explain."

Phillip shakes his head before he lowers it to his cuffed hands. "I cannot do that; it's classified."

Brandon rolls his eyes in frustration then paces the room for a moment. "One way or the other we're going to get to the bottom of what you do here, Mr. Stevens!"

Phillip watches the agent speaking with a slightly more composed Alfonzo. "What exactly are you telling Mr. Rodriguez?"

"We are going to tell him the truth."

Phillip eyes Brandon. He challenges his ability to provide a truth he could not possibly know. "And what is the truth, Agent Carter? Because if you are waiting for me to provide it, you're in for a long wait."

As if on cue, Darren produces the small document. Brandon takes the file and slowly flips through it. "Now, I admit that we are pretty much in the dark about what you do here, but we do have this! This is a copy of the only file we were able to retrieve from your hard drive. It wasn't destroyed because it was open and frozen."

Phillip looks up, unable to mask his apprehension.

"Your file on Mr. Rodriguez is very interesting." Brandon pauses for effect. "Enlightening, really."

"You cannot release that. It is classified."

"That's debatable, Mr. Stevens." Brandon drops the file on the table in front of Phillip. We're going to tell Mr. Rodriguez that apparently he was kidnapped, then drugged to think he had died and spoken to God . . . and that it was all set up by his stepson Paul.

Phillip passionately pleads his case. "You can't tell him that! You have to lie to him!"

"And tell him what?"

"Tell him someone else was responsible for what happened to him, not his stepson."

Brandon looks to Darren, and the two men share a regretful glance. "The NSA is not in the business of lying to people and making up stories. Apparently that's *your* area of expertise, Mr. Stevens."

Phillip leans forward with desperation, trying in vain to persuade these men to change their point of view. "Alfonzo is an evil man. He will kill his stepson!"

Brandon leans in close to Phillip's face and speaks conspiratorially into his ear. "Maybe if you cooperated more, you could help us come to a more complete understanding of the situation." Brandon leans back to his previous position, shrugging his shoulders at the possibilities in front of them. "Then maybe we could work together and alter our course to avert this impending travesty."

"I can't."

Brandon stares at Phillip and contemplates the impasse. He sees no options available without cooperation. "So be it. Just remember, Mr. Stevens, whatever happens, you could have prevented it." Brandon nods to the guard stationed outside the door. "Get him out of here."

Darren reaches for Phillip and pulls him to his feet, leading him from the room, Brandon looks from the file to where Alfonzo is still being debriefed. Brandon is in a dark contemplative mood. "What the hell have we jumped into the middle of?"

FIFTY-EIGHT

PHILLIP LIES ON the thin padding covering the solid metal bunk. He finds himself existing in a dark pit of depression. Running over the sequence of events that led him to this dark, dank cell, as nearly as he can tell, he has been confined for over thirty hours with no visitors except the guards who drop off his uneaten meals.

The loud clicking of a guard's shoes pulls him from his cycle of hopeless thoughts. Phillip slowly sits up from the bunk. He has learned that if he isn't quick to get his tray from the impatient guards, it will simply end up on the floor of the cell. While he has yet to find sufficient appetite to ingest the swill, the smell from the spilt food tray, along with having to clean up the mess, is enough motivation to get him to the cell window promptly. Click . . . click, click. The guard stops at his cell and peers between the bars.

"All right, Mr. Stevens. Here's your filet mignon." The guard laughs at his tired and worn joke. Phillip takes the tray just before the guard pushes it onto the floor. "You're learning."

Phillip sets the tray on the floor before calling out to the departing guard. He can't help but wonder why all the guards have the same body type: short and fat. "Officer Cates! What about my lawyer? I still have not heard anything!"

Cates turns and walks slowly back to Phillip's cell. He looks through the bars and stands in silence long enough for Phillip to begin to wonder if the man will ever speak. Finally Officer Cates beckons for him to move in closer. Phillip obliges the man. He puts his ear to the bars closest to Cates' mouth. Cates waits till he is fully in place then barks out a laugh as fake and ridiculous as it is loud. Phillip jerks away from the bars, grabbing his ringing ear. Cates carries on with his obnoxious fake laugh. Phillip quickly moves away, narrowly avoiding stepping in his tray of food.

"I didn't know you told jokes, Stevens, but I'll be damned if that was not a real side splitter." Cates slaps his leg, mocking Phillip's honest question. Phillip recovers from the cackling laugh and looks at the guard with more than a little hatred. He even surprises himself with the meanness in his response. "You don't have to be such an ass, Cates, though I should have expected it from someone with such questionable intelligence."

Cates approaches the bars with instant anger. "Did you just call me stupid? You better watch yourself, Stevens. I can make things a lot worse for you than they already are!"

Phillip backs away from the enraged guard, taking a seat on his bunk. "I really wish that was the case, Cates, because maybe then I would not be sitting so squarely on rock bottom."

Officer Cates stares at the dejected man, daring him to continue the altercation. To be honest, Cates enjoys the exchanges. They add spice to his otherwise boring days. He is slightly disappointed to see the fight gone from Phillip's eyes. He makes one final effort to provoke the man further.

"I'll tell you what, Stevens, I will check on your lawyer and see if I can't have him pay you a visit, say, right after hell freezes over."

Phillip keeps his head lowered, ignoring the comment. Cates spits a large glob into the tray of food sitting in the cell floor, then turns and continues down the hall.

"Enjoy your meal, Stevens."

Phillip lies back down on the bunk, more depressed than ever. The clash with the guard has done nothing to help his mood. The cycle of thoughts invades his mind once more. He tries to push the many recent events out of his head, not wanting to dwell yet again on his hopeless situation. Phillip closes his eyes to try and get some sleep. He begins to count sheep just to keep his mind from wandering to the endless dark places that now fill his aching brain.

***

Click, click, click. Phillip rolls over toward the concrete wall and away from the approaching steps of the mean-spirited guard. He is not sure if he slept or not, but the last thing he wants is to have another fruitless conversation with Cates. Phillip closes his eyes in order to pretend sleep. Sure enough, the footsteps stop at the bars in front of his cell.

"If I'm interrupting your rest, Phillip, I could come back later."

Phillip flips over with a start when he recognizes the voice. He looks up with shock and surprise mixed with happiness.

"Phillip, you look like crap."

"Senator, it's a relief to see you. I honestly didn't think you'd be able to make it."

Phillip stands up and quickly approaches the bars. The two men share a moment filled with too many emotions to allow expression.

Anthony breaks the silence. "How have you been treated?"

"All right so far, other than a jerk guard. Food's crap. I have no way of telling time, but by the meal count, I've been in here, about thirty hours."

"That's about right. It's 9:30 a.m."

"I didn't know if you'd come."

"Well, it took some doing, but I made it happen. I'm just sorry it took so long, and unfortunately, I don't have much time."

Phillip nods in understanding. "How bad is our situation?"

Anthony shakes his head negatively. "It's as bad as it gets—everything is compromised. In a matter of a week or two, everything and everyone in the program is going to be exposed."

Phillip shakes his fist in frustration and self-loathing. "This is going to destroy so many peoples' lives . . ." He paces the cell in frustration. "I should have told you about the president."

Anthony smiles with agreement. "In hindsight you probably should have. But don't beat yourself up, Phillip. You did what you thought was right."

"I followed protocol exactly!"

Anthony sighs at the hard lesson learned a little too late. "Phillip, in certain situations the right choices are the wrong ones. Hell, we all make mistakes; we just have to hope for the chance to atone when we do."

Phillip grabs the bars and lowers his head with regret. "How do you atone for something as big as this?"

Anthony shrugs. "God knows."

Phillip looks up with foreboding and asks the question foremost on his mind. "What about Sandra? Did she make it out?"

"She's safe. She made it out clean. With just a bit of luck, this whole thing could miss her."

Phillip exhales a huge sigh of relief. "Thank God. I was worried sick about her."

Anthony nods in agreement. "She's just as worried about you."

"Tell her not to. This is my deal."

Anthony laughs lightly at the absurdity of the statement. "If I thought it would do any good, I would, but that lady has a one-track mind, and it leads right to you."

Phillip blows off the statement as unimportant. "Right."

Anthony eyes Phillip with disbelief. "You really don't get it do you, Phillip?"

Phillip looks at Anthony with confusion. "Get what?"

"Phillip, for Christ's sake, the woman's in love with you! Has been for years!"

Phillip stands motionless, struck by what he feels to be true, but knowing he is realizing it far too late.

Anthony's frustration flows from him to be replaced by pity for an opportunity so badly missed. "If you somehow make it out of this, you better marry that girl."

Phillip laughs hollowly. "If I get out of this, then maybe I will. But I don't think that's something I'll have to worry about."

Anthony smiles broadly with the mischievous grin of someone possessing information not privy to the other. "You underestimate me again, Phillip!"

Phillip hangs from the bars with slight hope. "Anthony, what are you saying, man?"

Anthony looks swiftly back and forth down the hall before he reaches into his coat pocket and pulls out a plastic key card and hands it through the bars to Phillip. Phillip looks at it quickly then slips it in his own pocket. "That will open up every door in this complex, including your cell."

Phillip looks dumbfounded. "How did you . . .?"

Anthony quiets him with a wave. "No time to explain, just listen. Wait until thirty minutes after I leave." (Anthony takes the designer watch from his wrist and hands it through the bars while he explains the plan.) "Then when you leave this cell, take a right down the hall. There's a stairwell at the end. Take the stairs all the way to the basement. Once you get to the bottom, look for a green SUV with tinted windows. The driver will take you . . ."

Phillip excitedly interrupts Anthony's directions. "Listen, Anthony, I need to book a flight to Miami . . ."

Anthony again quiets Phillip but not so nicely this time. "Dammit, man, let me finish! The driver will take you to a private airport where a Learjet is already prepped and ready to take you to Miami. After you take care of your business there, return to the plane and Sandra will be there with everything you two will need to disappear off the face of the earth."

Phillip stares at his longtime friend in stunned silence, truly touched by the lengths the man has gone to in order to try and save his hide. "Damn you, Anthony, how will I ever repay you?"

Anthony smiles at the genuine appreciation he sees in Phillip. "Save that family, and then marry the girl. That will be a start. Anything else and I'll let you know." The two men hug each other through the bars then break apart.

"I've got to go." Anthony briskly walks away.

FIFTY-NINE

PHILLIP SPENDS THE next half-hour nervously pacing the cell, walking back and forth while trying in vain to calm the racing thoughts now whipping through his mind. He looks at the Rolex he now wears, easily worth five grand or more. *Only ten minutes have passed!* He struggles to control his excitement one minute, then the next minute fights just as hard to deny the fear he feels of being caught in his escape attempt. As the time slowly creeps past Phillip goes to the stainless steel sink and looks into the foggy metal mirror. It reveals the cloudy image of a much disoriented man.

"Jesus, I look like crap." He pushes the button to activate the five-second stream of cold water. He quickly splashes water onto his face, washing away the sleep. He pushes the button again and rubs water through his oily hair, slicking it back. Phillip grabs the small washcloth provided with his sheets and wipes away the water. He looks in the mirror into his own eyes and attempts to calm himself. He knows he will have to have a clear mind if he wants to succeed.

***

Phillip looks at the watch one final time then stands from his seat on his bunk and walks to the cell door. He quietly slides the key through the lock. Peeking out, he looks both ways down the hall. Seeing no one, he takes a right and slinks down the hall to the stairwell door. He enters and makes his way silently down the stairs.

Just as he begins to think he might make it, he hears someone enter the stairwell below him and start up. He looks over the stairrail and sees a guard coming his way. He starts to panic, watching the man approach from below. Phillip turns in a quick circle, trying to figure out a place to hide. He eyes the door into the stairwell with trepidation. It obviously leads to another part of the detainment center, but what choice does he really have: take a chance with the door or stay in the stairwell and be caught?

He steps through the door—opening onto the end of a hall identical to the one his cell was on—just before the guard comes into view.

Phillip looks down the hall and sees two guards going the other way. A couple seconds pass with him stuck in his precarious position, and then one of the guards turns and starts walking back his way. The guard does not see him because he is looking down at a file in his hand. Phillip is flooded with fear at being caught. All the man has to do is look and the jig is up: Phillip would go back to his cell, and Alfonzo would be free to do whatever he wants to his unsuspecting stepson!

He acts without thinking. He lunges back through the door, pushing it open with immense force just in time to hit the guard reaching for the door. The door smacks hard in the guard's face, breaking his nose and knocking him out. Phillip enters the stairwell and looks at the unconscious man at his feet with relief and surprise. He shakes his head not knowing if his luck was good or bad. He fights a compulsion to stop and see if the man is all right.

Phillip steps over the body then sprints down the stairs all the way to the bottom. He opens the door to see another guard, this one in the basement coming toward him. Phillip jumps back into the stairwell, looks around frantically then runs and hides behind the first flight of stairs. The guard enters the stairwell and starts up. Phillip waits for just a moment for the guard to pass, then creeps to the door and looks out cautiously; seeing no one, he enters the basement parking garage. He quickly spots the green SUV, jogs to it and jumps in the backseat, breathless and sweating with fear.

The driver looks over his shoulder, wanting to make sure he has the proper passenger.

"Good afternoon, Mr. Stevens."

Phillip is breathing too hard to reply. The driver starts the vehicle and drives up and out of the garage.

***

Officer Cates walks slowly down the hall; he has not seen his favorite prisoner since before he took his hour lunch break. Approaching the cell, he smiles gloatingly. He took the time at lunch to do a little research on Mr. Stevens. What he found out pleased him: this man is on the black list. The black list consisted of people the government wanted held but lacked the legal ability to do so. In cases like that they would send them here, and Cates knows of men that had spent ten years or more locked in these single cells, speaking to no one except the guards. He had even heard of one man who had spent twenty-seven years locked up before he finally died. This seems too much to hope for, but he figures he has at least a year or two to get to know Mr. Stevens.

It is with this knowledge that Cates reaches the cell. He cannot wait to see the look on Stevens' face. He looks between the bars, ready to gloat. His face suddenly changes from a cruel smile to one of confused alarm and anger. The cell is empty! He grabs his radio and speaks frantically. "Red alert! We have an escaped prisoner!"

Cates turns and sprints down the hall as fast as his short legs can carry his immense weight. He bursts into the stairwell clipping the bloody staggering guard, knocking him out again. Cates pulls his firearm and checks the guard for a pulse. He screams into his radio.

"We've got a man down in the stairwell to the parking garage! Send medical and shut the gate down now!"

***

Phillip hides in the floorboard as the SUV approaches the guard gate. The guards lazily wave it through and the driver waves back. The phone at the guard gate rings and sirens go off while the SUV slides by the gate. Phillip takes a peek over the backseat at the now closing gates.

"That was way too close!"

SIXTY

DANIEL SITS ALONE having a light dinner while watching CNN comment on his recent bizarre behavior. Daniel does not necessarily disagree with the opinion of the news anchor. Over the last several weeks, he has missed more meetings and functions than he has attended. It would not take long for the media to start asking questions, and with no answers forthcoming, to start making speculations as to the cause of his ever-increasing absences. The thing was, he had lost his drive and purpose. Daniel needed the *higher* purpose of a divine decree. The N.D.E.C. had taken that away from him along with his wife and daughter. Daniel dwells on this constantly. He finds himself reverting back to his old ways. Anger and hate assert themselves more and more firmly into his consciousness.

He listens to the anchor speak of a possible illness he might be suffering from. Daniel smiles at this. An illness might be just the thing. He has been contemplating on ways to smooth over his lapse in attending to his responsibilities. Lately he has been thinking whatever road he chooses to follow, he would be best served to continue to maintain his noble image as a humanitarian. Whether he actually remains a humanitarian he doubts very seriously. The more he thinks about it, the more he likes it; gone is the edict from God, proven to be nothing more than a cruel hoax designed by man. If man could be so callous and mean spirited, then so could the president.

Daniel returns his attention to the now cold plate of food. For the first time in a couple of months he feels well. As he raises a bite of the pasta primavera to his mouth, Josh Weedy bursts through the door in an extreme state of agitation and concern. Daniel eyes his chief of staff over the suspended fork.

"Will you be joining me, Josh? I can have another place setting set up."

Josh ignores the invitation. "Stevens has escaped from the detention center!"

Daniel slams the fork back onto the plate. He stares Josh down with anger and disbelief. "How did this happen?"

Josh continues into the small private dining room, shutting the door from listening ears. "The reports are still coming in, but it looks like he had some help from Senator Higgins."

Daniel wipes the food from his mouth while assimilating what Josh has said.

"That's not too surprising. I would have liked to have detained the senator, but there is no way of doing so until we trace the trail of evidence back to him. More importantly, where is Stevens now?"

"He has a hell of a head start on us. For some damn reason, the detention center waited more than two hours before letting us know about the escape. The one thing we do have going for us is that the lead agent from the NSA believes he knows where Stevens is *going*."

"Where does he think he is going?"

"Miami."

Daniel allows his confusion to show. "Why Miami?"

"Stevens believes there is a family there that might be in some kind of danger. Apparently he feels somehow responsible for this."

Daniel nods his understanding. "Josh, do whatever you have to do. I want Stevens back in custody. One way or the other, dead or alive. Do I make myself clear?"

"Crystal."

SIXTY-ONE

Paul sits tied up in a chair in a large guest bedroom on the first floor of Alfonzo's Miami mansion. He is badly bruised, bleeding and barely conscious. Kim hovers around her son, gently wiping his brow and face with a cloth. She is deeply concerned. She has no idea why Alfonzo has attacked Paul with such fierce anger.

***

Paul had returned alone from the weekend boating trip without Alfonzo.

"How'd the trip go?" Kim had asked.

"The trip was very eventful." Paul refrained from answering further.

Kim tried to pry more information from her son, who seemed more content than she had seen him in a long time. Gone was the brooding, angry teenager, replaced by a happy, if secretive, young man. He even dismissed her questions about Alfonzo's whereabouts.

"I'm not sure," he had said. "I think he went to Colombia on unexpected business."

It seemed to her the only thing he told her was not to worry; things were different now. So she let the trip go until Alfonzo came home this morning as secretive as Paul, but with a much darker demeanor.

"Where have you been the last three days?" Kim had asked.

He had ignored the question. "Where's Paul?"

"He went out early but said he would be back for lunch."

Alfonzo simply grunted and went upstairs to shower. Truth be told, he needed it. Kim had never seen him look worse or more disheveled. She reluctantly passed it off as "boys being boys" and went to prepare a light lunch in the kitchen. She very rarely cooked, but before he left, Paul had asked for a ham and cheese omelet like she used to make him when he was young. What mother could refuse? She quickly decided to make an extra one for Alfonzo; he looked like he could use a good meal.

Paul showed up in time to set the table in the private breakfast nook on the upstairs veranda just to the left of the kitchen.

"Sweetie, set up a third place," Kim said as she came out on the veranda.

Paul did so automatically without asking who she expected to join them.

At that exact moment, Alfonzo came out on the veranda. Kim did not know what was going on, but Paul's face told her something very bad had happened between the two men. Paul stood there with a look of shock and terror as Alfonzo stared him down with menacing anger. Alfonzo took a large swallow from the drink he held in one hand, the other hand remaining in the side pocket of his leisure suit.

"Daddy's home, Pauly boy! Kim, I need you to leave us alone!" Kim wanted to do no such thing, but Paul had recovered somewhat from his initial shock and persuaded her to go.

"Mom, it's all right. Why don't you go do some shopping, and we'll have dinner later instead?" Alfonzo nodded in grim agreement at the suggestion.

Kim left reluctantly and spent a couple very nervous hours roaming aimlessly over the outskirts of the city.

When she could stand it no more, she returned home to find Alfonzo well on his way to being drunk, and no sign of her son. When she asked, Alfonzo at first refused to allow her to see Paul, so she waited until he went upstairs to make what she assumed was another drink and then made her way into the first-floor bedroom, the one Alfonzo had recently not allowed her to enter. What she found inside was an unconscious Paul tied up in a chair and badly beaten.

Kim went quickly to the adjoining bathroom and grabbed a washcloth, wetting it with cold water. She returned to her son's side and gently began to wipe away the drying blood from his battered face.

***

Now, Kim tries hard to hold back tears, watching Paul regain consciousness.

"Oh, Paul, what have you done to make your stepfather so angry?"

Paul just groans at the words, not able to talk.

Alfonzo walks into the room, carrying a drink. He sees Kim attending to her son and explodes in anger. "What are you doing? I told you not to be in here!"

Kim turns and pleads with her husband. "Please, Alfonzo, let him go! Whatever he's done, you punished him enough. He's sorry; he won't disobey again!"

Alfonzo laughs grimly and then takes a sip of the drink he's holding. "If you knew what your little rat almost succeeded in having done to me, you wouldn't say that. No, you would say he hasn't suffered nearly enough."

Kim approaches her enraged husband and grasps him pleadingly. She cries in frustration for her son's release. "What more would you do to him? He's half-dead already!"

"Well then, we're halfway there, aren't we?"

Kim beats Alfonzo's chest with her fists at these heartless words.

"You bastard! You can't kill my son!"

Alfonzo grabs his wife viciously in anger and throws her to the floor. "I'm tired of your antics, woman! You don't have a clue what's happened here!" Alfonzo mulls over his own words. "Or maybe you do."

Lying on the floor, Kim trembles with fear and confusion. She looks back at her husband while she attempts to pick herself up. "Alfonzo, what are you talking about?

He shrugs with indifference. "It doesn't matter, Kim. There's no going back now."

Brutally, Alfonzo kicks his wife in the face, knocking her unconscious. He talks to himself, looking down with drunken satisfaction at his handiwork. "It's better this way. No loose ends."

SIXTY-TWO

PHILLIP STARES NERVOUSLY out the window of the descending plane. He waits with palms sweating for the plane to taxi to a stop. He worries he will be apprehended before he can leave the airport, but shakes off the useless fears. *If there are agents waiting on me there is nothing I can do about it.* The plane finally comes to a slow stop. Phillip is at the door before it fully opens. He exits the plane and jogs the few yards to a waiting car. He eyes the latest model cherry red Ford Mustang with approval and jumps in the car. As he pulls away, he can't help but notice the 9mm handgun in the passenger seat. Phillip sighs with extreme relief, leaving the airport safely behind him.

He looks at an address he has written down on a piece of paper and programs it into the GPS unit on the dash. The car gives him directions to his destination.

***

Alfonzo carries the bound and gagged body of his wife through the house and into the garage, struggling toward the back of his waiting Hummer. He drops her roughly next to her barely conscious son. Alfonzo tries to wipe away the copious amount of sweat from his face. He has thought more than once it would be nice to have a couple of his body guards help with the manual labor, but he has had no contact with any of them since his boat trip. He looks down at the unmoving bodies of his family and barks out a drunken laugh. Alfonzo slams shut the back hatch on the Hummer before deciding maybe he has had a little too much to drink. *Nothing a little stimulation won't fix.* He hurries back into the house to hit a line from his stash of blow. Plus he needs to get his gun. *I cannot forget that!*

***

Phillip speeds down the mansion-lined road. He approaches the address with mounting apprehension. He hopes he's arriving in time, but he cannot suppress the fear that he won't be.

Phillip pulls into the driveway indicated on his GPS, almost crashing into an exiting Hummer. Phillip stares through the windshields at Alfonzo. Alfonzo had jumped into the Hummer and slammed the door shut. He started the ignition and threw the vehicle in gear. He drove recklessly down his extended driveway, only to have to slam on his brakes to avoid hitting a fully loaded red Mustang pulling into his drive.

Looking through the windshields, Alfonzo sees a familiar face. His heart skips a beat as he throws the Hummer into park.

***

Jake Shields directs Will Cummings, his driver and long-time partner in the Miami unit of the FBI, to take the upcoming left—the final turn leading to the address he received from a very earnest NSA agent out of Washington. The agent had explained in no uncertain terms that he was to stop and apprehend a very dangerous criminal named Phillip Stevens, using any means necessary. He alluded this order came directly from the White House, possibly even the president's desk.

Jake sits in the lead car of an ever-growing line of police cruisers speeding to converge on the potential victim's address—the address of a man named Alfonzo Rodriguez. Jake had not had time to check if this was not in fact the same Alfonzo Rodriguez, a suspected Colombian drug lord operating in the Miami area. Jake holds tight as Will takes the left—tires squealing in protest—and accelerates dangerously down the oceanside boulevard. He looks ahead and notes an altercation in the driveway at the indicated address. Will screeches to a sideways stop a safe distance from the two men. Jake checks the mug shot provided and is not surprised to see the man holding the gun on the other is Phillip Stevens.

SIXTY-THREE

$\mathcal{S}$ANDRA HUNCHES DOWN, hurrying to the waiting helicopter. The door opens and she is helped in by Senator Higgins. She smiles a worried greeting, swiftly buckling herself into the already ascending chopper.

***

Alfonzo recognizes the man in the car blocking his path but cannot seem to place him. He grabs the handgun lying in the passenger's seat and gets out of the Hummer, brandishing the weapon.

"Move your fucking car! You're in my way!"

Phillip jumps from the Mustang with his own weapon in hand. Sirens sound in the distance. Trying to reason with the enraged man, Phillip knows he has little time to act. "Hold on, Mr. Rodriguez, I think you're about to make a terrible mistake!"

Alfonzo is sure he knows this man. "How do you know what I'm about to do? Who the hell are you anyway?"

"I'm Phillip Stevens."

The unfamiliar name does not help Alfonzo's memory. "So?" he asks.

"I'm the guy that ran the company who tried to have you brainwashed."

Alfonzo finally places the face; this is the crazy S.O.B. who pretended to be God! Alfonzo raises his gun, points it at Phillip and fires off several shots so hurriedly he never comes close to his target. Phillip jumps behind his car.

"Nobody fucks with Alfonzo Rodriguez and gets away with it!"

Phillip hears the sirens getting much closer. He looks behind him and sees the approaching police.

Alfonzo notices the police and lowers his weapon, hiding it from sight. "Shit!"

The agents screech to a halt and jump from their cars, pulling weapons and aiming at Phillip. Alfonzo sees he is not the interest of the agents and quickly speaks to aid his appearance as the victim.

"Hey, officer, this guy just showed up and threatened to kill me!"

Josh keeps his attention squarely on Stevens while addressing Alfonzo. "Sir, we'll handle this; just remain calm. Mr. Stevens, put the gun down and surrender or we'll be forced to fire!"

Phillip tries to plead his case, more to buy a little time than anything else. "But you don't understand. He's the bad guy; he's going to murder his family!"

Josh ignores the criminal's pleas as several more officers take up firing positions around him. "Mr. Stevens, we have a federal warrant for your arrest. If you don't surrender peacefully, we are authorized to use force!"

315

Alfonzo smiles smugly, knowing Phillip can't stop him. He decides to rub in the fact. "Surrender, Mr. Stevens, and let the agents take you in. Be gone from my house so I can go on with my day."

Phillip stands frozen. Everything seems to slow down for him. He raises his hands above his head but fails to drop the gun he holds. "Okay, officer, you win, I surrender."

Josh is inwardly relieved; he does not want to kill this man. "Drop the weapon and get down on the ground!"

A chopper approaches abruptly from a low angle and hovers very close at hand. Everyone's attention follows Phillip's gaze to the hovering craft. Josh is angered by the ill-timed arrival of what is sure to be a local news unit. He sneaks the quickest peek at the obnoxiously close helicopter.

Phillip had been watching the lead agent out of the corner of his eye. He takes his only chance, choosing to forsake his own life in the process. He turns and fires off three rounds, missing twice, but hitting the stunned Alfonzo squarely between the eyes with the final bullet.

Josh cusses himself, turning back at the sound of the shots.

"Take him out!" No less than six officers open fire, hitting Phillip several times, knocking the gun from his hand even before he falls to the ground.

***

Sandra and Anthony watch in horror.

"Oh, God, no!"

Anthony reaches forward and grabs the pilot's shoulder. "Land, damn it!"

The chopper lands. Sandra jumps from it and runs to Phillip lying on the ground. She pushes the agents to the side. "Get out of the way!"

The surprised officers let her pass.

Sandra grabs Phillip, holding him in her arms as he struggles for breath. He looks up at her with a bloody smile. "Hey, babe . . . I guess I really messed up."

Looking down on her dying love, Sandra cannot control her tears. "You did wonderful! You saved two lives today!"

Josh and the other agents jump into action. They check Alfonzo's body for a pulse without success. Will notices the Hummer rocking slightly and approaches the vehicle to check it out. He opens the hatch to discover the bound and gagged Kim and Paul. "Hey, Josh, you gotta see this!"

Josh walks over to where Will stands behind the Hummer. "Hell, anything for an excuse to get away from the sad scene with the lady. *Where the hell did she come from anyway?* He looks into the Hummer at the conscious but battered pair. "Well, what are you waiting for? Get them the hell out of there!" Will starts to untie the woman.

Josh returns from the Hummer to Phillip, now lying in Sandra's arms. *I think we might have screwed up.*

Sandra cries as Phillip begins to lose consciousness.

"Phillip, you know I love you, don't you?"

"I love you too!"

Sandra continues to cry, realizing Phillip's last words are the ones she has waited so long to hear.

SIXTY-FOUR

PHILLIP SITS UNCONSCIOUS in a chair in the solid gray room. The messenger stands in front of him, watching the motionless body.

"Phillip, wake up."

Phillip groans and opens his eyes. He looks around with first confusion, then growing awareness. "Are you kidding me?"

The messenger shrugs without emotion. "Maybe, maybe not. Remember you get to choose."

Phillip sits in silence; he looks at his arm and casually tests the invisible bonds. He smiles knowingly, watching the bonds appear to dig into his flesh. He relaxes and watches the wound and bonding straps disappear. He looks with curiosity at the messenger in front of him.

"Who are you?"

"Does it matter?"

Phillip contemplates the simple question a moment before he answers. "I guess not." He looks around in wonder, taking in the meaning of his situation. He begins to laugh in relief.

The messenger never moves. "What's so funny?"

"You, me." Phillip spins his head around to encompass his surroundings. "Hell, all this!"

The messenger continues to stand unmoving and not amused. "Do you think that you are not supposed to be here?"

Phillip sobers up at this. He thinks about his situation, going over all the events that led him to where he sits. He remembers the time in the cell, hoping for a chance to fix his mistakes and how hollow he felt knowing there was no opportunity. "No, this is exactly where I'm supposed to be."

"I'm glad you see that. Do you understand the mistakes you made?"

Phillip nods emphatically. "Yes, yes I do."

"If we let you go back, do you believe you would repeat them?"

"No, no I won't."

The messenger and Phillip stare at each other in silence for a moment before the messenger slowly nods in approval. "So be it."

Phillip loses consciousness as the room is sucked from his mind leaving only blackness.

EPILOGUE

PHILLIP SITS SLEEPING in his chair behind his desk, head bent awkwardly to the right. On the television hanging on the office wall, the same old man spouts the same heartfelt message about charitable need of the cause he fights so passionately for. Phillip wakes with a start. He looks around in wonder. He checks his body—everything is fine. He looks quickly at the date on his watch, not quite believing what he is seeing.

"Oh, thank you, God!" His office door opens and Sandra walks briskly across the office, dropping a large file onto his desktop. "Why are we thanking God?"

Phillip eyes Sandra curiously; she seems oblivious to the scrutiny. "Never mind."

Sandra looks at the TV. "Is he one of ours?"

Phillip just laughs, while Sandra looks at him confused.

"What's so funny?"

Phillip smiles broadly. "Hey, Sandra, you want to have dinner with me?

THE END . . .